Best Served Cold

H. A. BURTON

ISBN 978-0-9574147-0-9

For BB and SB

Prologue

She fell fast, hurtling backwards towards the hard surface of the ocean far below, her mind blank with terror. The surface of the water broke with a sharp crack as her flailing body plunged into the cold, dark depths. The smack to the back of her head knocked her unconscious.

She awoke, pain piercing her wrist and searing agonisingly across her back. The sky was still pitch black. She gasped and immediately drew in a lungful of saltwater. She started to splutter, crying out in pain through the coughing. Her mind felt fuzzy but a grim fear gripped her. 'Sharks!' she shrieked, her tongue feeling too big for her mouth. 'Oh please, no!' She wheeled round frantically, sobbing with the pain, splashing one-handed at the inky water, trying desperately to get her breath but feeling panic overwhelming her. She felt sure that at any second she would feel something grab her leg and pull her under. She sobbed uncontrollably, shivering with fear and cold. 'Help me!' she cried. 'Somebody help me, please!'

There was nobody. She was alone in the pitching sea under the night sky. 'Help me!' she screamed again. The pain in her wrist and her back threatened to overwhelm her. 'I'm so cold,' she wept. Her head pounded and the dizziness made her feel sick. She tried to continue to tread water but could feel her power over her limbs deserting her. 'So cold,' she mumbled. Her legs slowly stopped kicking and her eyes closed.

Part I

Six days earlier…

Chapter 1

A car crunched smoothly onto the gravel below. Dante dropped her fountain pen, leaped up off the carpet and rushed to the window, pressing her nose against the glass. Through the thick foliage on the branches outside her window she could just make out the rear of the sleek, black limousine. She tapped eagerly on her window pane as the chauffeur opened the rear door below, sighing in frustration when no-one seemed to hear her. Hurrying from her room, she dashed across the wide landing and flew down the curving staircase, just in time to intercept the front door bell. She flung it open with a flourish, shrieking at the sight of her friend.

'Paige!' She flung her arms around the young woman and received shrieks in her ear in turn.

'Dante! You look wonderful!'

'Thanks! I'm getting married tomorrow! I'm so excited!'

'I know! I'm so excited too!'

They danced around, hugging each other, the luggage at Paige's feet forgotten. An amused cough behind Dante brought them to a standstill. Her father stood in the doorway, eyes twinkling at the sight of their merriment. 'Hello Mr Kingsford,' smiled Paige. 'Thanks so much for letting me stay over tonight.'

'Well now my dear, it's a tremendous pleasure,' William Kingsford replied, gesturing both girls inside the house. 'However, I hope you're not too excited to be of any use to my daughter before the great day?' Dante rolled her eyes at Paige as she put an arm round her father. 'Daddy, behave yourself. I just know Paige is going to be the best maid of honour ever!'

'Sure am! As your older and wiser friend I guess I'll be advising and guiding you on this most solemn occasion....' Paige broke off with a yelp as Dante swatted her.

'Oh stop. Guidance indeed. From you of all people!' She grabbed Paige's hand and pulled her towards the staircase. 'Come up and see all the things I've been working on for tomorrow.' Mr Kingsford smiled and shook his head fondly as the pair headed excitedly upstairs. He called after them. 'Don't forget girls, we'll need to leave at 6:30 to be at the restaurant to greet everyone this evening.'

'Don't worry Daddy, we'll be ready, I promise.' Dante blew him a kiss from the landing.

Paige followed Dante into her bedroom. The afternoon sun spilled into the large room, caressing the well-loved treasures on the shelves. Small pieces of card lay strewn on the floor and Dante knelt to collect them up. 'I just have to finish writing out the place cards and then we can check our outfits.'

'Dante, why on Earth are you writing out place cards? Shouldn't the hideously expensive wedding planner have that all under control by now?' asked Paige, amused.

Dante grinned sheepishly. 'I said I wanted to do it. It makes it more personal for all the guests. This way I can write a happy little message to everyone from me on the back. I'm almost done.'

'You're too nice,' admonished Paige. 'And quite possibly a control freak. Let's get this finished so we can start your bridal pampering.' She waved a hand at the cards. 'Do you want me to write some?' she offered. 'I can do your handwriting.'

'Now that would be cheating,' laughed Dante. 'I won't be long.'

Paige sighed resignedly and sat down on the edge of the bed. 'When do the other bridesmaids arrive?'

'Oh, well they're arriving a bit later with my aunt and uncle so we're just meeting them at the rehearsal dinner, then they'll come back with us afterwards and stay over here too,' explained Dante. 'That way we can all get ready together in the morning. My dad has all the guest rooms ready – I think he's quite excited to have so many people in the house at the same time. It gets a bit quiet when it's just him. I think that's why he just stays in New York so much more often these days, even at weekends.'

She scooped up the cards and took them over to her desk, sorting them into piles. Paige wandered across the room. 'How's Blake?' she asked, looking out over the gardens.

Dante turned around, beaming. 'Oh, he's wonderful, as always. I think he gets more handsome every day. Well, you'll see tonight – you can tell me if you think so too.'

'You're a lucky girl Miss Kingsford. You really do have it all.'

Dante looked up from her cards, hearing an unusual tone in her friend's voice but Paige grinned at her. 'Come on, hurry up and finish those cards and let's have some fun!'

'OK,' agreed Dante, 'and then you have to help me finish my honeymoon packing. Blake won't breathe a word about where we're going, and I'm dying to know! He says he can't tell a soul.' She looked sharply at her friend as Paige remained demurely silent. 'Wait...you know where I'm going! You do, don't you?' she pestered.

Paige backed away, holding her hands up. 'My lips are sealed. But yes, I do know, and you will never make me tell!' she added, dashing behind a chair for protection. Dante remained at her desk, fiddling with her pen. 'Huh. Wow, I thought only Blake knew, but it feels a bit weird that you both know about my honeymoon and I don't.' She bit her lip and told herself crossly to get a grip. Paige saw the tears threatening in Dante's eyes and crossed quickly across the room to her.

'Hey, come on honey, don't be upset. He's keeping it from you so it's a surprise, but I had to know so I can help you pack exactly the right things, silly.' She stroked Dante's silky fair hair. 'You're probably just feeling a bit overwhelmed with the wedding. This time tomorrow you'll be Mrs Blake Harrington!'

Dante rested her head against Paige. 'You're right, I'm sorry. I do feel kind of overwhelmed. It's all starting to seem so unreal. ' She took a deep breath and grinned at her friend. 'OK. Let's get serious. Should we start on the Champagne now or later?'

Dante, Paige and Mr Kingsford arrived at 'The Lobster Shack' just before 7pm. The name fooled no-one; the 'shack' was in fact an elegant waterfront bistro, with white linen tablecloths, flickering candles on the tables and discreetly attentive waiters.   That evening it looked prettier than ever, with twinkling white fairy lights decorating the ceiling and lavish flower displays in bubblegum pink generously distributed around the dining area.

'Daddy!' gasped Dante when she saw it. 'This looks so beautiful! My favourite colour!' She held his arm, pointing at the roses and lilies. 'Did you do this?' William smiled benevolently down at his radiant daughter. 'I did, my darling. I want your last evening as Miss Kingsford to be perfect for you.' Dante reached up to hug him and he held her tightly, as if he never wanted the hug to end. Guests began to trickle into the restaurant.

'Excuse me sir, may I cut in?' a deep voice enquired. Blake Harrington stood beside William, devastatingly handsome in a dark grey suit that matched his eyes. He smiled down at Dante, leaning forward to kiss her lightly. 'Hello darling.'

Dante breathed in deeply, enjoying his subtle aftershave. 'Good evening sir,' Blake continued, offering his hand to William. 'The restaurant looks wonderful.'

'Hello Blake,' replied William, shaking hands firmly. 'Are your folks here with you? Have you all settled into your hotel?'

'Yes, thank you sir. Your recommendation was excellent.' He gestured towards two middle-aged ladies standing near the bar. 'My mother and aunt are keen to meet you, may I introduce you?'

'Of course.' William started to follow Blake but turned back towards his daughter. 'Dante, I see your aunt arriving, would you please go and welcome her?'

He raised an eyebrow and Dante nodded with a grin, knowing her father was trying to avoid his bossy sister-in-law for as long as he could. She watched happily as her father and fiancé made their way across the room together, two striking men. Turning, she found Paige at her side watching them too. Dante grabbed her hand. 'Come and meet my aunt and uncle and cousins, they just arrived. I want all my bridesmaids to be great friends.' She lowered her voice to a whisper. 'We're not actually all that close; my dad and my aunt don't get along too well – he thinks she's insincere and pushy – but my cousins are sweethearts.'

She led the way over to a slender lady in her late fifties who was shrugging off her exquisite mink coat. Her three slightly plump daughters and somewhat rounder father were being handed Champagne by one of the waiting staff.

'Hello Aunt Madeleine,' Dante greeted her warmly.

'Dante! Darling girl!' Madeleine swept Dante into a perfumed embrace, kissing her on both cheeks. She held her at arms' length. 'It's been so long! Let me look at you.' She took in Dante's perfect porcelain skin, freshly highlighted hair in its chic bob and laughing blue eyes. 'Well, you look like just the happiest bride to be, and so you should be.'

Holding Dante by one hand she gestured her daughters over. They chorused their hellos to Dante, trying to kiss her as their mother pulled them all into position around the bride. 'Let's see how beautiful you will all look together tomorrow.' Laughing, Dante beckoned Paige into the group too, introducing her to the other girls. Madeleine sighed dreamily, clutching her husband's arm. 'Look Cyril, don't our girls look wonderful. Dante, it's so fortunate that you're a wonderful height for a woman. Almost identical to your cousins, not too tall, not too short. With your father being so tall it's a mercy really.'

She surveyed the group with a critical eye. 'Paige dear, I assume you'll be wearing some higher heels tomorrow, and perhaps we can ask the hair stylist for an updo to add height.' Dante winced on her friend's behalf and smiled supportively at Paige as she saw her blushing fiercely.

'Ladies, you all look wonderful.' Blake appeared, smiling rakishly at them. He smoothly extracted Dante from the cluster of women and slid his arm around her waist. 'I'm going to steal my fiancée for a few moments, I hope you don't mind.' A chorus of 'Oh no' and 'of course not' followed the couple.

He led her outside onto the moonlit terrace and gazed down at her. 'That's better,' he grinned wickedly. 'You look even more stunning out here by yourself in my arms.' He bent his head and kissed her.

'Oh Blake, I've missed you the last few days.' Dante snuggled into his chest. 'I'm so happy; I can't believe we're actually going to be married tomorrow.'

'Believe it baby. I'm not letting a treasure like you go.'

Blake's mother joined them on the terrace, looking apologetic and holding a cell phone. 'Blake honey, I'm sorry to interrupt. You left your cell phone on the table and it was ringing. It's a man about some insurance?'

'Oh right, I'd better take that.' He took the phone quickly, frowning his annoyance at his mother having answered his phone. 'James? Blake. Would you hold for one moment?' He covered the mouthpiece and kissed Dante. 'Go on in Precious, I'll be there in a minute.'

Dante nodded and accompanied Susan Harrington back into the party. She looked at the older woman, noting her worried face. 'Is everything OK, Susan?' she asked.

They paused at the door and turned back to see Blake smiling widely as he listened to his caller. Susan sighed. 'He works so hard, he's just like his father. Driven. Ambitious.' She looked at Dante seriously. 'I need you to make sure that he's not like his father in every way. Martin died of a heart attack five years ago. He was only 50.'

Dante put an arm around Susan's shoulders, giving her a squeeze. 'I know, it must have been so awful for you, I'm so sorry.'

Susan smiled sadly. 'Don't let Blake go the same way. Promise me you won't let him work too hard.'

'I promise,' said Dante. 'We're going to look after each other for the rest of our lives.' Susan hugged her and they headed back in to join the other guests.

A couple of hours later the assembled friends and family were happily tucking into dark chocolate torte and sampling the aged port that was being passed round. William rose and tapped a few times on his wine glass with his fork until the chatter died out. All faces turned expectantly towards him.

'Unaccustomed as I am to public speaking...' he began, to peals of laughter from the room. He smiled, tucking his hand into his waistcoat pocket, a trait Dante knew meant he was about to enjoy making a speech. 'OK, OK, my we have a lively crowd in tonight. I can't fool you.' He smiled widely at his guests. 'In my long career as founder and CEO of The Kingsford Corporation I do of course find myself called upon to speak in public with flattering regularity. However,' he turned to Dante, 'having to make a speech about my beloved only daughter setting off on her journey into married life, well...That is actually hard for me to talk about.'

He smiled gently down at his daughter. 'Dante, you are the light of my life. You know I think that 22 is rather young to be marrying – I was almost twice your age when I married your mother! However, I'm assured by the gentleman opposite,' he raised his glass at Blake, 'that he will take good care of you. I don't want to say too much today or I will risk repeating myself tomorrow at the wedding itself, but I must at least say this.'

He took Dante's hand, his voice softening. 'If your mother were still alive and could see what a truly beautiful young woman you have become, both inside and out, she would be so proud of you my darling. As am I. You mean the world to me.' His voice trembled and Dante jumped up and flung her arms around him, swallowing hard to dissolve the sudden lump in her throat.

William cleared his throat and turned back to face his guests, keeping Dante held tightly against his side. 'Ladies and gentlemen, thank you all for coming to celebrate with us tonight. We will be delighted to enjoy your company at the wedding tomorrow. For now, let me ask you to send your best wishes to Dante and Blake and join me in toasting their happiness. To a happy wedding!'

'A happy wedding!' repeated all the guests joyfully.

The evening came to a close soon afterwards, the guests heading for their cars with eager chatter about the following day. Dante said her goodbyes to Blake and his relatives and waved them off to their hotel. She, Paige and her three cousins piled into the waiting limousine, chattering and laughing. 'Well, that was a fun evening,' smiled Dante, settling into her seat. 'I really can't wait for tomorrow now.'

'Blake looked very handsome,' giggled Rebecca. Her sister Claire pretended to swoon. 'He sure did Dante. Where can I find myself a fine figure of a man like that?' she asked. 'Remind me how you guys met? He's older than you, right?'

Dante laughed. 'Which do you want me to answer first? OK, yes, Blake is 29 – almost 30 - and Paige and I met him last year when we were starting our final year at college. He's already quite a successful businessman,' she said proudly. 'He came in to the business school to talk to us about risk management and we met at the drinks afterwards-'

'And couldn't keep their eyes off each other,' finished Paige, rolling her eyes. The cousins laughed. Dante laughed too. 'He took my number and we started dating. It's all been quite whirlwind really – he asked me to marry him when we'd been together for only six months.'

'And now here you are just a few months later, about to get married. How romantic,' sighed Claire. 'He must have known you were the one right away.'

'That's the way he tells it,' agreed Paige. 'He didn't have eyes for anyone else once he'd met our beautiful Dante.'

Eleanor looked at Paige. 'How did you meet Dante? Were you in the same classes in college?' she asked. Paige nodded. 'That's right. I'm a couple of years older than Dante but we met during Orientation Week and we've been friends ever since. We shared an apartment in our second and third years.'

Rebecca looked confused. 'How come you're older than Dante then? Shouldn't you be the same age? Were you kept back in school at some point? Ow!' she exclaimed as Claire pinched her.

Paige laughed shortly and flicked her dark hair away from her face. 'No, nothing like that. I decided to work for a couple of years before going to do my business degree. That way I'd actually have some real business experience first.'

'Very wise,' said Eleanor warmly.

'Yes, she is,' confirmed Dante, tucking her hand into Paige's arm. 'Paige is also a great listener and a great roomie. She always believed in me when others at college were dismissing me as just a silly little rich girl.'

They reached the house just moments after the car carrying William, Madeleine and Cyril had arrived home. The spry Scottish housekeeper, Mrs Craig, waited on the front steps to greet the party and show the guests to their various rooms. William wished everyone a goodnight and asked Dante if he could have a quick word with her.

'Of course Daddy.' She turned to Paige. 'You're in the room right next to mine, you should have everything you need in there. I've put some lovely goodies in your bathroom in case you want to take a bath or anything.'

'Thanks Dante, that's really sweet of you.'

'I'll pop in and say goodnight when I come up.' She followed her father across the hall and into his imposing study. She crossed to the large fireplace, glad to see that no fire had been lit on the warm evening. She curled up in her usual leather armchair, feet tucked under herself. William poured himself a measure of Scotch and sat down opposite her.

'Is everything OK Daddy?'

'Everything's fine my darling.' He swirled his whisky. 'I simply wanted to have a few minutes just the two of us because tomorrow you will, quite rightly, be the belle of the ball and quite impossible to talk to alone.' He placed his glass carefully on the mahogany table at his side and leaned forward to take Dante's hands in his. 'Dante, I know that you're happy but I do believe that 22 is very young to be marrying, I can't pretend otherwise. Marriage does take hard work at times, and I want you to know that if you ever need to talk about anything you can still come to me, you'll always be my little girl.'

'Oh Daddy, of course I will. But please don't worry about me. Blake is going to look after me really well. I'm very lucky to have two wonderful men in my life keen to take care of me.'

'Blake is a very ambitious man Dante.' William sat back in his chair, staring at a framed photo of his wife on the table at his side. 'I recognise much of myself in him at that age. I know that I was very driven. I'm not sure that I would have been a very good husband at that stage in my life. As you know, I didn't find the time to marry until I was in my forties. Your mother - and you - were the best things ever to happen to me but at 29... I'm not sure I would have recognised it. I was so ambitious, so determined to prove myself, I would have done anything. I see that same ruthlessness in Blake.' He frowned into his glass. 'One thrusts one's way forward, not caring who one hurts or how one gets ahead. And you, you're the last person I'd want to get hurt. I've always been so worried that my position has made you vulnerable. You hear such terrible stories of wealthy young women being kidnapped for ransoms, or taken advantage of by conmen, or worse...'

Looking up, he saw the troubled look on Dante's face and leant forward to grip her hands once more. 'Dante darling, I'm not trying to upset you, I'm so sorry, I got a little carried away there.' He laughed lightly and brushed a strand of hair behind Dante's ear.

'I just want to be sure that you understand. I know he loves you, but you may have some lonely times being married to a man as ambitious as Blake. And if you do, well, come and talk to me because I promise to understand.'

'I will. I think you're mistaken though Daddy. Blake tells me he really values the way you've involved me in your company my whole life, and the fact that I have my business degree. He feels like he can talk to me about work. We talk about the corporation a lot. He says I'm a real asset to him.' She smiled at her father. 'I know you've been hoping I'll achieve great things when I officially join the corporation after the honeymoon and I'm going to try not to let you down. I want to be an asset to you too.'

'You could never let me down. I'm excited that we'll finally be working together. You already know more about the company than most of my managers but-'

'I know, I know,' laughed Dante. 'You need to start me on something small, so as not to offend anyone.' She stood up. 'It's fine Daddy, and I'm looking forward to it. I'll try to be more ambitious myself, just like Blake. He can be a good influence on me. I'll prove to everyone that I'm not just some bleached blonde airhead, but the worthy heir of William Kingsford.' She leaned down to kiss him on the cheek. 'I love you Daddy. Everything's going to be just perfect.'

Dante left her father enjoying his whisky and padded upstairs. She popped her head around each of her cousins' bedroom doors to whisper 'Goodnight, thanks for being my bridesmaid!' then tapped lightly on Paige's door. Paige opened the door, dressed in her short white nightgown which set off perfectly her slim, tanned legs. She was speaking into her phone and smiled at Dante, waving her in.

'OK then sweetie, bye for now, good luck.' She pressed to end the call and turned to Dante. 'Sorry, I was just speaking to my cousin Bobby.'

'No problem! Hey, it's such a shame he couldn't come as your date to the wedding. You always said how close you guys are and I was really looking forward to meeting him at last.'

Paige shrugged, with a regretful smile. 'It can't be helped, he has something really important to do at work this week so he can't be here. I'll see him soon.' She crossed to the bed. 'Come and sit down,' she said.

'That's a cute nightie!' exclaimed Dante, sitting cross-legged on her friend's bed. 'You're lucky, you're so lovely and tanned.'

'I don't think you have anything to worry about,' replied Paige drily, getting under the covers. 'Remember when we did that test in Cosmo, and it turned out you had the 'perfect fantasy body'?'

'Oh yes: *"Womanly curves on a slim frame make your hourglass figure the perfect fantasy shape for men, and the envy of other women",*' Dante quoted with a giggle. 'I don't know about that. I still envy your tan. It takes me forever to be anything other than pale.'

'Not so envious of my short height and small breasts though, are you?' queried Paige, raising an eyebrow. 'And how do you even remember that article word for word anyway? You even have the perfect memory! Get out of my room, you annoying girl.'

They laughed, then Dante grew sombre. 'Seriously though Paige, is everything OK between us?'

Paige sighed and reached out her hand to Dante. 'I'm sorry, I know I wasn't really myself this evening. I guess I'm just jealous.' She saw Dante's querying look and hurried to explain herself. 'I'm jealous of Blake – he's going to have you all to himself and I'm losing my best friend.'

Dante leaned in for a hug. 'You're not losing me, silly! I'm still your best friend. I'll still see you all the time and you know you'll be welcome anytime at our place.' She rose and stretched. 'Get some sleep and we'll have a lovely girls' morning tomorrow being preened and pampered. Deal?'

'Deal.'

Dante slipped off to her own room. She changed into her night clothes but felt wide awake with all the excitement. She sat in the window seat, playing over in her mind all the happy times she had spent at the house with her parents when she was a young girl and, in later years, just her father. Their regular weekend escapes from the big city had been some of her favourite parts of her childhood. 'I love it here so much,' she thought, 'but I'm so excited to be living right in the heart of New York City now. It's going to be so much fun being married.'

Her thoughts turned to their wedding present from her father: an uptown penthouse apartment fully kitted out with beautiful furniture and appliances. She sighed happily. 'I'm so blessed to have such a generous father, and to have a fiancé so confident and secure in himself that he doesn't mind accepting such a gift,' she thought to herself. 'I can't wait to move in and play house!'

She tried to stem the giddy surge of emotion and calm herself enough to sleep. 'Dark circles under my eyes is not the look I want on my wedding day,' she told herself sternly. She climbed into bed and fell asleep dreaming of Blake.

Chapter 2

A burst of bright sunlight awoke Dante the next morning. She stretched luxuriously and allowed herself a few moments of perfect stillness, listening to the birdsong outside her window. A tap at her door made her sit up. 'Come in!' she called. Mrs Craig opened the door, carrying a tray laden with strawberries, French toast, scrambled eggs, honey and Dante's favourite granola. The housekeeper's eyes twinkled as she walked across the thick carpet. 'Good morning bridey!' she cried. She settled the tray on Dante's legs and dropped a kiss on the top of her head. 'Now I know you'll be excited, but I insist that you have a good breakfast.' She turned and beckoned to Paige who was hovering in the doorway. 'Come on in – there's plenty for you both here.'

Paige flew across the room and kissed Dante. 'Good morning you, it's your wedding day!'

Dante clapped her hands excitedly. 'I'm so excited! How am I going to eat?' She saw Mrs Craig's mock frown, and hurriedly made to pour some yogurt over the granola. 'I will, I will, I promise! Thanks so much Mrs Craig!'

Mrs Craig nodded merrlly at the two young women as they made a start on the food and left them to it.

'So,' said Paige, munching on a strawberry. 'What's first?'

'Well, the hair stylist is coming at 10am, so we'll all need to be showered and ready before then. Then we'll have our nails done, drink some more

Champagne, have our make-up done, the flowers will come, then-'

'-more Champagne,' cut in Paige. The girls laughed and Paige reached for some French toast. 'What flowers did you decide on for your bouquet in the end by the way?'

'There was only one choice for me - just a simple arrangement of English tea roses in a soft blush pink to match your dresses.'

'For your Mum,' acknowledged Paige.

Dante nodded. 'My dad always called her his beautiful English rose, and I always knew that's what I'd have on my wedding day.'

Paige patted her hand. 'It's lovely. It's like a little part of her will be here with us today.'

Dante smiled at her friend, blinking back her tears. 'You always understand, I'm so lucky to have you.' A shadow passed over her face. 'If it hadn't been for you, my time at college wouldn't have been half as great. Those awful girls...'

'Hey, let's not even give those bullies one second of air time. Not today!' exclaimed Paige. 'They were just jealous bitches who couldn't handle you being way richer than they were. Forget about them! Your true friends don't care whether you're rich or poor.'

'You're right, but you know I really am so grateful you were there to help me move away from that crowd and give me all your good advice. I felt sometimes like you were my only true friend.' Dante leant across the tray to hug Paige. Paige squeezed her tightly then shook her gently. 'Now come on lady, we've got a wedding to prepare for!'

The morning passed in a pastel blur of excited happiness and before she knew it, Dante was steadily saying her vows and then, what felt like only seconds later, leaving the church as Blake's wife.

'I feel like I'm going to burst with happiness!' she confided to him as they were pressed into the white Rolls Royce, the folds of her dress clouding around them. Blake smiled down at her and gripped her hand, sliding his thumb backwards and forwards along her shiny new wedding band. 'It's the perfect day,' he agreed. 'Perfect weather, perfect setting, and you – perfect for me.' He kissed her tenderly and Dante's heart fluttered.

She flitted from table to table at the reception between courses, chatting animatedly to her old school friends, politely schmoozing her father's business associates and receiving marriage advice from elderly distant relatives. Her father kept the tone light and humorous in his speech, entertaining the assembled guests, before handing the floor over to his new son-in-law to great applause.

Blake rose and all eyes turned to him, those of all the ladies particularly appreciative, admiring the dashing sight he made in his perfectly fitted tuxedo.

'Thank you. My wife and I....,' he paused, waiting for the cheers and applause at that opener to die down, '...would like to thank you all so much for coming here today and helping us celebrate our marriage. This has been a truly wonderful day in every respect and I am over the moon to have made Dante my

wife. As you can see, she is the most dazzling girl in
the world, a true diamond. I love you Dante.'

He stooped to kiss her and Dante beamed as the
guests applauded once more. Blake straightened up. 'I
can't possibly hope to follow my father-in-law's famous
speech-making so I'm just going to do two things. First
of all, I have to thank the bridesmaids for doing a
wonderful job today. Your combined beauty made the
bridal party just stunning and I know you've been a
great help to Dante. Ladies and gentlemen please join
me in a toast to the bridesmaids!'

'The bridesmaids!' chorused the room happily,
applauding again. Dante blew kisses to Paige and her
cousins.

Blake pulled an envelope from his inside jacket
pocket. He showed it enticingly to Dante and to the
guests. 'Secondly, I have the happy task of informing
my wife where we will be going on our honeymoon.'
Dante's heart leaped with excitement as a happy
murmur of anticipation ran through the crowd. 'The
answer is all in here my precious,' said Blake, handing
Dante the envelope.

Dante felt all eyes upon her as she prised open
the flap and pulled out a card. She read the words
written on it and her eyes widened. She looked up at
Blake unable to speak. Blake laughed, took her hand in
his and addressed the room. 'What my wife appears
unable to tell you is that we will be leaving this evening
for a month's cruise to and around the Mediterranean.'
The guests gasped and then clapped when they saw how
dumbfounded Dante was in her delight. 'I can't believe

it,' she managed to stammer. 'Blake! How amazing! Thank you!'

'You're worth it, darling,' he whispered in her ear. 'Let's go and cut our delicious-looking cake and then I want to twirl you around the dance floor in your beautiful dress before I whisk you away for good.' He pulled her up and Dante followed in dazed delight, certain that her heart could not possibly feel any more than it did at that moment without bursting.

'Good evening, welcome on board sir, madam.' The steward bowed slightly as Dante and Blake crossed the carpeted gangplank and stepped on board 'The Diamond Sunrise'. Dante beamed at him, feeling as though she were walking on air. 'May I take your names please sir?'

'Mr and Mrs Blake Harrington,' replied Blake, smiling conspiratorially at Dante. Her heart thrilled at her new title.

The steward instantly located their names on his list. 'It's my pleasure to meet you both and may I congratulate you on your marriage. My name is Hugh, and I am the chief steward on board.' He beckoned forward a waiting colleague. 'This is Francis, he will be your personal steward for the duration of the cruise.'

Francis smiled and gestured inside the ship. 'Hello, I'm very pleased to meet you both. Won't you please come with me and I'll show you to your suite. Your luggage will be brought along for you momentarily. We'll remain docked here tonight but by the time you wake up in the morning we'll be out at sea and on our way to Europe.' Dante squeezed Blake's hand excitedly at this news.

Francis chatted pleasantly to them as they followed him into the main atrium. He pointed out the way to the swimming pools, the gymnasium, the spa and beauty salon, the cinema, the numerous restaurants and bars and the various boutiques as they went. 'It's just like a wonderful luxury hotel, but on the water!' exclaimed Dante with a sigh of pleasure.

They eventually arrived in a wide corridor with tasteful artwork adorning the walls at appropriate intervals. They stopped outside a door, where a porter was already waiting for them with their suitcases. 'This is your room Mr and Mrs Harrington, allow me to open the door for you.' Francis slid a card key into the lock, and pushed open the door to reveal a large suite, beautifully decorated in shades of taupe and cream.

An oversized bed with opulent throws and cushions covering it was the main focus of the room. White roses spilled their delicate scent from the writing desk and from the low coffee table, which was nestled between squashy armchairs. Francis showed Blake where the temperature controls were and how to operate the discreetly positioned television and high-tech music system while Dante strolled around, taking it all in. A chaise-longue reclined gracefully underneath the large windows and Dante skipped over to kneel on it with a cry. 'What a wonderful view!'

New York City's night skyline glittered and sparkled at them in all its magnificence. Dante heard Francis and the luggage porter leaving the room and Blake shutting the door. She smiled as he came up behind her and slipped his arms around her waist, kissing her neck. 'So, do you approve?' he asked.

'Mmmmm, I approve of the room, and I approve of what you're doing.' She sighed happily as he kissed the nape of her neck and his hands caressed her hips through her silk dress. He brushed her hair to one side. 'We have some time before the cocktail reception,' he murmured in her ear. 'Why don't we try out that bed?'

The first few days passed in a whirlwind of excitement and activity. The lavish cocktail reception to welcome the guests on board that first night set the tone for the whole cruise. They were pampered and cosseted at every step. When they woke on the first morning Dante jumped out of bed to open the curtains and gave a squeal when she saw that, as promised, the dramatic stage set of New York had been replaced by a wilderness of vast grey ocean.

As newlyweds and suite occupants they were invited to dine with the captain at dinner on their first day. The captain and his other guests were charming company and seemed charmed in turn by the Harringtons. 'What a darling couple!' exclaimed Lady Harper to the captain, as Blake excused them from the table and led Dante to the dance floor after the meal. 'The girl is William Kingsford's daughter, did you know? Dear Billy, I had my eye on him at Oxford you know, many moons ago.' Captain Thomas stifled a smile and agreed that the Harringtons were indeed a charming young couple.

Blake made full use of the squash courts, ranking highly on the week's ladder. Dante then lured him to the spa for a couple's massage to soothe his muscles. She enjoyed the spa's tranquil atmosphere amid the orchid displays so much that she returned for a further massage on her own the following day.

As she approached her room she lost her sea legs and almost collided with a steward near her door. 'Oops! I'm so sorry!' she cried. 'No, it was entirely my fault, I do apologise,' said the steward. He gripped her arms, steadying her, looking intently into her face.

Dante started to feel a little uncomfortable, and stepped away. She laughed lightly. 'I think we're both OK, no harm done.'

She slipped into her room quickly, keen to change out of her spa bathrobe. Blake was using the telephone by the bed. ''No, that can't happen,' he said furiously. 'If that doesn't get finalised we're screwed.' He looked up and saw Dante. 'I'll call you back,' he said into the receiver and abruptly hung up. Dante smiled unsurely. 'Hi babe, is everything OK?' she queried.

He hugged her and kissed her on the forehead. 'Yes, of course.' He gestured impatiently at the phone. 'Just some business I was trying to finalise. I'll speak to them later.' Dante knew better than to complain about him trying to work on their honeymoon. Ever her father's daughter, she knew that business couldn't always wait. 'Anyway,' said Blake brightly, 'I guess we should think about dressing for dinner.'

They passed another enjoyable evening, talking mainly to an older couple from Oregon who were celebrating their 40th wedding anniversary and had saved up for the cruise for many years. Dante was touched to hear Blake tell the couple in great detail about their own wedding and how beautiful he thought Dante had looked.

'It reminds me,' he added, 'that I must never take my wife for granted. I plan to dance with her as often as possible. Shall we?' He stood up, holding out a hand for Dante, as the big band started a medley of classic love songs.

Edith slapped Art with her purse. 'Now look! That's romance. Don't tell me it's dead – take me dancing!' She winked at Dante and got up to join the other couples, Art grumbling as they went. Dante willingly followed Blake onto the dance floor and lost herself in the music. 'I always love dancing with you,' she murmured to him.

It seemed as if it was only moments later that the band announced their last song. Dante lifted her head from Blake's chest to find the dance floor nearly empty. Blake smiled down at her. 'We've out-danced everyone,' he said. 'They all drifted off to bed, I think it's quite late.' He looked at his watch behind Dante's head. 'Yep, it's getting late. Nearly 1am! How about a refreshing spell out on deck before we go to bed?' he suggested.

'Sounds good,' agreed Dante. 'The stars seem so bright out here in the middle of nowhere, it's amazing.'

They strolled arm-in-arm along the length of the deck, nodding at a couple of other strays enjoying the crisp night air. Meandering slowly, they eventually reached the very back of the ship and leaned together on the railing at the side. Even the other night owls seemed to have headed off to sleep now. Nobody else was around. Dante gazed up at the black velvet above them twinkling with its countless, priceless diamonds. 'So beautiful,' she sighed. 'I wish we could see them like this in New York. I can see the Milky Way and everything, look!'

'Mmmm,' replied Blake. 'It's quite stunning.' He stood close behind Dante and slid an arm around her waist. He stroked his other hand down her arm and held both of her hands under his against the rail, clasping her tightly in front of him.

Dante shifted uncomfortably. 'Honey, you're squashing me,' she complained. Blake didn't move, just clutched her hands more tightly. His voice was low, his mouth right by her ear. 'You know, people often go missing from cruise ships. No-one can ever prove what happened to them.' Dante shivered involuntarily. Her eyes were drawn to the heaving, choppy water churning far below around the back of the ship. Blake still gripped her hands tightly. Too tightly. Something wasn't right.

Dante was suddenly frightened. 'Blake, you're scaring me,' she said sharply. 'What are you doing?' She tried to push back against him to get away but he wouldn't budge. She strained to pull her hands from under his, frightened by his tight grip around her waist. She was deadly aware of his superior size and strength. The droning engine noise seemed suddenly oppressive. She was trapped. She couldn't take her eyes off the slate-grey water frothing sinisterly many metres below.

She felt a jolt of pure terror and struggled frantically, trying to free her hands so that she could hold on properly.

Blake's grip suddenly released her and she stumbled out of his arms. Two stewards strolled around the corner towards them. 'Good evening ma'am, sir,' they nodded. 'Good evening,' called Dante urgently. 'May I walk back with you? It's too cold to stay out here.' She caught up with them, her heart racing, not looking back at Blake. She walked with the stewards along the deck and back inside, through the empty bar and along to her floor.

Blake trailed a few steps behind, not catching up with Dante until she reached their room. She tried to get into the room before him and shut him out but in her nervousness she fumbled the key. Blake took it from her hands and opened the door for her. He followed her inside. 'Dante, I'm so sorry I frightened you. I wasn't trying to hurt you. As if I would!' he exclaimed, looking wounded. 'You're my wife. You're the most precious thing in the world to me. Why are you so frightened? I was just imagining how awful it would be to lose you and I held on too tightly. I'm sorry.' He held out his arms. 'Come here, let me give you a big hug.'

Dante backed away from him, her eyes as wide as saucers, her face pale. She shook her head. 'I just got a little frightened of being on the ship,' she stammered. 'Your story about people going missing was scary.' She felt the bathroom door behind her back, and grabbed the handle. 'I'm going to take a bath,' she gasped, rushing inside and slamming the lock closed.

She heard Blake pacing around the room. She ran the bath taps and sank down onto the floor next to the bath. Her heart was still pounding and her eyes filled with tears.

'Was that what I think it was?' she asked herself miserably, her recent conversation with her father instantly in her mind. 'Was Blake trying to kill me?' She remembered his steely grip on her hands and his arm around her waist. 'If he had wanted to, he could have thrown me overboard as easily as he liked.' She waited for her racing heart to slow down.

'He wouldn't do that though,' she reasoned. 'He loves me.' She shook her head. 'I can't believe I'm even having these thoughts. What's wrong with me?' She decided she would take the bath now that she had run it, and try to relax.

She poured in a plentiful gloop of satin cream and shook her hand in the water to froth up the bubbles. She shrugged off her cashmere sweater and slipped out of her dress and underwear before easing herself into the hot water. The steam relaxed her and she breathed deeply, trying to think calmly. 'Let's be serious,' she thought. 'I'm imagining there was something weird happening out there. I must be.' She watched some bubbles dissolve on her hand, trying to remember the stab of fear she had experienced. It all seemed so unreal now that she was in the warm luxury of the bathroom.

She leaned her head back against the edge of the bath, enjoying the warmth lapping around her throat. She thought of the way he had looked at her at their wedding. She remembered the way he had held her the night of their rehearsal dinner as he said that he would never let her go. She took a deep breath and relaxed her shoulders. She recalled all the lovely things he regularly said about her. 'He values me. I'm precious to him. I'm his asset, his treasure.' A whisper in her brain made her sit upright. She ran through his endearments once more. 'They're all about money,' she whispered fearfully. Her conversation with her father raced through her mind once again. 'Am I just another expendable heiress?'

Her blood ran cold as she recalled something else from the rehearsal dinner. 'He received a phone call about insurance and didn't want me to hear it.' Dante felt nauseous. Everything seemed unreal and yet blindingly obvious. 'Oh God,' she moaned. 'He's taken out an insurance policy on me, and now he's trying to kill me.' She felt light-headed, and rested her face on the cool edge of the bath tub. She groaned as she recalled his phone conversation earlier that day. 'It sounded like his business wasn't going well. Am I his way out of financial trouble?'

Her father's concerns about her marrying so young echoed around her head. She remembered her cousins' delight at the romance of Blake proposing marriage only a few months after meeting her, but now she felt only foolishness. 'I don't know enough about him. And now he's trying to kill me,' she thought dully. Her limbs felt like lead. She lay back in the bath, not moving.

Eventually she became aware that the water was cold and all the bubbles had long gone. There was no sound from the bedroom.

Dante dragged herself out of the bath and let the water drain. She wrapped herself in a fluffy towel and dried herself slowly, trying to delay opening the door. She caught sight of her frightened face in the heated mirror. 'It's OK,' she told herself. 'He can't do anything to me in our room, it would be too suspicious. He's not stupid. I'll just try and play along and hope he doesn't see that I'm suspicious of him. Then as soon as we reach Spain I'll get on land and report my suspicions and fly home. I just have to stay safe. Daddy will send someone to help me.'

At the thought of her father a wave of misery swept over Dante. She thought of all the trouble and expense he had gone to for her lavish wedding. Her wedding. A huge sob rose in her throat at the thought that none of it had been real and she wept quietly. 'I can't believe this is happening,' she whispered.

Eventually she wiped her red eyes and prepared to leave the bathroom. She tied a robe tightly around herself. 'I'll just say I feel much better after my bath and that I'm really tired,' she thought resolutely. 'Then I just have to get through tomorrow and part of the next day and it will all be OK.' She listened at the door. Nothing. She turned the lock and opened the door, trying to act naturally. To her relief Blake was already in bed, fast asleep.

She moved silently across the floor and changed into her night clothes. She pulled off her engagement and wedding rings as she did every night, not wanting to scratch herself in her sleep on any of the diamonds. Thankful for the enormous bed, she lifted the covers and climbed into her side without disturbing Blake. She reached out to turn off the light and lay in the dark, mind racing, ears straining for any sound. She felt entirely vulnerable.

'I have to talk to someone,' she thought. 'I can't do this alone.' She thought longingly of her father, but instantly worried about his age and stress levels. 'I can't worry Daddy just yet. Maybe I really am just worrying about nothing. I'll text Paige.'

She groped a careful hand down to where she knew her handbag lay. She eased open the side compartment and felt for her telephone. She turned it on, hiding the glow under the covers. 'Damn!' she swore, seeing that she had no signal. She slid the phone back into the bag and returned the bag to the floor. 'I'll have to try again in the morning.' She lay staring at the dark ceiling, trying not to think about the endless depths of cold ocean outside the window. It was only as the sky started to announce the dawn that she fell into a troubled sleep.

Chapter 3

Dante awoke what felt like only moments later. She could tell by the light that it was morning and that she had at least been asleep for a few hours. She wondered why her eyes felt so gritty and then she remembered the events of the previous night. Everything came rushing back to her and her heart lurched. She lay very still, listening for Blake. She heard the regular breathing that meant he was still fast asleep.

Gingerly she eased back the covers and slipped out of bed. She slipped out of her cobalt blue silky shorts and camisole and threw on some Capri pants and a vest top as quietly as possible. Grabbing her flip flops and her bag in one hand she stepped carefully to the coffee table to scribble a note to Blake. *'Gone to the spa again, I'll find you later, D.'*

She forced herself to add a kiss to the note, then tiptoed to the door. Blake stirred as she touched the handle and she stood statue-like, her heart pounding loudly enough to wake the whole ship. Blake turned over and resumed his sleepy breathing, and Dante slowly released the breath she hadn't realised she was holding. She turned the handle quickly and quietly and slipped out into the hallway, closing the door silently behind her. She slipped her feet into her flip-flops, shouldered her bag and hurried down the corridor.

The serene atmosphere of the ship reminded her that it was still very early and she realised that the spa would not yet be open. She headed instead for the coffee shop at the far end of the ship, well away from

43

where she and Blake usually breakfasted. Relieved to find it open, Dante entered and placed herself in a little nook behind a rack of newspapers. A smiling waiter came over and Dante ordered a cappuccino.

Delving in her bag for her phone, she checked to see if she had a signal. Still nothing. 'Well,' she reasoned, trying not to be too disappointed. 'It's still the middle of the night in New York anyway, so there'd be no point in texting just yet.' The waiter delivered her drink and she pensively stirred in some sugar. She glanced at her watch. 'Still far too early for the spa.' She beckoned the waiter back over and ordered a bacon and egg sandwich with plenty of tomato sauce. 'If ever there was a day for comfort food, this is it,' she decided.

She took as long as she could over breakfast, pushing the food she had no appetite for around her plate, dawdling until the spa was due to open. She arrived there, slightly out of breath from hurrying surreptitiously down the ship's corridors, just as the receptionist was opening the door. 'Good morning Mrs Harrington,' the receptionist said brightly, crossing to her appointments book. She frowned slightly, a crease denting her perfectly smooth forehead. 'Did we have you booked in for something this morning?' she asked anxiously.

'No, I don't have anything booked, but I so enjoyed my last couple of treatments that I'd like to try some more,' said Dante, glancing behind her.

'Of course, we'd be delighted. However,' the receptionist moved a manicured nail down the page, 'I'm afraid we're all booked up until midday.' She started to apologise but Dante cut in. 'That's fine, I'll take midday.' She quickly scanned the menu of treatments, noting the time allotted to each. 'I'll have a...um...full body massage. And a deluxe rose exfoliation. And a facial,' she added quickly. 'And may I wait in the spa until my appointment?'

'Of course madam,' said the receptionist, looking uncertainly at the clock, then at Dante. 'Won't you please follow me, and we'll get you settled in with some magazines and a lovely cup of herbal tea.'

Dante breathed more easily as she felt the now familiar jasmine-scented air of the spa envelop her. She changed into a fluffy, over-sized bathrobe and waffle slippers and shut her belongings in a bamboo locker, slipping her phone into her bathrobe pocket. She settled herself in a comfortable armchair in the heart of the sanctuary, soothed by the trickling water feature in the corner and the steam coming from her camomile tea. Other guests came and went before their treatments but nobody disturbed Dante. Eventually it was time for her first treatment and the therapist came to collect her.

Dante tried hard to relax but couldn't stop her mind whirring around. Between her second and third treatments she had to wait for a few moments while the room was prepared. She used the time to check her phone. 'Oh, thank God,' she breathed, seeing a solitary bar bravely shining on her screen. 'We must be just near enough land that I can pick up the signal,' she thought. Texting quickly, scared to lose the low signal, she selected Paige from her contacts and typed, 'Think B is trying to kill me. Really. Can't worry dad but scared. What shall I do? Help me xx'. She pressed send and waited what seemed like an age until the screen confirmed the message had been sent.

She could barely keep from checking her phone throughout her facial. She buzzed with anticipation. 'Paige will have a good idea, I know it,' she thought firmly. 'She'll know what I should do.' She thanked the therapist distractedly when her facial was complete and reached immediately for her phone. She opened it eagerly. Nothing. She swallowed hard, trying to smother her disappointment. 'Paige probably hasn't even received the text yet,' she rationalised.

She dressed slowly, signed for her treatments and stood outside the spa, unsure of what to do next. She looked at her watch. It was the middle of the afternoon. 'If Blake has stuck to his usual routine he'll be competing fiercely at squash around about now,' Dante thought. She decided it would be safe to head back to their room for a shower. 'Perhaps I can catch a movie after that,' she thought, 'and make it all the way to dinner without seeing him. By tomorrow lunchtime we should have reached Spain.'

She wandered slowly back to the suite, checking her phone every few seconds. Still nothing. She was just slipping her phone back into her bag and rummaging for the door key when she heard Blake calling her.

'Dante! There you are!' he cried. 'I've been looking all over for you.' He hurried up to her and hugged her. Dante tried not to hold herself too rigidly, but to act naturally.

'Didn't you see my note?' she asked, trying to smile at him.

Blake looked confused. 'Well, yes, but I didn't think you'd be at the spa all day. Were you?' he asked incredulously. Dante turned and let herself into the room. 'I decided I'd get my spa addiction out of my system and try out everything I wanted to all in one day,' she improvised, dropping her bag onto the coffee table. 'Now I'm free to try some other things too, maybe the climbing wall.'

'Well, OK then. Climbing it is for us tomorrow! You don't need any beauty treatments anyway, you already look like a million dollars.' Dante winced at the term but Blake didn't seem to notice. He moved closer to her. 'I thought maybe you were avoiding me,' he said playfully, with a smile that didn't reach his eyes.

'Of course not, don't be silly,' stammered Dante. 'Why on earth would I be avoiding you on our honeymoon? I thought you'd be playing squash and I wouldn't be missed. I guess it all took longer than I thought.'

She dropped into an armchair to stop Blake's advance. He looked at his watch. 'Well, I could make the last matches if I leave now, if you're sure you're OK?' he asked.

'Of course! You should go, honestly,' Dante urged. 'I have a headache coming on, so I think I might just spend the rest of the day quietly in here.'

Blake grabbed his gym bag and dropped a kiss on the top of her head. Dante flinched and immediately hoped he hadn't noticed. Blake paused, staring at her intently. Dante stared at her hands. 'Maybe it is best if you have some time to yourself,' Blake murmured. He hung back at the door, smiling concernedly at her. 'Take some painkillers – there are some in the bathroom. You can't have a headache tonight, we've been invited back to the captain's table. Quite the honour, twice in one cruise!' He pulled the door shut behind him.

Dante was surprised to see that she was trembling. She cursed the captain's invite. She had wanted to stay safe and alone in her own bedroom all evening. She shook herself. 'Pull yourself together Dante. Maybe it's for the best. Nothing can happen to me in front of all those people and if Blake suggests another 'romantic' moonlight stroll I'll refuse. I just have to keep my wits about me.'

She checked once again to see if she had any text messages, slamming down her phone in frustration when she saw that the signal had now disappeared again. She felt very alone.

By 7pm Dante had put a brave face on things quite literally, applying her make up with care so that she looked her best. 'Maybe I can seduce Blake into not wanting to kill me,' she joked to herself hollowly. She made up her eyes slightly more heavily than her usual fresh-faced look, emphasising their brilliant clear aqua shade. She wore a sapphire-coloured sheath that clung to her curves and set off her caramel blonde highlights to perfection. An appreciative whistle made her jump. She turned to see Blake leaning nonchalantly in the doorway, his eyes running hungrily over her shape in the clingy satin.

'You look good enough to eat,' he purred, strolling towards her and running a finger across her neckline. Goosebumps rose on Dante's skin. She smoothed her hair and smiled up at him. Her usual low heels didn't do much to counteract the height difference between them.

'You look pretty great yourself,' she replied. She didn't have to lie. It gave her a wrench to see just how overwhelmingly masculine he looked in his black tie, his dark hair tousled and still slightly damp from the shower. She squashed the thought and tried to concentrate. 'We'd better go if we don't want to keep the captain waiting,' she said lightly. She grabbed her clutch and Blake shepherded her from the suite.

Blake was incredibly attentive at dinner, more so than usual. Several of the couples at the table were openly envious of the attractive young couple. More than one wife pinched her husband for staring at Dante, while secretly wishing that her husband was as handsome and charming as Blake.

Dante tried hard to be vivacious and witty so that the meal would last as long as possible. She had determined not to drink but Blake had proposed toast after toast to various silly topics, leaving their table in fits of laughter, and had insisted that she join in. She struggled not to feel oppressed by Blake's arm on the back of his chair, his hand casually caressing the back of her neck. The Champagne was going to her head really quickly, she could feel it. Her water glass was empty and she looked around the table to see if she could see any more.

'Allow me madam.' A low voice spoke discreetly in her ear and she recognised the steward she had nearly bumped into outside her room the previous day. He poured her a full glass of water from the bottle he was carrying and moved away to the next table.

Dante drank gratefully, trying desperately to clear her head. She tried to join in with the rest of the table, taking another small sip of Champagne to hide her plan not to drink. Her head felt fuzzier by the second. She couldn't focus properly on what her neighbours were saying to her and she had an overwhelming urge to lay her head down on the table. Her head started to droop, and she heard Blake's concerned voice. 'Sweetheart? Dante, are you OK?' She sat up, feeling hot and feverish, aware of the knowing glances that some of the women were sharing over their Champagne flutes. 'I don't feel well,' she mumbled.

'You don't look well darling,' agreed Blake. He started to support her up from the table. 'Captain Thomas, please excuse us from the table, my wife isn't well. I think I should take her on deck for a breath of fresh air.'

'No!' burst out Dante, panic-stricken, wind-milling her arms as best she could to shake Blake off. An embarrassed hush fell on the neighbouring tables, as long necks craned to see what was happening. 'OK, OK, we'll go back to our room, shhhh, it's OK,' soothed Blake. Dante swayed ominously. The captain stood up to help Blake. 'Is there anything I can do Mr Harrington?' he enquired. Blake shook his head as he swung an unwilling Dante up into his arms. 'No, thank you sir. I'll take her back to our room. I know she had a headache earlier on – perhaps her painkillers are reacting with the alcohol. I'm so sorry that we've disturbed your dinner.'

'Don't mention it at all. I hope Mrs Harrington feels better, and we'll look forward to seeing you both tomorrow. If it's anything more serious please do ring for Dr Haines, he's available at any hour.'

'Thank you sir.' Blake strode off to their suite, Dante mumbling and shaking her head in his arms as they went.

Back at their room Blake sat Dante gently on the edge of the bed. He stared down at her for a moment before easing her shoes off her feet and placing them neatly on the floor. Dante felt as if her head were in a vice. Her vision was blurred and furry but she could make out Blake holding a glass of what looked like water in front of her. 'Drink some,' he directed her. Dante clamped her lips shut and shook her head woodenly. The movement hurt. 'Dante please!' urged Blake. Dante kept her lips shut tight and closed her eyes. 'Drink it!' said Blake, his voice suddenly fierce. He grasped Dante's jaw with one hand, trying to force it open and pour in the liquid. Dante squirmed away, sobbing in her throat.

Exasperated, Blake shoved the glass onto the bedside table and pulled Dante to her feet. He yanked down the zip at the back of her dress and pushed it off her with one hand, holding her upright with the other. Dante moaned, not wanting him to touch her. She fumbled his hands away as he tried to remove her underwear, starting to cry. 'Fine,' sighed Blake. 'Keep them on.' He felt under her pillow and pulled out her camisole and shorts, helping her into them. He pulled the covers back for her and lay her in the bed, before tucking her in. Dante felt her face was burning. She felt hot all over. She writhed under the covers, pushing them off her hot skin.

She heard Blake talking quietly into the phone, then felt him stroking her hair as she lay on the bed, finally still. 'Don't worry my darling,' he murmured. 'By tomorrow this should all be over.' Dante tried weakly to struggle up but sleep took her and she collapsed back against the pillows.

Snatches of reality came to Dante and then flew out of reach as she tried to hold onto them. 'Am I dreaming?' she wondered. Her head felt heavy and her limbs were wooden to match. She felt carpet under her bare feet as she stumbled along. 'Why aren't I walking properly?' she pondered slowly. She tried to concentrate on her left side. It felt warmer than her right. She realised that somebody was helping her along, her left arm flung over their shoulders. She took a deep breath and registered the scent of Blake's aftershave. She turned towards him but encountered only darkness as she was marched swiftly along. 'Why can't I see anything?' she asked.

She became aware that she was being carried upstairs and then wind suddenly whipped around her. 'I'm on a boat,' she thought groggily. 'I like boats.' Now her feet were sliding on damp wood. Salt air was on her lips. Still she was being helped relentlessly forward by her unseen companion.

She stumbled as they came to a stop and her arm was suddenly dropped to her side. Large hands on hers roughly forced her fingers to untie the robe knotted around her waist and she shivered as the robe dropped to the ground.

Something rang a warning in Dante's brain as the fresh air started to revive her. 'What's happening Blake?' she asked fearfully. 'Where am I?' No answer. The sound of waves below made her heart bang like frantic jungle drums in her chest. 'No!' she cried helplessly. 'No! I'm on deck! Don't do this Blake! I can't-'

A hand was clamped harshly over her mouth and muffled her cries. She writhed frantically, aware now that she was blindfolded, aware that she was in terrible danger. She tried to bite the hand but it just gripped her face harder, hurting her mouth. She tried to kick her captor but he was too big to care. Suddenly, in one fluid movement Dante felt herself lifted up, heaved over the railings and then dropped into mid-air.

The breath flew out of her lungs as the sea rushed up to claim her. She didn't even have time to scream.

Chapter 4

The canvas sail flapped noisily in the breeze. A gull squawked insistently overhead in the cloudless sky. The young woman stirred on her thin mat on the small deck as spray misted her bare legs. Moaning with pain she woke abruptly. She stared about her, not knowing where she was, eyes squinting painfully in the bright sunlight. She could hardly move. Her entire back felt like one enormous bruise, as if she had been repeatedly slammed into a wall. Her right wrist throbbed painfully. She turned her head slowly, her temples exploding, and whimpered faintly when she saw her wrist jutting out at entirely the wrong angle. She tried to speak but no sounds came to her parched throat. Her face burned and stang whenever spray landed on her from over the low side of the boat.

A thin man, dressed in a once-white tunic over filthy brown trousers popped his head up on deck from below. Seeing her awake he called to her. She had no idea what he had said. He clambered onto the deck and crouched next to her head, offering her water from a jug. She opened her mouth and yelped with pain. She tried again, opening her mouth only a small amount to avoid antagonising her aching jaw. He poured slowly and she relished the water trickling down her throat. He spoke again - a question judging by his quizzical expression - but she simply stared at him in confusion. 'I don't understand,' she managed to croak. He smiled tentatively, his teeth yellow against his black skin, seeming at a loss as to what to say to her.

Revived slightly by the fluid, she slowly surveyed the rest of the deck. She noted with surprise half a dozen other people lying together on the other side of the deck all staring at her listlessly.

Two more men arrived on deck, hurrying to pull down the flapping sail. They stared with eyes full of curiosity at her as they made their way back across the deck, picking their way over legs and bodies, before ducking below once more. The water-bearer walked to the back of the boat. He threw out some large nets to be trawled along in their wake. He sat low on the floor, mostly hidden to any passing boats, one hand on the nets.

She turned her face out of the blazing sun and tried not to focus on the searing agony in her wrist. Lying perfectly still to avoid any twinges tormenting her back, she allowed the gentle rocking of the boat to lull her to sleep once more.

She awoke to urgent whispers around her. It was pitch black, but someone was shining a small beam erratically around the boat. The light shone in her face and she shut her eyes against the glare. 'Bien. Vamanos,' she heard in a low voice. Her mat was lifted by its four corners and she cried out in pain. Several voices shushed her, their anger evident even in their whispers.

She struggled not to make any more noise as she was carried joltingly off the boat and onto the shore. She could hear many feet splashing through shallow water, then muffled steps on sand. The men carrying her grunted with the effort and she had the sense that they were walking uphill. It was as if the moon had never existed. Not a scrap of light assisted their progress other than the one small torch at the front of the procession.

She heard a slight clunk ahead as a door opened. Moments later she was lifted roughly into the back of a van. The doors clicked shut quietly, and the van pulled away. She gasped as she rolled against the doors. Pain shot from her wrist and every muscle in her back screamed in agony. She could feel people squashed up against her left side and she strained her eyes in the darkness, trying in vain to see another face. 'Where are they taking me?' she wondered. 'Is this a dream?'

The van drove for what seemed like hours, every minute like torture to her injured body. At last they came to a stop and the rear doors were flung open. Once again her eyes flinched away from the torchlight shining in her face. Someone she couldn't see dragged her mat out. She caught a glimpse of a rotting wooden door in the torch's beam as she was carried into a building, before being placed on the floor. She felt so strange, and in so much pain, that she started to sob quietly. No-one came to her aid.

She heard other people filing in and shuffling around before the door was closed. Only then was a light switched on – a bare bulb hanging from an exposed wire. Its dim light revealed some sort of outhouse, totally bare apart from the 15 or so people blinking confusedly in the light and several thick cobwebs clustered in the corners.

The young woman recognised all the people she had seen on the boat deck, plus a handful more. About ten were men, the rest were women. All looked pitifully thin and horribly dirty.

She became aware of an older woman near the door, her hand on the light switch. She said a few words and the men followed her obediently from the room. The young woman looked at the other women in the room. One stared sullenly back at her, the others stared carefully at nothing, some looking frightened, some tired.

The older woman returned, carrying a plastic bag. She handed a bread roll to each of the women then disappeared once more, turning off the light as she went and locking the door behind her. The young woman could hear the other captives tearing into the bread like hungry wolves. She felt too strange and flimsy to consider eating. The pain in her wrist was unbearable. She slipped in and out of consciousness.

Some time later there was a rattling as the door was unlocked and the light was flicked on once more. The older woman was now accompanied by a well-dressed lady wearing a hat with a lacy black veil which obscured most of her face. She peered intently at each of the women before pointing to the tallest of them and announcing something out loud. The older woman instantly beckoned the tall girl forward but another girl rushed forward with her, her sister judging by their near identical faces, thought the young woman. The sister fell on her knees in front of the visitor, imploring her in a strange language.

The visitor seemed not even to notice her, simply summoned the tall girl and made to leave the room. The sister started to scream and plead, trying to grab onto the visitor's skirt. A loud crack exploded across the room as the older woman smacked the back of her hand hard into the sister's cheek, shocking her into silence. The three women left the room.

Almost immediately the older woman returned, accompanied by a squat man in suit trousers and rolled-up shirt sleeves. Sweat had left dark stains under his arms but he looked otherwise presentable. His black hair was slicked back with grease. He surveyed the room for a few moments, then spoke quietly in the older woman's ear, looking over as he did so at the young woman lying on her mat. He reviewed the other three remaining women and approached the youngest one. He pushed back her matted hair, holding his fingers under her chin to look at her filthy face more clearly in the dim light. He said something sharply to her and watched her closely as she turned in a slow circle. He snapped his fingers and nodded, turning back to the older woman. She pushed the girl to follow the man then bent down to the young woman on the mat. Taking hold of her good arm, she yanked her up into sitting, then into standing. The young woman cried out in pain, and received a slap in the face. The older woman hissed some words at her that she didn't understand and dragged her outside. The young woman could barely walk, but stumbled slowly in agony alongside her jailer.

A small van waited outside the building. The two young women were shoved towards it, and made to clamber awkwardly into the back. The older woman covered them both with rugs and blankets.   Just before her head was covered the young woman heard crying from the other girl. She blacked out again, nauseous from her wrist pain as the van bumped over deep pot-holes in the roads.

She revived a little as the road surface changed. Now the van was gliding at speed along much smoother roads.   After some time she felt the van slow, then stop completely, then start up again on what sounded like gravel. The engine was turned off and for a moment all was still. 'Where am I now?' wondered the young woman.

The van doors were wrenched open. The rugs and blankets were peeled back and the squat man peered in. He gestured to another man to lift the young woman out. He peered more closely at the other girl and swore quietly, calling out a sharp order. He turned to the young woman, noting her pallid face and drooping stance.   Supporting her with one arm, he half carried her towards the house. The young woman noted flaming torches illuminating a large driveway area leading to an imposing villa, mostly in darkness. She whimpered, wondering where she was being taken now. She couldn't hear the other girl following.

She was half dragged around to the side of the house, dropping with pain and exhaustion.   A heavy door was pulled open from inside and she was helped along a well-lit corridor. She took in large terracotta tiles on the floor and white-washed walls before she was dragged through another doorway and down some stone stairs. Her eyes adjusted slowly to the dimmer lighting on the lower floor as they descended.

A slender woman who looked to be in her late forties, with long dark hair and kind eyes, met the man at the bottom of the steps and preceded him into a room on the left. The man lowered the young woman onto a mattress on the floor, muttered something to the other woman and left the room abruptly.

The young woman moaned deliriously, feeling feverish. She felt the room slipping away from her. She tried to hold on to the image of the dark haired lady bending over her, but the waves of pain battered her into submission.

Chapter 5

She dreamed of boats. Water splashed onto her face and wet her lips. She put out her tongue but couldn't taste salt. Groggily she opened her eyes.

The dark haired lady was sitting on the edge of the mattress, dipping a cloth in cool water. Seeing that the girl was awake she smiled, offering her a glass of water. The young woman realised she was incredibly thirsty. She leaned up, clutching greedily at the glass and slurping down the water. 'Tranquillo, tranquillo,' murmured the older woman, easing the glass away with a smile. She turned to a side table and carefully turned back with a bowl full of soup. The young woman's senses were overwhelmed at the delicious scents of spices rising from the bowl. Her stomach growled like an accelerating motorbike. Sitting up stiffly, she automatically reached out her right hand, then stopped in surprise to see it encased in plaster. 'El doctor,' explained the lady. 'Esta bien ahora. Solo seis semanas.'

She spooned the soup into the young woman's mouth. Her taste buds burst into life as the meaty broth slid down her throat. She devoured the bowlful and felt life flooding into her. She lay back on the mattress. 'Thank you,' she whispered to her carer.

'Inglesa?' enquired the other lady. 'Americana? What your name?'

The young woman stared at her. Her mind was completely blank. 'I don't know,' she faltered. 'I don't know what my name is.' She tried to remember who she was, casting her mind back for clues. All she could remember was being on a small boat with people she didn't know. Before that, nothing. Her memory was blank. 'I don't know who I am,' she moaned, shaking her head. She sat up, breathing heavily. She felt disorientated. The older woman patted her soothingly on the shoulder and gestured to her to lie back down. 'Is OK.' She thought for a moment, then pronounced, 'You Aurelia. Si?'

She realised the older woman was trying to help her and she smiled faintly. Aurelia. It was a pretty name. It would be OK for now. She tried the strange name, trying to roll the r in the same way the other woman had done.

'Speak Spanish?' the other woman now enquired. Aurelia shook her head. 'Is OK, I learn you.'

'You speak English.'

'A little,' the woman waved her hand modestly. 'I learn on radio. You learn me more.'

'I'll teach you more,' smiled Aurelia. 'What is your name?' she asked.

'My name Maria.'

'Thank you for the soup Maria, it was delicious.' She pointed at the empty bowl. 'Delicious.'

'Gracias,' smiled Maria.

'Where are we? Is this a hospital?' Aurelia asked. A troubled look passed fleetingly across Maria's face and she turned to pick up the empty bowl. 'I come back.' She crossed the room quickly and closed the door behind her.

Aurelia lay back on her mattress, trying again and again to remember something more than the boat.

She strained her mind but came up with nothing. She had no idea what time it was as the room she was in had no windows. She looked around. The room was very small. Her bare single mattress lay on the floor. She was covered with a sheet. Next to her head was a small table made of uneven wood, and another mattress lay on the far side of that. A small home-made wooden crucifix hung on a nail above each mattress. A simple wooden chair sat next to the door, with a small pile of what looked like clothes on it.

Aurelia looked down at herself, noticing that she was wearing a silky blue camisole top. She pushed the sheet aside and saw matching shorts. Both the top and the shorts looked soiled and frayed. She saw that her skin looked sunburnt and she touched her face as the observation triggered a burning feeling there.

As if she had read Aurelia's thoughts, Maria reappeared with a small dish. 'You put,' she said to Aurelia, gesturing at her skin and making rubbing motions. She handed the dish to Aurelia. 'You put,' she repeated. 'Esta muy bien.' Aurelia sniffed the lotion in the bowl. It smelled of plants and fresh air. She scooped up some lotion with her good hand and rubbed it onto her legs. Almost instantly the sunburn was soothed enormously. Eagerly she smoothed some onto her parched face, enjoying the relief from the tightness and burning. She continued moisturising her collarbone and shoulders, luxuriating in the cool lotion until it had all gone. She lay back gratefully, feeling refreshed. Maria left another glass of water on the table for her and gestured for her to sleep. 'You rest. Later we speak.'

Aurelia drank the water then dozed. She felt much more peaceful now that her skin felt better, her stomach was full and her wrist was finally pain-free. The muscles in her back still ached painfully but manageably so. In her waking moments she heard noises from beyond the closed door and entertained herself by trying to decipher them. 'Pans clattering, heavy chairs scraping on stone and dishes being washed,' she decided sleepily. 'I must be near a big kitchen. It sounds like a restaurant.' The noises died down and soon there was silence.

The door swang open and Maria popped her head round, checking to see if Aurelia was awake. On seeing her charge looking more refreshed she helped her up from the mattress. 'Come,' she said. 'Puede lavarse.' Aurelia looked questioningly at her, following her out of the bedroom, but the meaning became clear when she crossed the hallway and found herself in a tiny, very basic bathroom. Aurelia guessed that the hole in the floor was meant to be the toilet. A rusty sink clung to one wall, seemingly propped up by its own brown pipes. A tin bath stood in an alcove opposite the door. It was partially filled with water.

'No es muy caliente,' said Maria, dipping Aurelia's hand in to show the water was only tepid and wouldn't hurt her skin. She pointed out a well-used bar of soap and a small, tattered blue towel and tactfully withdrew, pulling a curtain across the alcove as she left.

Aurelia stepped out of her shorts, camisole and underwear and climbed into the bath. There was no room to recline but the water still felt divine to her. She sat with her knees bent up, leaning back on the edge as

66

much as she could, enjoying the water on her body. She rested her cast on the edge of the bath. Maria's hand groped under the curtain and whisked away her discarded clothes. 'Voy lavar!' she called in. Aurelia now recognised the word for washing, and smiled.

She wet her hair and clumsily cleaned her face with one hand, feeling the best she had since being on the small boat. She sent up a grateful prayer for Maria. 'I don't know why she took me in, or where I am, but thank goodness I'm with her,' she thought. She reached for the soap and slowly washed herself as best she could, enjoying feeling properly clean.

As she leant over to replace the soap she heard a sound at the curtain. She caught a glimpse of dark hair and a beard as she saw an eye looking at her around the side of the curtain. She instinctively covered her breasts with a cry. She heard a man's quiet laugh, then the face disappeared.

Apprehensive now, Aurelia sat for a moment without moving. Then, hearing no further sounds, she hurried to step out of the bath and dry herself off. The towel was not large enough to wrap around herself afterwards. She peered around the curtain to see if her clothes had been left anywhere nearby. There was no sign of them.

She tiptoed across the small room and peeped outside the bathroom. Outside was some sort of hallway, devoid of furniture. She could see daylight dimly filtering in from what she presumed was a window hidden around the corner to her right and a closed door right at the end but there was no sign of anyone.

She held the towel tightly over her front as best she could, took a deep breath and scurried across the hallway into the sanctuary of her room. To her relief the room was empty, and she saw a set of clothing on her mattress. She coated herself in more lotion from the dish that had been placed on the table then dressed in the white cotton skirt and pale coffee-coloured top. 'This is exactly the same as the outfit Maria was wearing,' she noted as she dressed. She slipped her feet into the cork flip-flops which had been left out for her.

Now dressed, she decided to try and find out where she was. Stepping out into the hallway she flip-flopped along the smooth tiles, wincing as the muscles in her back ached. Rounding the corner she found that the hallway opened up into a large kitchen. Dozens of blackened pots and pans hung from ironwork strung in a grid across the ceiling. Late afternoon sun crept down through the window high up on the far wall, catching the motes dancing in the air. Aurelia sensed that she was on the lower ground floor from the angle of the sun's rays. Two large sinks stood under the window, a pile of clean dishes next to them as if they had recently been washed.

Maria stood at the large table in the centre of the room, chopping a huge pile of tomatoes, her long hair tied back in a loose plait. Two other young women kneaded dough listlessly at one of the work counters, wearing identical outfits to Aurelia. Seeing her, Maria put down the knife, wiping her hands quickly on her apron. 'Hola Aurelia,' she said quietly. She pulled her forward to sit on a stool at the counter next to her.

She gestured at the other girls. 'Sofia y Ana,' she explained. Aurelia smiled over her shoulder at them but they just carried on kneading their dough. Maria continued her chopping. Aurelia rested her cast on the table and looked earnestly at Maria. 'Please tell me where we are,' she requested. Maria hesitated before answering.

'We are in Spain,' she said eventually, confirming Aurelia's guess. 'In the very South. We are in the house of Señor Luis Jose Alvarez.' Aurelia noticed a tension in the air at the mention of her host's name. 'We work here.' She glanced at Aurelia quickly. 'You work here. We are his...' Maria paused, grasping for the correct word in English. 'Como se dice esclavos in ingles?' she asked Sofia. Sofia shrugged, neither knowing nor caring. 'Ah, lo se,' Maria said, remembering. She looked down, continuing to chop. 'We are his slaves.'

Aurelia laughed. 'You mean you are his servants,' she corrected. Maria stared sadly at her. 'No. We are his slaves.'

Aurelia's heart thumped in her chest. 'Slaves? What kind of a place is this?' she wondered. 'This can't be true.' She looked again at the window and noticed the thin iron bars on the other side of it, decorative yet effective. She looked more closely at Sofia and Ana, noting their thin frames and miserable, drawn faces, their dejected posture. She noticed the heavy door at the end of the room, closed firmly.

She turned despairingly to Maria. 'I can't be a slave,' she pleaded. 'I don't know who I am, but I know I'm not a slave. I'm sure of it.' She shook her arm. 'You have to help me get out of here, please!' Maria frowned with the effort of following Aurelia's rapid English. She shook her head sadly. 'You work here,' she repeated. 'I learn you, you work.'

Aurelia didn't bother to correct Maria's language this time. Her mind raced. Didn't slaves work on chain gangs, doing hard labour? What was she expected to do? Maria saw her confusion and patted her hand. 'We be OK,' she nodded. 'You sleep now.'

Aurelia saw that she wasn't really wanted in the kitchen when they were busy. She trundled back to her room, feeling confused. She closed the door and eased herself back down onto her mattress. She tried desperately to remember anything she could about her real life. Nothing. Nothing at all. Sobbing in frustration, she cried herself to sleep, only remembering just as sleep eventually claimed her that she had not asked Maria about the strange man spying on her in the bath.

Chapter 6

Over the next week it became clear to Aurelia that Maria was trying to keep her out of sight of anyone else. She encouraged her to stay in the bedroom, sneaking bowls of soup or the occasional thin sandwich to her. Aurelia never had enough to eat but was grateful for the food she was given, and for the snatches of company that Maria offered her. Nothing further was mentioned about her being a slave.

They began to teach each other their languages, Maria building quickly on her basic knowledge of English, Aurelia determined to learn Spanish just as quickly. 'You are good at learning,' Maria smiled admiringly one morning, after more proof of Aurelia's good memory. 'Maybe I'm really Spanish,' joked Aurelia to cover the anguish that always came with reminders that she didn't know who she really was. Maria stood to return to the kitchen.

'Can't I help you?' asked Aurelia. 'I know I only have the use of one arm, but I'm sure I could do something. I'm feeling much stronger.' She stood up. 'You and the other girls always seem so busy in there, bustling about, and I just lie here wondering who I am and listening to you out there. Let me help,' she urged the older lady. Maria smiled, although her eyes remained troubled. 'You can help,' she agreed. 'But the small work only, and exactly as I say.'

'Deal,' smiled Aurelia, feeling a strange sensation as she said it. 'Deal,' she said again to herself, as she followed Maria to the kitchen. 'Why does that sound so familiar?' She felt as if something were tugging at the edge of her memory. It slipped away as fast as it had arrived, and Aurelia shook her head to clear it. 'Maybe it will come back to me later,' she thought hopefully.

In the kitchen Maria briefly showed Aurelia where everything was kept, before hurrying over to join Sofia who was expertly gutting and descaling a sizeable pile of fish. 'You stir?' she called back to Aurelia, nodding at a steaming pan on the stove. Aurelia nodded, glad to have something to do at last. She found a wooden spoon and started to stir the rich tomato sauce, finding it slightly awkward with her left hand. Keeping an eye on the pan she looked over at the other two women. 'Where's Ana today?' she asked.

Sofia shot a quick glance at Maria, but Maria just concentrated on decapitating another mackerel. 'She work this week in different part of the house,' she said. Her tone did not invite further enquiries.

Aurelia turned back to the stove, determined not to make a nuisance of herself. 'Maria and Sofia are clearly busy,' she said to herself.

As the morning when on it became clear to Aurelia that the work in the kitchen was non-stop. Maria and Sofia were like a well-oiled machine, albeit one running too fast and with not enough steam. They rushed to and fro, Maria calling out directions and orders, building up between them a veritable mountain of delicious looking food.

The smells tormented Aurelia and her mouth watered. 'Surely it can't be too long until lunch,' she thought. 'I can't wait to try this. Maria is some kind of culinary genius.' She stirred and washed items as

72

directed and tried to squash her stomach rumblings. The kitchen became quite unbearably hot as they worked, the ovens combining with the burners on the stove and the heat of the day outside to make an impromptu sauna. Sweat trickled down Aurelia's forehead and spine.

Eventually the crescendo of frenzied activity began to slow as everything was ready. Maria critically eyed the table as it groaned with food. She expertly added garnishes to certain dishes to complete them – a sprig of parsley here, some chopped chives there.

A bell jangled on the wall near the door, making Aurelia jump. Maria gestured at Aurelia. 'Go to your room,' she hissed. 'Go now.' Aurelia was puzzled but obeyed the urgency in Maria's voice, hurrying down the hallway.

As she reached her room she heard bolts being drawn back on the other side of the kitchen door and the voice of a man speaking harshly to Maria. She heard him climbing back upstairs. Peeping round the corner of her bedroom door she saw Maria and Sofia carrying large, heavily-laden trays of food up the stairs. A few moments later they reappeared and repeated their actions, dishes clinking on the trays on their way up.

When they hadn't reappeared after five minutes Aurelia slipped along to the kitchen. She saw that all the food had gone. She looked around for something to eat herself but saw nothing. 'Don't tell me there's nothing left!' she thought in despair. 'I've been looking forward to that all morning,' she thought as she recalled the amazing dishes that had been concocted before her hungry eyes. She sloped dejectedly back to her room and lay on her mattress, trying to ignore the hunger pains in her stomach.

After some time she heard Maria and Sofia returning to the kitchen. Aurelia peeped out once more and saw them laden down with heavy trays of dirty plates and serving dishes. The kitchen door slammed shut behind them and Aurelia could hear bolts being drawn across on the other side once more. She considered it safe to return to the kitchen, so she made her way there.

Maria and Sofia were stacking the huge pile of dirty dishes next to the sink and preparing to wash them. Sofia ran water and piled crusty serving dishes in to soak. Maria spotted Aurelia hovering uncertainly and smiled at her. She beckoned her over to the large table. 'Come. We eat.' Aurelia felt relief flood through her.

'Oh, thank goodness!' she exclaimed. 'Is there some left for us? I thought it had all gone.' Her voice faltered as she saw Maria collecting up scraps of ham and a few slithers of cheese and trying optimistically to make them spread over three pieces of left over bread. She grated black pepper over them then passed a piece to each of the young women. Taking a bite, she chewed and swallowed before answering Aurelia.

'We cook for the men up there. There are many men who work for Luis. Every day we must serve the breakfast. Every day we must cook the lunch.' She waved a hand at the sink. 'Then we clean, and we start once more to make the dinner. Then we clean again.' She took another bite of her bread.

Aurelia had devoured her scant sandwich and watched hungrily as Maria chewed. 'But what about all the food we just made?' she blurted out. Maria patted her hand. 'Is not for us. Is for them. Many men. They hungry.' She sighed. 'I try keep us food but if they want they take.'

'But you – we – don't have enough to eat,' protested Aurelia.

'Nobody care. We manage. Sometimes, if we lucky, some food is leftover. Then, we eat! If not,' Maria shrugged, looking resigned, 'then we eat only these little...how you say?'

'Scraps,' sighed Aurelia. Sofia had bolted her food down in her usual sulky silence and was back at the sink, clattering dishes. Aurelia stood up and started putting herbs and spices back on the shelves, tidying up as best she could one-handed. 'I wish my plaster was gone so I could help you both more,' she said.

'Do not wish it,' warned Maria. 'With the break in your arm I keep you down here. If your arm good you work upstairs as well.'

'Why is that so bad? Maria?' asked Aurelia. Maria clattered pans at the sink frowning darkly and pretended not to hear the question. Aurelia retrieved a damp cloth from Sofia and started to wipe down the kitchen surfaces. 'Well, maybe I could take cooking lessons from you while my arm is still in a cast,' she suggested brightly. 'You seem to be an amazing cook, I'd love to learn. And then when my wrist is better I can help you properly.'

Maria smiled at her, pleased by the compliment. 'Thank you, that will be nice,' she said. 'We learn cooking, we learn English, aprendemos español - it will be a busy kitchen,' she laughed.

75

'Por que te ries? No es divertido,' spat Sofia suddenly, glaring at Aurelia. Maria paused, pushing her hair back into a tidier knot. 'Sofia wonders why we laugh,' she explained. 'She says living here is not funny. She is right, of course.' She patted Sofia's arm placatingly. 'Tiene razon.' Maria sighed, gazing up at the window, before looking at Aurelia. 'I like to try be happy though still,' she smiled.

'Who are you Maria?' asked Aurelia, suddenly needing to know some answers. 'Why are you here like this?'

Maria nodded, gesturing to Aurelia to stand near her while she started to dry the dishes that Sofia placed on the rack. 'I explain you before,' she began, 'that this the house of Luis Jose Alvarez. Luis is my cousin. My mother was his mother's sister. Luis is not a nice man. He was not a nice child – spoilt by everyone for being the only boy in our family. I am two years older than him and this house should be mine.'

Her eyes flashed as a frown crossed her face. 'We all lived here - is traditional in families in this region before marriage – my family, my aunts, uncles and cousins, our grandparents when they were alive. I was the eldest of the cousins and my father should have left this house to me. Instead, he was tricked by Luis. Tricked in his desire to have a son into believing that Luis really cared for him, and cared for the family. He made my father – a weak man – believe that the house should only be in a man's hands and that if he was made head of the family and the house was left to him he would take care of me and all the other female relations.'

She placed a plate sadly on the counter. 'It was all lies,' she said flatly. 'As soon as my father died Luis show his true self. He keep my mother locked in a room alone, until she die of loneliness and a heart broke soon later.'

Maria's English disintegrated under the weight of her emotion. She sobbed quietly for a moment. Aurelia patted her shoulder until Maria collected herself. She wiped her eyes and continued. 'Is a long time ago now, but still I hurt...He send my sister away but keep me because I like to cook and he need me. I try to run away but he catch me and force me down here. He make the cellars into rooms next to the kitchen. He put bars on the window and bolts on the doors. I am allowed outside only sometimes, and only when watched by one of his guards in the courtyard. He think he is very important, he think people want to kill him. Probably they do. I do not know how he make his money but he a very rich man. Probably he lie and he cheat. He change the house into his own palace he call it, and he keep his friends staying with him. All the time, more friends, more parties. I am here only to cook and to clean.'

'How long have you been down here?' Aurelia asked quietly, not sure she wanted to know the answer.

'Fifteen years,' whispered Maria. Aurelia could not believe her ears. She stated in wonder at Maria. 'Fifteen years?' she repeated incredulously.

'Si. I was 31 when my father died. I was working in the chemist shop in the village and I was to be married.' A sad smile crossed Maria's face. 'Felipe was so handsome. He was in the army and we were

77

engaged already for five years. We were to be married that year when he finish his service but when Felipe returned Luis tell him I had run away with another man in the village.' Maria's voice was low and hollow. 'Felipe left the village and moved away, believing I had betrayed him. Luis was very pleased to tell me this.'

Aurelia was horrified. She felt her eyes welling up in sympathy.

'Without Felipe my life is nothing. I knew I would not escape Luis. But with Felipe gone, there was no reason even to try. I have stay here, feeling thankful at least that I have my cooking, which I have always loved. And I always have some company.'

Both women glanced at Sofia who was sweeping the floor, her face surly.

'Any company is better than none,' said Maria quietly.

'Well, and so who is Sofia? And Ana?' asked Aurelia, puzzled.

Maria gathered up a large bowlful of potatoes and started to peel them. 'For a long time I told Luis that looking after his house and his stomach was too big job for just one person. He ignored me until his many friends started to move in – then he saw that they were not happy with the delays for food, and the cleaning of their bedrooms and so he found others to help me. Sofia and Ana arrived together one day, about eight years ago.' She lowered her voice conspiratorially. 'They tell me they came from Romania, thinking they would find a better life in Spain but they too were tricked and brought here to Luis and now they cannot leave.' She shrugged. 'Ana try to make the best of it and be friendly but Sofia, she just want to be at home. I think her heart also is broken and she not like to talk to anybody.'

She looked with curiosity at Aurelia. 'And now you are here too.' She took in Aurelia's fair skin and light hair. 'You are a mystery. I had convinced Luis that even with Sofia and Ana's help we struggle with the big meals and he said he will get two more girls to help me. From things I overheard I believe he was going to buy two girls from Africa. He is a bad man. But then you arrive, only one person and I think not from Africa!'

Aurelia remembered the other girl. 'I think there was supposed to be another girl, she was in the van with me, but I don't know what happened to her,' she said. She shook her head, confused by Maria's earlier words. 'Did you say he was going to BUY two girls?' she asked, certain she had heard wrong.

'Si. Unfortunately many people are try to come to Spain and they come here against the law. People like my cousin take advantage of them. He buy people like they are cattle,' Maria said in disgust.

Aurelia's mind went back to the dismal shack where she and the other girl had been chosen from the group in the middle of the night. The sweating man had been buying her. Her heart contracted at the thought. She looked at Maria with panic in her eyes. 'This isn't right,' she said. 'I was on a boat, a small boat with lots of other people. I think they were African. I couldn't understand them and I don't know why or how I was on their boat but I wasn't like them.' She took a deep breath, trying to calm herself. 'I thought I would remember who I was and then I could go home, but now you're telling me that Luis will keep me here anyway!' She clutched at the counter as a wave of light-headedness swept over her. Maria gripped her shoulders.

'No!' she said fiercely. 'We will not let that happen. We will try and find your lost memory and until then I will keep you hidden downstairs.' She stroked Aurelia's soft hair. 'It is better if Luis does not see you, does not know you are here. He may forget and then you will be more easily able to escape.' She sighed. 'The first thing is to help you remember, and keep you safe until you do.'

Chapter 7

Aurelia was silent for a moment, trying to take it all in. 'It wasn't Luis himself who...bought us then?' she asked, stumbling over the word. She remembered the greased back hair and sweat stains.

Maria laughed harshly. 'No, Luis does nothing for himself. That was Paolo, one of his men. Luis pays people well to keep them loyal. He has a strong band of staff and followers around him, enjoying his wealth,' she said bitterly. 'Anyway, enough for now,' she said, noting Sofia starting to drag a large tureen onto the stove. 'Now, we cook. Come.'

Aurelia watched in wonder as the other two women started to turn basic ingredients into plentiful dishes full of tantalising aromas. 'It's like magic,' she said to Maria admiringly. She helped wherever she could but mostly tried not to get in the way.

Before her eyes another bountiful feast was prepared as the afternoon drew on, the centrepiece of which was a succulent roast lamb. It looked like far too much food even for a room full of hungry men to devour. 'Sometimes we try make too much on purpose, and hope they will leave some. If so we can eat it,' confided Maria. 'Normally they just carry on eating until all is gone. They are ignorant and greedy.'

Aurelia sighed. 'Couldn't we just take a small amount of something now, while we're cooking it? Would they really notice?'

Maria looked troubled. 'Sometimes we are so hungry we have to –we take a little and eat it very quickly. But they can come in at any moment,' she whispered. 'I never know if someone sits outside the door all the time, or if they stay away from the cellar level until they need our food. In the morning is OK, they never come in early, his men like to sleep. So while we prepare breakfast we can take some extra bread and jam and eat it. Sometimes though they come in later in the day when it is not a mealtime, and if we are eating then they say we are thieves...it is not good for us.' She broke off, shaking her head, lips firmly together.

Aurelia suddenly remembered the man who had spied on her in the bathroom. 'There was a man down here!' she exclaimed in a low voice. She blushed. 'He came into the bathroom while I was taking my bath, I saw him looking around the curtain at me.'

Maria put down her vegetable knife and stared at Aurelia. 'What did he look like?' she asked.

Aurelia considered. 'I only saw him for a second, but he had a beard, with dark hair. Small, very dark eyes and thick eyebrows,' she added, thinking back. Maria started chopping again. 'That is Jorge,' she said contemptuously. 'He is one of the gardeners. I do not think he will tell Luis that you are here because he would have to explain why he had been in the kitchens, and he is not supposed to come in here.'

The room was growing dark and Maria had switched on the lights by the time the bell jangled for dinner to be served. Glancing at the small clock on the wall Aurelia saw that it was 8pm. As before, she ran back to her room so that no-one would see her, keeping her fingers tightly crossed the whole time the others were away that they would bring back some leftovers.

It had been such an enormous meal, she felt sure there would be some for them. She heard the others returning and the door being bolted behind them. She glided along to the kitchen, her mouth watering expectantly. All she saw was a heap of empty dishes. Her heart sank and she felt like crying.

She looked at Maria in despair but Maria's eyes were dancing at her. She beckoned Aurelia over to the table and lifted up the lid on a serving dish. Inside were two perfect roast potatoes, glistening crisply in the already setting fat. Aurelia's eyes widened.

She glanced at Sofia and saw that she was energetically chewing as she stood at the sink. Maria popped one of the remaining potatoes into her mouth and Aurelia did the same. An explosion of flavours burst into her mouth as the warm fat hit her taste buds followed by a hint of rosemary and salt. She chewed hurriedly, torn between wanting to savour the delicious flavour and wanting to get the food into her stomach. Her hungry stomach won, and she was left running her tongue around her mouth wishing for more.

'Thank you,' she whispered gratefully to Maria. 'That was the best potato ever.' Boosted by their illicit treat the women went back to work on the dirty dishes.

Over the next few weeks life settled into a routine. Aurelia remained hidden in the kitchen, helping the other women wherever she could and learning how to cook from Maria. Aurelia wished she had the use of both hands so that she could practise preparing the dishes herself. She was fascinated by the wonderful creations that seemed to come from nothing.

At times she forgot she was imprisoned in the lower floor of the house. Maria was wonderful company and very kind. She found food for the four women whenever she could and her positive nature helped to keep Aurelia's spirits high. Some days Aurelia enjoyed herself so much teaching English among the delicious aromas that she forgot that she wasn't there by choice. Ana too had decided that she would like to learn English and the informal tutoring was sometimes surprisingly merry.

Her wrist started to itch under her cast. Maria noticed her trying to insert a skewer down the inside of the cast to scratch her skin. 'It has been nearly time,' she said. 'We will need to take your wrist out of the plaster.' Aurelia was relieved to hear it. 'At last,' she said. 'Who will do it?'

Maria looked worried. 'One of Luis' associates is a doctor. He stays at the house sometimes. He was here when you were brought in and he was able to mend your arm.' She drew in a breath. 'I will have to get word to Luis that one of us needs to see the doctor and ask that Dr Magri be sent down to us when he is next here. Let us hope that Luis will not ask too many questions.'

Aurelia spent the next week in a state of anticipation. Every day when Maria returned from serving meals Aurelia asked if the doctor had been there. Each time she was disappointed. One afternoon she sat dejectedly in her room trying to resist the awful urge to scratch when Maria popped her head round the door. 'Dr Magri is here,' she said. 'He will come down to us before the dinner. Luis did not even see me asking him.'

'Wonderful,' exclaimed Aurelia. 'I can't wait to have both arms free!' She waited in her room a little apprehensively, wondering if the procedure would hurt. Maria and Ana were still clattering in the kitchen when Aurelia heard the door bolts being undone. 'Buenas noches señoritas,' said a man's voice. Aurelia couldn't hear Maria's reply but she heard footsteps approaching her door. A tall man in his early forties appeared, stooping slightly as he entered through the low doorway. 'Hola señorita.'

'Hola doctor,' replied Aurelia, smiling apprehensively. She held out her arm as he sat next to her on the mattress. He turned her arm backwards and forwards, checking Aurelia's face for signs of discomfort. Seeing none, he opened his black leather case and drew out a small hack saw. Aurelia gasped and drew back.

'Esta bien. Tranquillo,' the doctor soothed, reaching for her arm. His hands were cool and gentle. Aurelia looked on in fascinated horror as he placed the teeth of the saw on the edge of her plaster and started to saw, holding her elbow firmly in his other hand. He worked swiftly and in just a few moments the cast was split in two. He pulled it apart fully and prised it from Aurelia's arm, seeing her wince as a few downy hairs were trapped in the plaster. Finally her arm was free.

She gingerly rotated her wrist in both directions, noticing how thin and wasted her right forearm looked compared to her left. A vivid scar ran along the top of her wrist. The doctor took her hand and helped her circle her wrist, his eyes never leaving her face. She smiled at him, her feminine instincts flattered by the close attention of a handsome man. 'Gracias doctor,' she murmured. 'Con mucho gusto,' he replied gallantly. He ran his eyes over her body. 'Otra cosa?' he asked.

'No, gracias,' replied Aurelia firmly, refusing his offer of further help. The doctor shrugged and gathered up his bag. Nodding to Aurelia he left the room. She held her breath until she heard him being let out of the kitchen and then she gave a small squeal of joy. 'I can use both my arms again!' she thought with glee. She ran out to show Maria. Turning the corner into the kitchen she came face to face with Paolo.

He looked her up and down and smiled maliciously before leaving the kitchen. 'Diez minutos,' he reminded Maria gruffly as he passed her.

Maria called to Aurelia. 'We have only ten minutes to finish preparing dinner. I must hurry. Is your wrist well?'

'It's fine, thanks,' said Aurelia. She moved forward to help Ana collect up a large amount of cutlery. 'Why was Paolo here?'

Maria disappeared behind a cloud of steam for a moment as she drained the water from a vat of pasta. 'I do not know,' she confessed. 'He came down with Dr Magri. I have a feeling Luis sent him to find out who needed the doctor.' She turned to Aurelia, looking harassed. 'I am afraid our secret might be a secret no longer. Luis knows that you are here.'

Chapter 8

The next morning Aurelia woke earlier than usual. Maria was shaking her. 'Get up, you need to bathe today before we go upstairs.' Aurelia shook her head to clear the sleepy fog from her brain. 'Upstairs?' she asked in confusion.

'It is as I thought,' said Maria. 'Luis has been reminded that you are here. He has asked that you deliver the meals today with me.' She watched as Aurelia dragged herself up off the mattress. She led her across the hallway to the bathroom. 'When we go upstairs Luis insists that we are clean and well-presented.' She laughed harshly. 'He does not care what happens to us down here, but when we are in front of his friends...well. I have a clean uniform for you and you must bathe. Here is soap, here is shampoo. Hurry now.' Maria left the room, pulling the door tightly shut behind her.

Aurelia was wide awake now that her curiosity about upstairs was about to be answered. She hurried to take off her simple cotton night dress and splashed into the tepid water. 'This is much better than the bowl of cold water I normally have to make do with to wash,' she thought. Delighted to be able to use both hands she quickly wet and shampooed her hair, enjoying the feeling of a truly clean scalp at last. She soaped her body and rinsed off, then quickly dried herself. Her clean set of clothes was waiting in the bedroom and she dressed, glad of the fresh cotton.

She floated down the hallway into the kitchen, unable to contain her excitement at the change in her routine. Maria caught her by the shoulders. 'Be calm, child,' she warned her. 'Please do not make the mistake of thinking it is an adventure upstairs.' She started to tidy Aurelia's hair with the comb she kept in her apron pocket. 'You must stay behind me as much as possible. Try to make yourself invisible.' She put the comb away and shook Aurelia's shoulders. 'I know you will want to look about you, but do not. Do not look at any of the men. Keep your head down.'

Aurelia was frightened by the intensity in Maria's tone. 'You should be frightened,' Maria warned, seeing her face. 'These are not nice men. Try to be invisible,' she repeated.

'What on Earth goes on upstairs?' wondered Aurelia. The other women had appeared in the kitchen by now and were preparing the first loaves of the day for baking. Aurelia and Maria joined them in the preparations for breakfast.

An hour later all was ready, and the bell had sounded. Aurelia gripped the handles of her tray as she heard the bolts being slid back, her stomach knotted with tension. She lifted the heavy tray off the table and followed Maria through the doorway and up the curving stone steps. She concentrated on placing one foot in front of the other, not used to carrying such a heavy tray, not used to using her right wrist anymore. She focused on the floor and on Maria's back in front of her, but couldn't help noticing that they were in the wide terracotta-tiled passageway with whitewashed walls that she had glimpsed on the night she arrived.

They entered another room, Paolo just behind them. Aurelia was aware of sunshine streaming in through two sets of French windows on one side of the room. Her eyes were drawn to the beautiful sunny day on the other side of the glass. She saw manicured gardens, and lemon trees laden with large fruit within reach just outside the windows.

'Hurry,' whispered Maria, recalling Aurelia to the moment. She saw that the room was currently empty but a long table was laid with ten places. The women placed their trays on the sideboard against the far wall, and unloaded their fare quickly and efficiently onto the middle of the dining table – loaves of warm bread, plates of pastries, dishes of jams and butter, hard boiled eggs, slices of ham, hot coffee and milk.

Maria glanced round to make sure that all was in order then hustled Aurelia from the room. They walked with their empty trays back down the hallway, Aurelia's eyes wide, taking in avidly the many dark wooden doors, the large terracotta urns with tumbling plants, the decorative woven wall hangings and the feeling of light and spaciousness before she was ushered back down the dimly lit stone steps and into the kitchen.

Maria breathed a sigh of relief and shook her head at Ana's raised eyebrow. 'No,' she confirmed. 'Nadie.'

Aurelia realised her heart was beating fast and tried to calm her breathing. Maria patted her arm. 'Sometimes it go like that for breakfast. Nobody there when we arrive. Is nice.' The women cleared up what they could while they waited for the signal that the dishes upstairs were ready to be removed. 'Is different at lunch and dinner,' explained Maria. 'Then we have to wait and serve the food.' Aurelia nodded, her apprehension starting to get the better of her.

When the bell rang once more she accompanied Maria and Paolo back upstairs to the dining room, certain that this time she would come face to face with her captor. Her heart was in her mouth as she cast her eyes down and followed Maria into the room.

It was something of an anti-climax for Aurelia to find the place deserted once again, although the room had definitely been used. Maria tutted impatiently at the state in which the men had left the table. 'They are pigs,' she muttered, hurrying forward to collect up dirty plates and cups. Aurelia joined her and they stripped the table of everything, before wiping it clear of crumbs, butter smears, great blobs of jam and scattered piles of egg shell. They made it back to the kitchen once again without seeing anyone other than Paolo. Aurelia's head was pounding with the stress of it all.

The morning was a whir of making spicy chicken pies, pork fillets in a sherry sauce and tuna and potato casserole. Now that Aurelia had two hands again she was a full member of the kitchen chaos, rushing from dish to dish. She followed Maria's orders carefully, delighted to see the wonderful creations blossoming under her own hands. 'Very good, tomorrow I start you learning to make the bread,' said Maria. Aurelia beamed at her.

In no time at all the morning had vanished and the bell was announcing 1pm. Aurelia waited for Paolo to arrive then began the already familiar routine. On reaching the tiled corridor she knew that this time was different. A hum of harsh male voices spread from the dining room right down the hall. The hum grew louder as Aurelia followed Maria into the room, her feet feeling suddenly heavy.

As soon as she crossed the threshold she knew that she had been noticed. She could feel eyes boring into her and she felt her face flush in response. She obeyed Maria's instructions, keeping her eyes firmly on the tray in front of her. Placing her tray on the sideboard she fled the room behind Maria to collect their second load of trays. On their return to the dining room she did exactly as Maria had suggested in advance, unloading the dishes at the sideboard while Maria took them round and served the men.

Aurelia kept her back to the room, turning only to give a new dish to Maria or take an empty one from her. She heard a deep voice speaking sharply and Maria answering in a low voice. Aurelia had a dish of peas ready to hand to Maria but Maria spoke in her ear. 'Luis wants you to help me serve. Is OK. Keep your eyes down, take the peas round with this spoon and just hold it out for each man to take what they want. Start with Luis.'

Heart thumping, Aurelia did as she was told. She made her way to the head of the table and offered the dish to the man who sat there, keeping her eyes lowered. She had an impression of a large, well-fed man with a deep tan sprawling in his chair. She made her eyes focus only on his weighty gold watch, lurking in the thick, dark hair of his forearms.

Luis took a spoonful of peas but watched Aurelia. She could feel his eyes on her. He said nothing to her but let her continue around the table. She completed the circuit and made her way back to Maria, not quite sure why she had found it such an ordeal. All the men seemed well-behaved in Luis' presence – raucous and loud but well-behaved. Aurelia glanced at Luis and saw that he was staring straight at her. His podgy face was topped with greasy black hair and his small eyes looked intently at her. She cast her eyes back to the floor and waited quietly next to Maria.

Eventually the men had eaten their fill. They left the room in twos and threes, spilling out through the French windows into the gardens. Luis was in their midst, lighting a fat cigar. He appeared to have forgotten that the women were still there.

'You did well,' whispered Maria. 'Hurry, let's go.' They collected up all the dirty dishes and headed back downstairs with their ever-present guard Paolo right behind them. The endless washing up started immediately and Aurelia felt a wave of weariness come over her. 'I suddenly do feel like a slave,' she thought resentfully. 'It's just constant work.'

What felt like only minutes later Aurelia trudged once more up the stairs with trays loaded with dinner, her eyes on Maria's back. Now that she knew what to expect in terms of numbers of people and how the room was set out she felt slightly more prepared, but she still found it intimidating walking into the room full of laughing men. She coughed at the thick cigarette smoke and instantly could have kicked herself when all eyes turned to her.

She scurried after Maria, her face flaming. She tried to blend into the background but at a barked command from Luis, Maria nudged her and nodded for her to start handing dishes round too. Luis watched the women from under hooded eyelids. After the meal he waved Maria over, gesturing at Aurelia. 'Ella limpia mañana. Que se arriba esta semana.'

'Luis, she doesn't know what to do or how to do it,' implored Maria in English.

'You will teach her tomorrow,' he said peremptorily. 'Then she will know.' Aurelia's eyes widened at Luis' good English. Maria started to protest but he raised the back of his hand at her as if he would strike her and she backed away. 'Come,' she beckoned to Aurelia. We clean up now.'

She translated for Aurelia when they reached the kitchen, as they started to unstack the plates. 'Every week Luis makes a different one of us work upstairs, cleaning the rooms, making the beds, arranging the flowers, tidying up in the lounges after his guests.' She looked at Aurelia with concern. 'This week he has asked for it to be you. I tell him you don't know how to do it but he say I teach you. I am to go with you tomorrow to show you what to do and then the rest of the week you will be alone up there. You will have a break from the cooking but I am afraid it will be an even busier week for you. The men are pigs and not nice to look after. I hope he will treat you well. It is what I did not want to happen, that he would see you and want to have you upstairs with him.' She looked as if she might add more, but then decided not to.

Aurelia shrugged. 'Well, if the other girls have to do it, I guess I should take my turn,' she said, trying to sound braver than she felt. 'How come he speaks English?'

Maria frowned again. 'Darling Luis was given an education worthy of the favourite child,' she explained. Aurelia considered this as she unloaded dishes into the sink. 'How come you're never upstairs?' she asked. 'I've seen Sofia and Ana missing each week in turn, but never you.'

'He needs me in the kitchen more than in the house. And he does not like his servants to answer back to him. I know him too well.' She looked Aurelia frankly in the eyes. 'You will need to do exactly as he tells you. It will not be well for you if you do not do what he wants.' She looked down at the crusted dish in her hands. When she continued speaking it was in a whisper. 'I did not tell you before as you did not need to know but...the reason we needed more help is that Luis killed another girl who worked here.'

Aurelia gasped. 'He killed her?' she asked, fear gripping her at the thought of working near him all week. 'Why?'

Maria shrugged. 'She did not obey him in everything he asked. He has a temper. He is a bad man. I tell you this to protect you – do as he tells you.'

Aurelia could feel her headache returning. She nodded, her thoughts whirring.

She barely slept that night due to the apprehension she felt about working upstairs. She lay, staring at the ceiling, wondering how badly the other girl must have antagonised Luis to end up dead. 'If only I could remember who I really am,' she thought wretchedly. 'Maybe then I could see some way of getting out of here.'

The next morning after a hasty but delicious piece of freshly-baked bread with plum jam she accompanied Maria upstairs, carrying her spare clothes and toothbrush. Maria's words from earlier on echoed in her head. 'When you work upstairs you stay upstairs. You bring what you need.' She followed her to a small room off the hallway, more like a cupboard, with a mattress on the floor and a small sink in one corner. Maria gestured to her to leave her things there and follow her. Aurelia noticed on the way out that the door locked on the outside. She would be a prisoner up here too.

'Does Paolo always come with you when you work up here?' she asked Maria quietly, flicking her eyes towards their silent shadow. Maria shook her head. 'No, normally up here you are completely alone. I think today he does not trust us as we are together. Maybe they think two women can escape from ten men and the other staff outside.' With a small smile, she showed Aurelia where to collect cleaning products, a broom, a bucket and cloths.

They spent a hard morning cleaning the dining room and large lounge in the main section and then moved round to each the wings of the house in turn. The wings contained the bedrooms – room after room of simple whitewashed walls but luxurious, ornate bedsteads and fittings, designed for comfort. As Maria had predicted, the rooms were left in varying states of filth and mess. They bustled round, tidying and cleaning. 'It is difficult to have all this done in time, especially with just one person,' huffed Maria, expertly tucking in a sheet. 'Luis insists that all the bedrooms are cleaned in the morning. After lunch the men may take a siesta. Sometimes, on the rare occasions when Luis does not have many guests, then it is a lucky week and the work can be done more easily.'

'Where are the men now?' asked Aurelia. Maria paused for a breather, hands on hips. 'They ride, they hunt, they play golf, they attend cattle markets, they discuss business in town. Always they have something to occupy themselves. Life is like a holiday for them.' Aurelia looked longingly out through the large windows onto the gardens beyond.

She trudged into the first bathroom that she had to clean and stopped dead as she saw herself in the mirror. She took in her reflection, feeling odd. 'So that's what I look like,' she thought to herself. She saw bright blue eyes in a lightly tanned face. Her hair was mostly blonde, but darker roots were starting to grow out. She looked thin.

Maria found her standing there. 'What are you doing? We must hurry,' she said. Aurelia nodded. 'I haven't seen myself since I arrived here,' she said slowly. 'I didn't even know what I look like.' She felt the whisper of a memory stirring at the edge of her brain as she stared at herself, but then it was gone. 'Think! Think!' she urged herself. 'Who are you?'

After the rooms were done, the women moved back to the main area to clean the library. Brandy glasses littered the small tables in the library, and cigar stubs were prolific. 'There is a small laundry room on this floor,' Maria informed Aurelia. 'There we can wash the glasses and return them to the crystal cabinet without needing to go downstairs. We will also wash all the bedding and towels we just removed.'

Paolo had melted away. 'He goes to fetch Sofia and Ana to serve the lunch,' explained Maria. 'Come quick, I show you the laundry.' They slipped along the corridor and into a small and very basic kitchen. The sunshine burst in through the small window above the sink. They loaded bedding into the large washer and set the machine in motion.

Maria checked that Paolo was still nowhere in sight before shutting the door tightly. 'It is time for us to eat too,' she said, eyes twinkling at Aurelia. Opening the cupboard below the sink she pulled out a hessian bag that appeared to be full of cleaning rags. Moving the rags to one side she revealed several bananas, oranges and apples. She offered the bag to Aurelia who grabbed a banana hungrily and started to devour it.

'Where's this from?' she asked with her mouth full, delighting in the delicious fruit.

'Whenever we can take some fruits from the bowl in Luis' library or the dining room we do so and we hide them here. Then the cleaning girl that week have something to eat. Otherwise food for the girl up here is forgotten,' she said, her eyes darkening as she crunched into an apple. They bolted down their fruit, terrified of being discovered. Aurelia stuffed the banana peel into her apron pocket for disposal in the bins later.

Back in the corridor they could hear the men enjoying their lunch. They set off to clean Luis' study.

It was a beautiful room, with mahogany furniture, rich rugs and a large drinks cabinet. 'We do not spend long in here,' explained Maria. ''Luis does not like to find anyone else in here. We just dust and take away any dishes and no more.'

Aurelia tried to remember all the instructions for the different rooms, and the order in which she had to clean them. 'So, every day I repeat these steps?' she asked as they made their way back to the dining room to clean the room after the men had finished lunch.

'Si,' confirmed Maria. 'After this, we go back to the laundry room and we finish the washing. It is done twice a week.' Aurelia's heart leaped as she polished the dining room table. 'I didn't see a dryer,' she thought. 'Maybe we'll have to go outside to hang out the laundry.' She rejoiced at the thought of being outside for the first time in over six weeks.

Hardly daring to believe it might be true she tailed Maria back to the laundry room, Paolo now with them once again. They dragged the damp sheets and towels out of the machine and loaded in some more. Maria called out to Paolo. He entered the laundry room, pulling a key on a chain out of his pocket. 'We're going outside,' thought Aurelia. 'We really are.' As if in a dream she saw Paolo unlock the door. He beckoned Maria through. Aurelia stepped forward, already imagining she could feel the sun on her skin, and the fresh air on her face. She smiled slightly then realised Paolo was shutting the door in her face. 'Stay,' he grunted at her. The door closed.

Aurelia moved to the window. She could see Maria crossing the lawn of the large enclosed courtyard and starting to hang out the laundry. A sob rose in her throat. She pressed her hands onto the work surface. 'I will not cry,' she thought fiercely. 'I have to be strong.' She swallowed again and again until the lump in her throat disappeared, but she could not stop a tear escaping. She was angrily wiping it away when Maria and Paolo returned. He sneered at her forlorn face and brushed past her.

Maria dropped the large laundry basket, sweating slightly even from only a few minutes in the hot afternoon sun. Seeing Aurelia's face she gave her a quick hug. 'Did you want to go outside, querida?' she asked gently. 'Well, don't worry. Paolo never lets more than one person outside at the same time but there will be more laundry to do during your week up here, you will go outside then.'

Aurelia sniffed, smiling back at Maria. 'That's true, I forgot about that,' she said, brightening up. Her face clouded over again instantly. 'I'm worried I won't remember everything that needs doing or how to do it or what order to do it in,' she confided miserably.

'Yes you will,' said Maria firmly. 'I explain you everything again this afternoon while we work, and tomorrow you see it will all be clear to you. I know you are good at learning things.'

They spent the rest of the day hard at work in the remaining parts of the house, sweeping, dusting and polishing. They moved furniture, cleaned fireplaces and shook rugs, trying always to be in whichever part of the house the men were not. Aurelia was exhausted. At last the men finished dinner and she heard Sofia and

Ana taking the dirty plates back downstairs. She and Maria returned to the dining room for the final cleaning of the day. The crumbs and mess were a cruel reminder of the feast that the men had just eaten. Aurelia's stomach grumbled. She was so used to it by now that she just ignored it.

'I can't imagine doing all this by myself for the rest of this week,' she thought in dismay. The familiar lump rose in her throat as she imagined having this week every few weeks for eternity. 'I have to get out of here,' she thought dejectedly, swiping at some crumbs in the middle of the table. 'I need to find out who I am and how I got here.'

She saw from the clock on the sideboard that it was nearly 10pm. Paolo entered the room, swinging a large set of keys like the jailer he was. He jerked his head for the women to follow him. They reached Aurelia's cupboard and he jerked the door open before pushing her in. 'Good night Aurelia, I knock in the morning, you will be fine, remember-' Maria's words cut off as Paolo slammed the door shut. Aurelia heard the key rattle in the lock, then silence. Shivers of apprehension tickled the back of her neck as she groped in the pitch black for the light switch. 'Please be no spiders, please be no spiders,' she repeated, sighing with relief when her fingers found the switch and the dim wattage weakly warmed the room.

She forced herself to brush her teeth in the small sink, then collapsed gratefully onto the mattress. Every muscle ached. Her head buzzed with all the new information she'd taken in that day. She tried to run through in her mind what she needed to do first in the morning, but within seconds she was asleep.

Chapter 9

The next day was a blur of activity for Aurelia. She awoke to a quick knock on her door and realised that it must be Maria and one of the other girls on their way to deliver breakfast. She turned on the light and washed as best she could in the sink before dressing hurriedly, not sure when her door would be opened.

From the moment that Paolo wrenched the door open it was action all day. As she cleaned up after breakfast she found a slice of buttered bread underneath a napkin on the table. She sent up a silent thank you for Maria's kindness. She slipped the bread into her apron pocket to eat it in secret as soon as she could.

Maria had been right – Paolo checked on Aurelia from time to time but did not shadow her all day. She was glad of the freedom from watching eyes as she stumbled nervously around all the bedrooms, feeling all day as if she were against the clock. She hurtled from one task to the next, not having time to slow down for a second. She was careful to sneak a piece of fruit into her apron and add it to the items hidden in the laundry room to keep up the supply. By 10pm she was locked back in her room, wondering where the day had gone. Apart from a quick glimpse of Maria and Ana when they had arrived to clear away the lunch dishes she had not seen the other women at all.

She lay down on her mattress, glad that the day was over and she was one day closer to escaping back to the relative calm of the kitchen. She shivered as she thought about Luis. 'He was staring at me all through lunch and dinner,' she thought. 'I don't like him at all.

I can feel him watching every move I make, it's intimidating.'

Her thoughts broke off as she heard slow footsteps outside in the corridor. They stopped outside her room and she held her breath, wondering who was outside. After a moment or two, the footsteps carried on down the hallway and Aurelia slowly released her breath. 'Who was that?' she wondered. She had a feeling it had been Luis but told herself not to be ridiculous. 'Why would he be lurking outside my door?' she scoffed, trying to ignore the seed of fear that had lodged in her mind at the thought.

The next two days followed the same hectic yet ultimately monotonous pattern. On the fourth day on her own upstairs Aurelia was determined to step outside. 'Maria told me I would wash the men's bedding another time in my week up here, so today's the day,' she thought, feeling optimistic at the thought of breathing in the fresh air outdoors. She hurtled through all her normal chores, bundled the first load of washing into the machine and counted the seconds until it was finished.

When Paolo came to check on her she told him that she needed to hang out the sheets. He nodded and followed her to the laundry. Aurelia gripped the heavy laundry basket, keeping her face down so that Paolo would not see the excitement in her eyes. She passed through into the garden as soon as he had opened the door, making her way straight over to the washing lines.

As she walked she took in lungful after lungful of sweet air, savouring the scent of jasmine and citrus fruits in the air. She fought hard to resist the urge to spin round and round in the warm autumn sunshine. She wanted to run and dance, free from the confines of the house. She hummed quietly under her breath as she started to hang out the sheets. She could see Paolo back at the house, lighting a cigarette while he waited for her.

The grass was hot and dry under her bare feet and the sun caressed her shoulders through the cotton as she pegged the sheets on the line. She stretched and breathed deeply, enjoying the scent of the freshly washed laundry. She closed her eyes for a moment, delighting in the warm sun on her face.

Turning to pick up the empty laundry basket her skin prickled. She saw a movement at the study windows. Luis was staring right at her. Aurelia moved back to the house, all pleasure in being outside gone.

Aurelia was not able to shake a sense of foreboding for the rest of the day. She passed Maria in the hallway as dinner was being brought in and tried to speak to her but Paolo just barked 'No,' at her and urged Maria and Sofia into the dining room with their trays of food.

She could feel Luis' dark eyes on her at all times and her hands shook as she served out the food. 'He seems to be trying to intimidate me and it's working,' she thought. 'He never says anything to me but his staring is awful.' She tried to be extra efficient and prompt in her serving in the hope that he would leave her alone. She couldn't forget the girl he had killed.

She was relieved to escape Luis' brooding gaze and make it back to her cupboard that night. 'I'll be glad when this week is over,' she thought. 'His staring is making me really uncomfortable.' She turned off the light and lay down to sleep.

Just then she heard the footsteps again. They came slowly down the hallway and stopped outside her door. She held her breath again, waiting for them to move on. She shrank back against the wall as she heard the key turning smoothly in the lock. The door was pushed open. Luis stood in the doorway. Aurelia sat up and stared at him, her heart thumping, unable to see his face properly in the dim lighting of the hallway at night.

'You have not finished your work,' he stated. His eyes flicked over her. Her thin cotton nightgown suddenly felt invisible. She pulled her sheet up to her chest.

'I haven't?' she said in surprise, still finding it odd to hear English coming from Luis' mouth.

'No, you have not finished,' he replied, not moving.

Aurelia scrambled to her feet. 'I..er.. I thought I had... I'm sorry-' she stammered. She glanced at her uniform on the floor.

Luis followed her glance and smiled sardonically. 'You will not need that. It is a new job. Come with me now,' he ordered. Aurelia followed him unsurely, feeling woefully underdressed in her nightgown and bare feet. 'Why don't I need my uniform?' she thought with dread.

The house was in darkness apart from the low lighting in the hallways. 'His friends must have decided on an early night,' she thought. They turned towards the library and Aurelia could see light spilling out from under the doors. The sound of faint music reached her ears. 'Or maybe they're all just in the library,' she thought miserably. 'Why am I here?'

She started to walk more slowly. Luis did not look back, just grabbed her wrist in a vice-like grip and yanked her forward. Aurelia whimpered, fearful of what was going to happen to her.

Luis pushed open the heavy wooden door to the library. Aurelia blinked in the light after the dim glow of the hallway. Luis' friends were sprawled in armchairs and lounging on the sofas. Cigar smoke hung thickly in the air, mingling with the earthy scent of whisky.

A cheer went up from the men as Luis thrust Aurelia through the doorway. She half stumbled into the middle of the room and stood looking fearfully back at Luis. He calmly closed and locked the door. He turned to her and ran his eyes over her body. 'You have not finished your work,' he repeated again. 'Now you will earn your keep.'

Aurelia felt faint, imagining the worst. 'What do you mean?' she asked.

She watched as one of the men got up and changed the CD. A sultry beat filled the room and the men started to clap expectantly, grinning widely.

'You will dance,' said Luis.

'Dance?' repeated Aurelia, unsure that she had heard correctly, and struggling with a combination of embarrassment and relief.

'Dance,' stated Luis firmly. 'Dance now.'

Heat leaped to her face and she felt as if her body was not her own as she started to move awkwardly. 'This is so humiliating,' she thought, closing her eyes so that she would not have to look at the men's leering faces.

'Dance more sexy,' called Luis imperiously. Aurelia bit her lip and tried to sway her hips, feeling more and more uncomfortable, aware that her thin nightgown was quite revealing. 'I said more sexy,' growled Luis, his face now near hers. Revolt welled up in Aurelia and she shook her head.

Luis grabbed her arm tightly with one hand and cracked her across the face with the other, his mouth leering maliciously at her. Stars flashed across Aurelia's vision and she cried out in pain. 'You're an animal,' she hissed, tasting blood on her lip.

'You will obey me,' he whispered fiercely. He grabbed both her wrists, standing behind her and forcing her to sway in front of him. She tried to squirm away, mortified, her eyes filling with tears at the sight of the cheering men. In a flash, her tormented mind remembered.

'I know who I am!' she cried. 'I remember!'

'Be quiet!' barked Luis in her ear. She tried to focus on the images coming back to her, to blank out what was happening. She shut her eyes tightly, wishing herself back in the kitchen. Luis' cigar glowed in his fingers and bumped against Aurelia's arm. She yelped in pain but Luis did not move away. Aurelia pulled away as much as she could to avoid the burning tip touching her again.

The song finished and Luis pushed her away. She half fell onto the lap of one of the guests, clutching at the burn on her flesh. He tried to put his arms around her but she fought him off and sprang up, backing away towards the door. 'You go,' said Luis, waving her away. She turned to see Paolo waiting to accompany her from the room. She darted out as soon as he opened the door, and stood panting in the hallway.

Her cheekbone ached where Luis had hit her and her raw arm was sore. She touched a hand to her face and felt the swelling. She felt filthy after the men's ogling eyes. Yet in the midst of her pain and misery she felt a kernel of truth blossoming in her mind. 'I remember,' she whispered to herself between her sobs.

Paolo led her to the nearest bathroom and pulled a towel from the cupboard. He sat down heavily in the chair in the hallway, not looking at her. 'Ducha. Tres minutos,' he barked, jerking his head towards the bathroom.

Grateful for this unexpected and welcome chance to wash properly she ran into the bathroom. She started to shut the door but Paolo called 'No!' so she left it ajar. 'At least he's not spying on me,' she thought, glad to see his chair facing the other way. 'I believe he doesn't enjoy this part of his job very much.' She felt warmer towards Paolo than she had up until that point.

Aware that she only had three minutes she dropped the towel and her nightgown and stepped into the large shower enclosure. Her head was banging behind her temples but the warm water was soothing. She soaped her whole body, scrubbing at it fiercely to try and feel cleaner. 'I feel like a stripper,' she thought. She tried not to think about what had just happened to her, focusing instead on the memories that had returned to her.

She had flashes of her wedding day, a happy, sunny day in beautiful gardens. She could see the handsome face of her bridegroom, smiling warmly down into her eyes. 'Blake,' she whispered weakly, leaning for a moment against the shower wall.

She turned off the water and stepped out to dry herself. She pulled her nightdress back on and wrapped the towel around her wet hair, watching her image appear in the enormous mirror as the steam cleared. She saw a swollen cheek and the beginnings of a black eye decorating her frightened face. But underneath all that, the bright blue eyes and full lips were unmistakable.

'I'm Dante,' she whispered.

Chapter 10

Paolo led Dante back through the dark house to her cupboard without saying a word to her. Behind her she heard shrill, chattering women's voices as they were let into the house and shown to the library. 'Prostitutes no doubt,' she thought, under no illusions about the men in the house. 'I'm so proud that I could be the warm up act,' she thought bitterly. 'At least it wasn't worse.'

She had never been so glad to be locked alone in the tiny space. She turned off the light and lay staring up into the darkness, gently fingering her swollen face and trying to ignore her sore arm. The shock of the last hour meant that sleep was impossible for her. Adrenaline rushed through her veins.

'My name is Dante,' she repeated to herself out loud. 'I am married to Blake. We were married in the Hamptons on July 25th. My father is William Kingsford.' Her voice trembled at the thought of her father and tears stung her eyes. 'Oh Daddy, what's happened to me, and where do you think I am?' she wondered. She took a deep breath and continued trying to put together what she could remember. 'My best friend is Paige Osborne. She was my bridesmaid along with my three cousins.'

She trailed off. 'So how on Earth did I end up here?' she asked herself in bewilderment. She willed herself to remember more. 'Come On Dante, think!' Despite her best efforts, no more information came to her. The stress and horror of the day took their toll and eventually she fell asleep.

The next day she was determined to remember more. More and more details started to trickle back into her brain and she snatched hungrily at each one. 'I have a business degree,' she remembered. 'I met Blake at college.'

She carried out her chores on autopilot, glad to see that Luis and the other men seemed to be determined to ignore her completely, as if they had never seen her before. 'Fine with me,' she thought, refusing to let her mind wander back fully to her humiliation of the night before. She swept her hair back from her bruised face defiantly, pleased to let all Luis' friends see how he had hurt her. 'Let them remember what kind of a man he is,' she thought contemptuously. Dr Magri had returned as a guest at the house and he looked curiously at her face and the burn on her arm as she served breakfast. She boldly looked right into his eyes, feeling defiant, before turning away, hating them all.

'I must find a phone,' she thought intently as she started her rounds of the men's bedrooms. Paolo was shadowing her again. 'As if he thinks I might do something desperate,' smiled Dante bitterly. 'Well, he's half right. I do desperately need to find a phone.' She surreptitiously inspected every room she entered for a telephone but saw no landlines at all, even in the study and the lounge. 'They must all use cell phones,' she thought in frustration.

She watched them at dinner and noticed a couple of the men talking on their phones, always returning them to their pockets when they had finished. 'I have to find a way to get hold of one,' she decided.

She wondered as she returned to her cupboard that night if she would be able to steal one the next day. She stopped at the door but Paolo just muttered 'No,' and kept on walking. Her heart stopped for a moment in sheer dread of being taken back to the library.

With relief she saw that she was being returned to the kitchen instead. 'Pero, no es una semana ahora,' she said to Paolo, querying why she was not required to stay upstairs for the remaining seventh day.

'Mañana no Luis, sin invitados,' confirmed Paolo, ushering her downstairs. 'Necesitan solo el desayuno.' He unbolted the kitchen door, hustled her inside and shut her in.

Dante smiled at the familiar kitchen smells, her hand on the locked door, glad to be out of harm's way. Turning, she saw Maria, Sofia and Ana staring at her in horror. 'Aurelia!' gasped Maria, rushing towards her. 'Your face! Querida, your poor face!' She took Dante's hands, noticing the burn on her arm and inspecting the damage to her face and the spreading black eye. She looked at Dante frankly. 'Was it Luis?' Dante nodded, suddenly unable to speak. Maria saw the tears welling. 'What did he make you...?' she started softly, stopping as Dante suddenly broke down sobbing

Ana nodded and waved them away, motioning that she and Sofia had the kitchen under control. Maria nodded gratefully and led Dante gently to her room, her arm round the younger woman's shoulders. 'Is OK, is OK,' she murmured as they reached her room. 'You safe now.' She sat Dante on the mattress and sat down next to her, rubbing her hands between hers.

Dante sobbed as if her heart would break. Maria soothed her and let her cry, holding her closely. Eventually Dante stopped crying and Maria handed her a tissue. 'Tell me what happen Aurelia.' Dante didn't know where to start. She stared at Maria, her eyes wild.

'My name is Dante. My memory is coming back. I'm Dante.'

Maria beamed at her. 'This is wonderful! Dante,' she repeated. 'Good. It is a lovely name.' She nodded encouragingly.

Dante rocked backwards and forwards as she spoke. 'It was such hard work, and I was so tired all week and so hungry and then just when I thought that was as bad as it got, last night Luis- ' she swallowed, before continuing in a low voice, eyes on the floor. 'It sounds so ridiculous. He made me dance for him and his friends. I was only wearing my nightdress and they were all so disgusting. It was humiliating, I was so embarrassed.' Her face flushed at the memory of her awkward moves in front of the noisy men. She glanced at her arm. 'Luis' cigar burnt me and he didn't care.' She looked at Maria with suddenly angry eyes. 'Why didn't you tell me?' she cried. 'Why didn't you warn me that I was to be their seedy entertainment?'

Maria sighed heavily. 'I'm so sorry Dante. I did not know for sure that he would do anything and I did not want to frighten you if it was not necessary.' She passed a hand tiredly over her eyes. 'Even if I warned you, he would make you do it anyway if he was going to, there was nothing you could have done. You would just have been more terrified and perhaps made mistakes at your work and angered him. You are lucky that it was just dancing. Others are not so lucky. Sofia...' She stopped and gripped Dante's hand. 'If I could stop this happening to you I would,' she promised. 'You do not belong here, and now Luis has treated you like...'

'Like a prostitute,' finished Dante. She smiled bitterly. 'I head a posse of women arriving for the men after they'd watched me. How charming.'

Maria sighed again. 'I hoped you might be different and you would not be treated as the other girls are. He is despicable. A pig.'

Dante could not remain angry in the face of Maria's obvious distress. 'So, this happens to all of the girls when they work upstairs?' she asked in disgusted wonder. Maria nodded sadly. 'Ana will talk to you about it now that you know. She will be glad of someone to discuss this with. Sofia prefers just to block out what happens to her and talk to nobody.'

She sighed. 'He leaves me alone of course – trapping me in the kitchen of my own home is punishment enough for his cousin – but the other girls, yes. He seems to think it is part of the work of the house when a girl is upstairs cleaning for him to have her entertain his friends in this way. He likes the power. He is despicable,' she repeated. They sat together in silence for a moment. Maria stood up wearily. 'I want to hear everything you have remembered about your other life,' she said, 'but first we must clean you up. Come with me.'

Dante took Maria's outstretched hand and heaved herself to her feet, wincing at her aches and pains. She followed Maria back to the kitchen. Sofia and Ana seemed to have gone to bed; the room was deserted. Dante sat on a stool by the sink with cold water running on her arm as Maria bustled around. 'It is late for ice to help but we try,' she said, bringing a cloth-wrapped bunch of ice cubes to Dante and holding it against her swollen face. 'You hold that please,' she directed. She smoothed some drops of lavender-scented lotion around Dante's bruised eye. 'This will help it heal quickly,' she explained, dotting another lotion on her burn. 'Come, we go back to your room and we talk.'

Dante trailed Maria along the corridor. 'Oh!' she remembered as she entered her room. 'Luis only wants breakfast tomorrow, he's not going to be here for the rest of the day.'

'I know. Paolo told me we are only needed first thing.' Maria grinned wickedly. 'We serve breakfast and then we have a day of peace. They are rare, believe me!' She sat opposite Dante on the spare mattress, perching on the edge in anticipation. 'So! Tell me what you have discovered!'

'Well,' began Dante, 'not everything's come back to me yet, but more comes back every minute.' She took a deep breath. 'My name is Dante Kingsford and I'm 22 years old. I'm American, I live in New York City. My father is William Kingsford, the founder of the Kingsford Corporation.'

She took a tangent, seeing Maria's blank look. 'It's one of the most successful consulting companies in New York. We trouble shoot in other companies – we analyse their working procedures and advise them how to be more successful in their own businesses. We train up staff to be experts in all kinds of fields and we place them where they're most needed and best able to advise,' she explained briefly. 'My father has been preparing me my whole life to take over the company one day. I've had holiday jobs there for years, since as soon as I was old enough to be useful. I went to university and studied business and I was about to start working at the company full-time for the first time.'

'So you are rich!' exclaimed Maria. 'It is like a fairy tale!'

Dante laughed, embarrassed. 'Yes, I guess you could say so. My father is a very wealthy man, and a very generous man too. I'm his only daughter and he's always treated me like a princess.' Her eyes clouded over and she looked earnestly at Maria. 'He'll be so worried. They'll all be so worried. I have to find a way to contact them,' she said quietly.

'We think about that later. Tell me what else. What about your mother?'

Dante looked down. 'My mother died when I was eight. Since then my father and I have been everything to each other.' She smiled. 'Well, until I met Blake.'

Maria smiled. 'Aha! A man?'

'The most handsome and brilliant man I ever saw in my life. We were married. Our wedding day was July 25th. He looked so wonderful – so tall and strong. It was such a wonderful day. I had four bridesmaids, including my best friend Paige, and an enormous chocolate cake and dancing and fireworks, it was just wonderful.'

'It sounds beautiful,' agreed Maria. She looked puzzled. 'And so what then? You were married to this very handsome man but now you are here.' She shrugged apologetically, as if hating to remind Dante of her current fate. 'What happened in between?'

Dante sighed. 'I can't remember it properly,' she said frustratedly. 'I can remember nearly everything about the wedding. And then...,' she paused, thinking. 'And then we went on honeymoon!' She sat bold upright. 'I remember! It was a surprise from Blake – he bought me a luxury cruise to Europe! We sailed from New York and then-'

'And then?' asked Maria, leaning forward with concern as she saw Dante's face drain of colour. 'Are you OK?' Dante shook her head, clutching her stomach. 'Oh God, I remember,' she whispered hoarsely. 'I remember everything.' She looked up at Maria, her face stricken.

'We went on our honeymoon and Blake tried to kill me.'

Chapter 11

There was a shocked pause as Maria took in what Dante had just said. Her white face and dead eyes told Maria that she had been deadly serious. 'What do you mean?' she asked. 'What did he do?'

'He drugged me, and he pushed me over the side of the ship,' said Dante in a daze. 'It's all come back to me so clearly now.' She pulled her knees up to her chest and covered her face with her hands. Her voice when she spoke was muffled. 'I thought he loved me, but he wanted me dead.'

'But why?' wondered Maria. 'Why would he want to kill you?'

Dante looked up at her. 'For money,' she said flatly. ' I think he took out an insurance policy on me before our wedding and then he wanted to kill me so that he could claim on it.'

'Does this really happen outside of books?' asked Maria incredulously.

'Apparently so,' confirmed Dante. She toyed with her fingers, remembering her last days on the boat. 'Everything was perfect at first but then one night Blake really scared me out on deck – I had the strong feeling that he was going to push me overboard. Suddenly I couldn't see him in the same way, I was really suspicious of him. It felt like everything he'd ever said to me was all about me being wealthy. I think his business was in trouble too.' She shook her head sadly. 'It suddenly all fitted together in my mind – he just saw me as a quick way to become very rich.'

'But if you were suspicious of him didn't you tell somebody?'

Dante sighed. 'It seems stupid now that I didn't. I didn't want to worry my father and I thought if I could just avoid Blake as much as possible until we docked in Cadiz I could get safely on shore and then get away from him and fly home.' She frowned. 'I did try and contact my friend Paige, but I don't think my text ever got through. The signal was really weak.'

'So what exactly happened?' asked Maria.

'I don't remember exactly, but I'm sure he drugged me.' Dante thought back. 'I spent the day trying to stay out of his way after his weird behaviour the night before. I wanted to stay in our room that night by myself but we'd been invited to eat at the captain's table which was an honour we felt we couldn't turn down.'

She pictured the dining table in her mind. 'I was trying not to drink so that I could stay alert, but Blake kept making toasts and I had to keep taking sips of my drink so it wouldn't look like anything was wrong and then I started to feel really ill.' She touched her stomach, remembering the nausea. 'I'm sure it was in my Champagne. Suddenly I couldn't sit up straight and I felt awful. Blake wanted to take me out on deck. I didn't want to go with him and I was struggling against him but I remember him taking me back to our room and putting me to bed.'

Her voice started to crack as she focused on her memories. 'It must have been later that night that he took me out to the deck again. He had me bundled up in a robe and I was still completely out of it, I had no

120

idea where I was being taken. Before I knew it we were outside, on the edge and then...Then he threw me overboard.'

Maria crossed to take the shaking girl in her arms. Dante clung to her, weeping. 'I thought he loved me,' she sobbed. 'I thought he wanted to be with me. How could he do that?'

Maria sighed, stroking Dante's hair, her eyes full of pity. 'Money can make men do very strange things,' she said resignedly. 'What a terrible time you are having these last two months,' she sympathised. 'You are very strong to get through it all.'

Dante laughed harshly through her tears. 'I'm not through it yet,' she said. Her thoughts raced around in her head. She wiped her eyes and stared at Maria. 'They all think I'm dead,' she whispered. 'I have to find a way to let them know I'm here. I have to tell my father. He'll be so worried.'

She stood and started pacing up and down her small room. 'I have to get word to my father and I have to escape. I can't let Blake get away with this.' She turned to Maria, her eyes blazing with determination. 'I have to escape.'

'We will find a way,' vowed Maria, 'I will help you. It is really a milagro – a miracle – that you survived. How did you come from falling from the ship to being here? You should be dead.' She hugged Dante closely, seeing her pale face and wounded eyes. 'I am so glad that you are not dead, but it is really a miracle.'

'I think the people on the small boat I woke up on must have found me in the sea,' considered Dante slowly. 'Think about it – it all fits! Blake tried to do it the previous night when we were still way out at sea, but a couple of stewards disturbed us and I got back inside. By the next night we must have been closer to Spain than he had originally planned and by some amazing chance, ' Dante shivered at how lucky she had been, 'that other boat was crossing from Africa and found me.'

She leaned against the wall. 'I wonder how long I was in the water. I should have drowned! Just the impact alone should have smashed me to pieces.' She fingered the scar on her wrist. 'There could have been sharks and all sorts. By rights I should be dead.' She shuddered and dragged her mind back to her rescue boat. 'I think those poor people were trying to escape to Spain from Africa and they were sold to people traffickers. I think I got mixed up in it all.' She shook her head. 'I can't really remember it too well. I was in so much pain.'

'I am not surprised, if that is what happened to you,' whistled Maria in amazement. 'You really are a little milagro.'

The women talked long into the night, discussing details of Dante's real life and tentative escape theories. Eventually, Dante's eyes started to droop and Maria left her to sleep.

The next day, Maria and Ana took the breakfast trays upstairs and then waited tensely below with the other women, hoping that Luis' plans had not changed. They heard car engines starting and then the noise of several cars pulling out of the grounds. The women shared relieved smiles.

When they returned from collecting the dirty plates Maria and Ana's smiles were even wider. They waited until Paolo had locked them in again and plodded back upstairs, then Maria lifted the napkin covering two dishes. 'Look!' she exclaimed. Dante's eyes widened at the pastries, several hard boiled eggs and leftover bread and ham. Ana grinned at her and Sofia. 'They must have been in a hurry to get to wherever they are spending the day. They hardly touched anything!'

The four women ravenously tucked into the food, for once eating their fill, hardly believing their luck. Maria wrapped a loaf in a tea towel. 'We save for later too,' she said sensibly. She patted Dante's hand. 'You see – you are my little miracle. We find out who you really are and already our luck has changed.' She took off her cooking apron and put on rubber gloves, looking businesslike. 'Paolo say we are meant to use today to clean the kitchen from top to bottom as we will not need to prepare any meals.'

Dante stretched and nodded, feeling as if she would happily do any chore now that she had a full stomach. 'I'm just glad not to be seeing any of the men,' she said, still embarrassed by them leering at her. She took one corner of the kitchen and started to pull pans out of the cupboards. As Maria passed her she spoke in an undertone to her. 'I'm going to find a telephone next time I go upstairs,' she said. 'Whatever it takes, I am going to use a phone and I'm going to call my father.'

Dante spent the next two weeks in a conflicted state of mind, feeling physically sick at the thought of more abuse from Luis but knowing that she would not have a chance to find a phone unless she went back upstairs. She saw Sofia return to the kitchen after her week upstairs, and noted the unhappy woman's closed face. 'Don't think about it,' she advised herself. 'Anything could happen before then.'

She tried to occupy her mind in the meantime with more cooking lessons from Maria. 'I never knew how much I enjoyed cooking,' she confided to her friend one day as they made grilled sardines and a rich stew of chickpeas with chorizo. 'I really find it very comforting.'

Maria nodded. 'For me as well. It is one of my joys of life, and one that Luis has not tried to take away from me, thanks be to God.'

'When we get out of here you should open a restaurant,' said Dante seriously. 'People would pay a fortune to eat meals like this.'

Maria waved away the praise, smiling. 'I think my chance to run a restaurant has passed, but thank you.'

Dante looked at her frankly, putting down the fruit tart she was latticing. 'Maria, have you not thought of trying to escape?' she asked.

Maria smiled sadly. 'Of course I have! I used to think about it every day. The chance to be free, the chance to be outside, to eat, to hear music, to see friends.' She paused. 'I tried many times to escape when I was first imprisoned,' she confessed. 'Each time Luis caught me and beat me. When he told me what he

124

had told Felipe, and that Felipe had left forever, I gave up,' she said simply. 'My reason for being outside was gone, and I just gave up. I believe I was depressed for a long time, many years, but now, I try to be thankful for my cooking and I try to be thankful that I am still alive.'

She patted Dante's hand. 'Now that you are here, it is different. You have made me think again that we should not be here, that we should try to find a way out. Especially you,' she added. 'You do not belong here.'

'None of you do!' exclaimed Dante. 'We have to think of a plan.'

As the days ticked down to Ana returning to the kitchen and Dante's turn upstairs loomed, she started to feel a sick knot in her stomach. She woke several times in the night, frantic and sweating, trying to fight her tangled sheet. By the time she actually accompanied Maria upstairs on her first day, loaded down with her tray of breakfast goods her hands were trembling. 'I think I'm going to be sick,' she mumbled to Maria. 'I feel awful.'

'You can do it, stay calm,' soothed Maria out of the side of her mouth. Paolo tutted at them and they scuttled forward, not speaking anymore. After breakfast was cleared away, Maria and Sofia disappeared with the dishes and left Dante upstairs, Maria giving her an encouraging smile as she left.

Dante was determined to do an extra thorough clean, and find a phone in doing so. After cleaning the dining room she went straight to the lounge. She opened all of the cupboards and cubby holes she could find one after the other under the pretence of dusting. No telephone. Heading round to the wings to clean the bedrooms she tried to picture in her mind places where the men might keep their phones. 'I bet they take them with them when they go out,' she thought, 'but you never know.' She made a thorough search of each room but found no phone. Discouraged, she set off to serve lunch.

The men were already seated and Maria and Sofia were bringing out the food. Dante couldn't look at Luis. She felt hatred boiling inside her as she stalked over to the sideboard to collect a dish to hand round. 'I hate him,' she thought fiercely. 'I hate them all. I hate that they won't lift a finger to help themselves, they just sit there waiting for me to do everything for them.' She clattered a pot a little sharply onto the table and was waved away in irritation by one of the men. She was glad when lunch was over and the men trooped out. She continued her cleaning, noticing that her hands were shaking, but able to breathe more easily without Luis in the room.

She searched fully in the library, the study and the other remaining rooms. 'There must be a phone somewhere!' she reasoned. 'What if there's an emergency, or their cell phones don't have a proper signal?' Her search didn't turn up anything. She stood, hands on hips, surveying the sparkling library surfaces. No landline. 'I'm going to have to get hold of one of their cells,' she realised.

Her intense desire to find a phone helped her get through the week. Every day she kept a sharp eye on the men and on their rooms, to see if they had left their phones out. Nobody ever did but Dante's new mantra was 'Maybe tomorrow,' muttered under her breath over and over. The nights were the worst. Every night she reached her cupboard and lay in fear that Luis would come for her. When he didn't, she began to suspect that he was deliberately tormenting her. Whenever she did glance at him during mealtimes his eyes were fixed on her as usual. 'He's a vile animal,' she thought, with a shudder as she slipped away from his end of the table. 'He's treating this like some kind of hunting game.'

On her last night upstairs Dante was dreading the day ending. 'It has to be tonight,' she thought unhappily, her pulse quickening at the thought. Her feet dragged as she followed Paolo to her room. She grabbed his arm as he opened the door, her face pleading. 'Please don't let him do this,' she begged. Paolo shook her hands off and pushed her inside. Hearing the door lock, sobs rose in Dante's throat. She fought hard to stop them, wiping her face with her hands. 'I will not let him see me cry again,' she promised herself as she changed out of her uniform. She wondered desperately how she could get out of this.

'Maybe if I pretend to be asleep he won't make me go,' she thought hopefully. Flicking off the light, she lay down facing away from the door and tried to breathe regularly. The blood pounded in her ears as she listened for footsteps. Eventually, there they were. She fought to keep her breathing deep and regular as the key turned and the door was opened even though her heart was banging in her chest.

'Come with me,' said Luis at her back. Dante lay still, her rib cage rising and falling. 'Do you think I cannot tell that you are lying to me?' he asked, his tone icy cold. 'And do you think I would care about waking you?' Seeing Dante unmoving he laughed humourlessly. 'Very well,' he growled, bending down and wrenching her to her feet by her arm. She cried out in pain at his tight grip. 'You should not have tried to lie to me,' said Luis coldly.

He marched her along to the library, gripping her arm fiercely in his large hand all the way. She was moving so fast that her feet barely touched the floor. Luis flung open the library door and practically threw Dante across the room. Not taking his eyes off her, he clicked his fingers at the CD player. One of his guests scrambled to put on the same sultry music. As the first notes sounded he growled at Dante. 'Dance.' His tone left no room for argument.

She tried her best to move sensually to the music. 'I just don't have it in me,' she thought. She tried to pretend she was dancing at a party in front of a man she liked but Luis' angry face was in front of her whenever she opened her eyes.

'I just don't have a good enough imagination,' she thought in despair, seeing Luis' face growing colder and more angry. Her limbs felt awkward and gangly. Luis stepped towards her. 'You are making me angry,' he hissed at her. 'You will not embarrass me. You will dance properly for my friends.'

He reached out a hand and yanked her head by the hair, pulling her around the room. She yelled in pain, hurrying to keep up with him so that her hair would not be pulled from her head. The assembled men cheered at the show of Luis' strength. He gave a vicious tug of her hair before letting go as the song finished. 'Get out,' he spat. He shook his head at Paolo and Dante was returned to her room without a chance to shower. She cried herself to sleep, her head aching from the stress.

The next day she was pale and drawn, aching all over. Luis' rough fingers had imprinted purple bruises along her upper arm. Her scalp was tender and sore. She stumbled silently through the day on autopilot, counting the minutes until she was allowed to rejoin Maria in the kitchen that night. Slipping gratefully down the stone steps around 10pm she heaved a sigh of relief, before dropping to the floor in exhaustion as Paolo bolted the door behind her.

Maria helped her into the tin bath and tried to soothe her. Dante sat in the lukewarm water, her eyes glazed. 'Are you OK?' asked Maria worriedly. Dante didn't seem to hear her.

'Maybe we could poison him,' she suggested slowly, as if in a trance. 'Maybe we could poison them all.' She stared off into the middle distance.

'You do not want to become a murderer,' said Maria gently but firmly. 'If you act against your good nature, against your morals, you are lost forever. You are a good person. We will find another way.' She helped Dante out of the bath and into bed, stroking her hair soothingly until she fell asleep.

Chapter 12

Over the next two weeks Dante and Maria plotted as they cooked. 'You seem to have thought of most possible escape plans and discounted them all for one reason or another,' said Dante in frustration, pounding at some dough.

Maria nodded. 'I spent a lot of time when I was first here working out how I could escape to have my revenge on Luis. Unfortunately he prevents any of my ideas from working.' She gestured towards the door. 'We are locked in here at all times, unless we are serving or cleaning upstairs. When we serve we are accompanied by Paolo, when we clean he checks on us regularly.'

She looked up at the window. 'Even if we got out of the house we would find ourselves only in the garden in the middle of the courtyard –all inner doors only lead there so you would still be trapped, but in the open air. It is only the front door which opens to the outside world. But even then you would still be in his grounds for a long time. We are well outside the nearest village. And beyond that there is no other town for many miles. It would be impossible to make a proper escape on foot.' She looked at Dante. 'Luis is never alone – he always has friends or business associates here, so there are always plenty of people who would chase after us if somehow we did get out. In addition there is a security guard with a dog outside, patrolling the grounds.'

She stirred her tomato sauce briskly. 'In any case, I fear for the remaining girls if one of us got out.

Luis' rage would be immense. He would take his temper out on the rest.'

'But what if we strike all together when Luis and all his friends were out?' asked Dante. 'What if we ganged up on Paolo and got the key to the front door and-'

Maria laughed. 'Have you not noticed that Paolo does not come down here when the other men have gone out? I am sure he fears that happening. We are allowed out only when the other men are here, and only then in twos at the most. In any case, it is only Luis who has the key to the front door.'

'What about one of the guests?' suggested Dante. 'Maybe they don't know we're prisoners down here. Maybe we could approach one of them and ask them to help us!'

Maria snorted. 'You have too much faith in human nature,' she scoffed. 'They know exactly what is going on. They would love slave girls in their own homes if they could get away with it. I hear them sometimes at dinner, making comments. Some of those guests were friends of my family – they know who I am and that this should be my house, but they ignore me and flatter Luis because they like his hospitality and his playboy lifestyle and they want to be a part of it. He is a powerful businessman and they need his contacts and his business.'

Dante thought for a moment then looked at Maria, her eyes bright. 'I know! What if one of us pretended to be really sick, and we'd have to be taken to hospital, and then while we were there we could raise the alarm?'

132

Maria laughed again as she placed some loaves into the oven. 'Do you think Luis cares enough to send us to hospital if we are unwell? It is best for us if we are never sick. We can count on no assistance from him.'

Dante lapsed into thought. 'I'm sure there must be a way.' She shaped more loaves carefully, decorating the tops as Maria had shown her. She looked at Maria with determination in her eyes. 'I am going to find a phone this time,' she said. 'All of our discussions about escaping will be irrelevant – I'm going to get through to my father and he'll rescue us all, and then we'll be free and Luis will be in jail where he belongs. I won't rest until all four of us are out of here.'

Dante spent her next week upstairs obsessed with watching for phones. Every time she saw one of the guests talking on his phone during a meal she prayed that he might drop it, or leave it on the table by mistake. She tried not to make it too obvious, knowing that Luis' eyes would be upon her as always. She rummaged in pockets of discarded clothes in every room she cleaned, terrified of being discovered but intent on finding what she needed. Exasperated, she wondered if the men ever let their phones out of their sight for a second. 'Probably not,' she sighed. 'Luis no doubt orders them to keep them close by at all times.'

As she made her way down the hallway one afternoon late in the week after hanging out a load of laundry she heard voices in the library. 'No,' she thought to herself. 'It's just one voice.' She glanced in as she passed and saw one of the guests pacing up and down, talking on his phone. 'I wonder why he isn't out with Luis and the others?' she thought, crossing to the study and beginning to polish. She heard him finish his call and then the rustle of a newspaper. Dante chanted to herself 'Please leave your phone,' over and over again, listening for sounds of him leaving the room. Eventually she heard him crossing the hallway, then his footsteps died out.

She flitted silently into the library, hardly daring to look. 'Yes!' she exclaimed quietly, a jolt of adrenaline hitting her. There on one of the leather sofas lay a black phone. She darted over to it, slipped it into her apron pocket and tried to walk unsuspiciously towards the laundry room. Nobody was in the hallway. Rushing into the room she shut the door and leaned on the back of it. Her hands shook as she snapped open the phone and dialled the code for the USA, then her father's cell phone number. Every sense was strained as she listened for noises outside while she waited for the call to connect.

'This number is no longer in service,' came a tinny automated voice. Dante's joy at hearing an American accent was immediately squashed by puzzlement at her father's phone not being picked up or transferred to his voicemail. 'I'll try the Hamptons house,' she thought, redialling quickly, her fingers fumbling. 'Come on, come on,' she urged, listening to the ringing.

'Hello?' came a small voice.

'Um, hello?' asked Dante quietly, confused by the young child's voice. 'Who's this?'

'Henry. Who are you?'

Dante paused, thrown by this development. She heard a woman laughing at Henry and taking the phone of him. 'Thank you darling, I'll take that. Hello?'

'Yes, hello,' stammered Dante. 'May I speak to William Kingsford please?'

'Ah. That was the previous owner. Um, I'm afraid he died. Didn't you know? We bought the house a few weeks ago.' The lady paused at the silence on the other end of the phone. 'I'm so sorry to be the one to tell you,' she added gently.

Dante reeled, the room spinning. She mumbled a goodbye and hung up, struggling to take in what she had just heard. Forcing it to the back of her mind with the determination born of necessity she redialled once more with shaking hands. 'Please be home Paige,' she pleaded quietly as the call connected. The phone rang twice. There was a click as it was picked up and then an unmistakeable deep voice answered. 'Hello, Paige's phone?'

Blake. Dante hung up, her face white. 'What's he doing on Paige's phone?' she thought frantically. 'Is he going to get rid of her too?' Her knees buckled and she slid to the floor, her mind racing. 'My daddy's dead,' she moaned, feeling like her heart was breaking.

'I have to pull myself together,' she mumbled. 'I have to call the police.' She opened the phone once more and started to push in numbers.

Brisk footsteps in the hallway outside made her start. She jumped up off the floor, shoving the phone inside her skirt waistband. She was rinsing the crystal glasses at the sink when Paolo opened the door to check on her. 'What have you got in there?' he asked, gesturing at her apron pocket.

'Nada,' stammered Dante. 'Nothing.'

'Show me,' he commanded gruffly. She crossed to him, holding her pocket open for him to check, thankful that she had not kept the phone in there. She broke into a sweat with fear that the phone might beep or ring at any moment.

'One of the guests has lost his phone,' he told her in Spanish, watching her carefully. 'He believes he left it in the library. Did you see it?'

Dante shook her head. 'No, I didn't.'

Paolo shrugged. 'No matter. I will fetch my phone and call his phone from mine and we will find it when it rings.'

Dante felt sure her pale face would give her away. 'Has he really searched properly?' she asked. 'Shall I help look?'

She piled the glasses quickly back onto her tray and left the room, heading for the library. The guest was in there, kneeling to look under a sofa. He looked up, glowering at her as she entered.

'Buenas tardes,' she murmured politely, setting down the glasses. She made a show of looking thoroughly behind scatter cushions and under magazines on the coffee table, shaking her head. As she pulled up the sofa seat cushions to look underneath them she managed to slip the phone out from under her shirt and grab it as if she had just found it. 'Ah!' she cried, brandishing it, hoping the heat from her hand would explain why it felt so warm.

The man took it from her, his eyes appraising her, running over her face and body. 'Gracias señorita,' he murmured close to her ear. Dante shivered at his powerful presence so close to her. 'I don't trust him,' she thought. She scurried out of the room under Paolo's watchful eye and continued her chores, longing for the day to end so that she could try and take in the enormity of the information she'd learned on the phone.

At dinner that night she was aware of two sets of eyes on her constantly – those of Luis and the guest. The latter smirked at her as if he knew a secret, his strong hands playing idly with his teaspoon. Dante tried to ignore him at the same time as trying to ignore all the other information hammering in her head. She tried to shut out the images of her father that kept crowding in on her mind. A lead weight sat in her chest when she thought about Blake possibly hurting Paige. A headache started to press in on her as she tried to focus only on serving the meal. The men's eyes bored into her and she felt like she needed to scream.

She fled as soon as she could to her cupboard and sank gratefully onto the mattress as Paolo locked her in. At last she was alone and could think in peace. She felt numb. She replayed her phone conversation in her head and suddenly reality hit her. She cried for what felt like hours. 'He's dead,' she sobbed. 'I'll never see him again.' The pain in her chest grew and grew and she knew instinctively what had happened. 'He died of a broken heart, I'm sure of it,' she wept. 'Blake tried to kill me and now he's killed my father too.'

At the thought of Blake her heart hardened. 'What's he going to do to Paige?' she wondered. 'Is he pretending to comfort her and then he's going to kill her too? Maybe he knows about the text I sent her. Maybe it did get through after all,' she thought, horrified. 'He'll need to get rid of her to cover himself.' A thought nagged at her brain. 'What if Blake and Paige are in this together? What if she got my text but ignored it?' She banished the thought immediately, hating herself for having even considered it. 'Paige wouldn't do that,' she thought stoutly. 'She's my best friend. It must all have been Blake's doing and now she might be in danger.' She sat bolt upright. 'I have to find a way to warn her!'

Footsteps in the hallway outside made Dante start. They were slow and quiet, as if someone was trying to walk without making any noise. She held her breath and listened. The footsteps drew closer and then stopped right outside her door. 'Who's out there?' Dante wondered, frightened. 'It doesn't sound like Luis.'

She heard the key turning quietly in the lock and then the door was pushed open. The guest from earlier stood there in the dim lighting of the hallway. He smiled wickedly at her, shutting the door behind him.

'I want to talk to you,' he said.

'You speak English too!' exclaimed Dante in surprise.

He squatted down next to her, his eyes raking over her curves in her thin nightgown. She felt uncomfortably as if she were naked, and crossed her

138

arms across her chest. He smiled. 'Yes, I speak English.' The smile vanished from his face. 'I also recognise international phone numbers on my phone. Who were you calling, my pretty?'

Dante froze. 'I didn't delete the numbers I called,' she thought in horror. She shook her head and tried to look puzzled. 'I don't know what you mean.'

'Oh, I think you do,' he said menacingly. 'Why did you steal my phone?' He moved towards her.

Dante backed away until she was up against the wall, feeling threatened. 'I didn't. I promise. I don't know what you mean.'

'Very well,' he purred, kneeling on her mattress and unbuckling his trousers. 'I will make you remember!'

She cried out as he lunged heavily on top of her, pinning her underneath him and pushing up her nightgown with one hand. 'No!' she cried. 'You can't do this. Stop! Help!' She fought to get out from under him, squirming as best she could under his weight. He clamped a large hand hard over her mouth, hurting her neck as she tried to twist away from him.

'I will do this,' he hissed. 'You must be punished.' He grabbed at her breasts with his free hand, laughing into her terrified eyes as he felt her skin. Suddenly his hands were gone and he was being flung off her. She grabbed to correct her nightgown and whipped her head up to see Luis. Roaring with rage he was shaking his guest like a rat.

'Nobody touches her!' he yelled. 'Do you understand me? Nobody!' He wrenched the guest's arm behind his back and marched him from the room.

He paused in the doorway to look at Dante. 'Only I will touch her. After we are married.'

Chapter 13

Luis roughly pushed the guest out of the room and slammed the door. Dante sat shell-shocked on her mattress. 'Married?' she said, in disbelief. 'What new horror is this?' She felt woozy and her hands trembled. The inside of her cheek hurt where the guest had squashed her mouth.

Feeling like her head would explode with all the strange and upsetting information she had gathered that day, she lay down and stared into the darkness, praying in vain for sleep.

The next day, she apprehensively served the meals. She noted that the guest had gone. She waited in fear for Luis to make some reference to the previous night but he ignored her completely.

That night when she returned to the kitchen she sank down onto a stool and stared blankly at Maria.

'What is it, querida?' asked Maria, with concern. 'Was it a bad week?'

Dante blinked, wondering where to begin. 'I found a cell phone,' she stated. Maria clapped her hands and jumped up. 'You did? Did you call your father?' she asked excitedly.

Dante's eyes filled with tears. 'He's dead,' she cried, burying her face in her hands. Maria crossed quickly to hug Dante's heaving frame. 'He's dead,' she wailed, 'and I'm sure it was the news about me that killed him.' She clutched Maria, sobbing her heart out.

'Tell me what happened on the phone,' said Maria gently. Dante explained how she had borrowed the phone and spoken to the new owners of her father's house, then the fresh horror that she had felt on hearing Blake's voice answering Paige's phone. Finally, she confided what had happened with the guest and how Luis had saved her. 'He frightened me,' she said, her eyes troubled. 'As he left the room he said that I was going to be married to him. Surely he doesn't mean that?'

Maria laughed humourlessly, shaking her head. 'Ah Luis! It seems he can still be a good Catholic boy.' She took Dante's hand, her eyes frank. 'Luis wants to sleep with you I think. I have seen him watching you.' Dante's mind flinched away from the thought and she forced herself to listen. 'We were raised as very strict Catholics, it is common in Spain, particularly in this area. Luis picks and chooses which parts of his faith matter to him and I am surprised he is doing it this way but still...' She sighed. 'He must have decided that he will keep you chaste until after you are married to him. Perhaps to make himself feel better about the rest of his treatment of you, of us. It does explain why so far you have only been asked to dance.'

Dante stood up, pacing the kitchen, her heart racing at Maria's matter of fact tone. 'I can't marry Luis,' she cried. 'I won't! Chaste? I'm already married for God's sake and in any case Luis is...repulsive. I won't do it.' She turned pleading eyes to Maria. 'You have to help me!'

'Of course,' agreed her friend. 'We have to get you out of here before he can do this. I am just so glad he stopped that man hurting you.' She hugged Dante tightly.

Their plotting about ways to escape stepped up another level in the following weeks, but still they could not find a way to do it. Dante was frantic about Paige and desperate to call the police but despite her best efforts could not find another phone to use.

'I should have called the police first, as soon as I got the phone,' she angrily berated herself. 'We'd all be out by now.'

When she took her turn upstairs she spent the week in a state of panic and apprehension in case it should prove to be her wedding week, but Luis never mentioned it again. He continued to stare at her and continued to make her dance for him and his friends.

'Cut my hair off,' she begged Maria in desperation one night when she returned to the kitchen. Maria stared at her in confusion. 'Please,' urged Dante, handing her the scissors from the drawer. 'Cut my hair off. Maybe he won't like the look of me with no hair, and he'll change his mind about wanting to marry me.' She laughed bitterly. 'Even if not, at least he won't be able to drag me round the room by my hair anymore.' She touched her tender scalp and grimaced.

Maria took the scissors, looking uncertain. She stroked Dante's soft hair gently. 'Are you sure?' she asked.

Dante blinked back her tears angrily. 'I'm sure,' she said huskily. 'It's not like there's anybody that I need to look nice for.' She sniffed and tucked back her shoulders. 'Please.'

Maria sighed and started to chop.

On her next visit upstairs Dante waited in nervous anticipation to see Luis' reaction to her dramatic hair cut. All of her blonde highlights had been chopped out, leaving only a shorn head of very dark blonde roots. She did not have to wait long. Arriving for lunch Luis saw her at once. He gave a roar of rage and leaped across the room. He slammed her by her throat high against the wall. 'Who told you that you could do this?' he shouted in her face. 'How dare you do this without my permission?' He dropped her, leaving her gasping for breath and shaking on the floor. Some of his guests sniggered at her distress.

She was not called upon to dance that week and her heart leaped, thinking that the pain of being thrown against the wall had been worth it. Her joy was short-lived though as everything returned to normal on her next visit upstairs and her ritual humiliation in front of the men continued.

Christmas and New Year came and went, celebrated lavishly by the men upstairs, but barely noticed by the imprisoned women downstairs. Winter turned to spring.

Before she knew it, eight months had passed since Dante had first arrived at the house. She no longer cared or even noticed that she was permanently underfed; her appetite had disappeared at the same time that she learned that her father was dead. As the months passed she began to lose hope of ever escaping. 'What is there to escape for anyway?' she asked herself dully. 'My life as I knew it is over.'

She looked critically at herself in the mirror as she cleaned one of the bathrooms. She noted how thin she had become, her once shapely frame now simply skinny. Her stomach was concave, her hip bones jutted out alarmingly and her full breasts had shrunk almost to nothing.

She took in the dark hollows under her eyes and her sallow complexion, gained from spending too much time indoors. Her shorn hair was starting to grow out into a short crop. 'I look like a street urchin,' she thought. 'Straight out of Dickens.' She thought with a by now familiar pang of all the wonderful books in her father's library back home. 'What has happened to all of his belongings?' she wondered. 'If he left everything to me in his will, what happens if they think I'm dead too?'

She was called that night to dance once more for Luis and his friends. Tiredly she dragged herself to the library and forced herself to move to the music, closing her eyes as usual so that she wouldn't have to see any faces. Part way through, the music was turned off. Luis barked at Paolo, clearly displeased about something. Paolo led Dante back to her room and shut her in. 'What was that about?' she wondered, bemused. Glad that her usual ordeal had been cut short she put it out of her mind.

The next day at lunch Dante saw Luis filling up two plates. As his guests started to leave the room after the meal he pointed at the untouched second plate and gestured to Dante to take it. 'You will eat,' he said. Dante was instantly wary of this unusual kindness. She hesitated. 'Eat,' he repeated firmly. He watched her cross to the table and start to eat, before leaving the room. Alone with the food Dante gobbled it down as fast as she could, her starved stomach rejoicing. 'If only it was later in the week and I could save some for the other girls without it spoiling,' she thought, as she chewed hastily.

A horrible thought suddenly hit her and she pushed her plate away, her appetite gone. 'What if Luis is trying to fatten me up?' she thought. 'I've lost a lot of weight while I've been here. What if he wants me 'curvy' again before marrying me?' The thought turned her stomach. 'Oh, here we go,' she thought, seeing Paolo enter the room. As she suspected, he seemed to have had his orders from Luis. 'Eat,' he told her. Dante forced herself not to think about Luis but to enjoy finishing the first decent meal she had eaten in a long time. 'It's all giving me good energy to help me escape,' she reminded herself.

Dante shared her fears with Maria when she returned to the kitchen. Maria bit her lip apprehensively. 'You could be right,' she said. 'You are extremely thin now and I know Luis likes his women to be more shapely.'

'I can't marry him Maria,' said Dante defiantly. 'I won't. Even if I did marry him it wouldn't be valid as I'm already married but even without that, he's just so...' She shuddered.

'Like a fat, angry pig?' suggested Maria.

'Exactly,' grimaced Dante. 'He is keeping us all prisoner here, malnourished, starved of daylight, humiliated whenever he feels like it, beaten whenever he is in a bad mood and yet now I am supposed to marry him? And how would that even work? Would he still keep me locked in the kitchen or-?' Her voice trailed off as a thought occurred to her. 'Maybe I can go through with it,' she said slowly. 'Maybe it would give me the chance I need to be upstairs and to escape!'

She thought for a moment but then shook her head, sitting down heavily on a stool.

'I just can't do it,' she said. 'I can't let him touch me.'

Maria sighed, her eyes troubled. 'We have to find a way to get you out before he marries you. Otherwise you will have no choice.'

Chapter 14

Despite their best efforts, Dante and Maria came up with no ideas for escape. The only positive outcome of those weeks was that Luis insisted that Dante should eat. He ensured that sufficient leftovers were sent down for her with the plates. Dante shared the food with the other three women, glad to see them eating and hopeful that she could avoid regaining her curves if she herself ate very little.

Maria warned her to be ready at any time for Luis to put his plan in place. 'He is a devious and selfish man,' she said. 'He will not consider your feelings or give you any time to prepare yourself. Be ready for him to descend on you at any time with a priest.'

'Surely we'll need to go to somewhere official,' said Dante hopefully, 'and then maybe I can run away from there?'

Maria shook her head. 'He will not risk that happening. It will happen here. He has enough friends in high places to make sure he gets a valid marriage certificate without leaving the house. This delay worries me – he is up to something I feel.'

Dante's heart skipped a beat in the familiar way it did whenever she thought about being forced to marry Luis. 'It's just to get upstairs,' she told herself repeatedly. 'I can do it.' She tried to use her days upstairs looking for any information that might be of use to her in plotting an escape route. She memorised the layout of the house, where the windows and doors were, how many staff members she could count and the timings of the household.

'My big chance is going to be the marriage day itself,' she confided to Maria and Ana. 'It will be a break from the normal routine, I might be able to catch Luis off guard.'

'Mmmm,' said Maria, unconvinced. 'Luis is not a man to let down his guard. Be careful.'

On Dante's next turn upstairs she was preparing to hand round a dish of fish stew for dinner when Luis got up from his chair and grabbed her wrist. Surveying the room with a wide grin he addressed his guests in Spanish. 'My friends, do you know what day this is?'

The men shook their heads, laughing, expecting a great joke.

'It is my wedding day. Earlier today I received my official certificate proving my marriage to Aurelia.' He turned to Dante and kissed her hand with wet lips, his eyes mocking.

Dante felt the room spinning. Her mind reeled. 'No!' she shrieked inside her head. 'There was supposed to be a wedding day, I was supposed to be able to try to get word to the priest, I was supposed to be able to try and escape!' She stood frozen to the spot, staring at Luis.

'After dinner you will come to my room,' he stated before sitting back down, to cheers and whistles from the men. Dante's face flushed and she felt a cold sweat breaking out on her forehead. She felt sick.

She barely knew what she was doing as she proceeded round the table with the stew. 'I'm not prepared,' she thought in panic. 'I can't do this.' The men on either side of Luis were chinking glasses with him and telling bawdy jokes, looking over regularly in her direction. She felt hot and ill. She mechanically finished serving, trying to collect her thoughts. Some of the men called for more wine and she moved to pour glasses out for them, topping Luis' glass up at the same time.

'Perhaps if he gets drunk he won't be able to do anything,' she thought. Clutching onto that thought she topped up his glass as often as she could during the meal, trying not to be noticed.

Her hands felt clammy and she cast desperately around for an idea. All too soon dinner was ending and one of the men at the foot of the table was standing to make a toast to Luis and his new bride. Loud guffaws rang around the room and Luis' eyes glittered at Dante. Pushing back his chair, he stood. 'My friends, join me in the library for a digestif while my wife finishes her work.' He shepherded them from the room, turning to Dante before he closed the double doors on her. 'Paolo will bring you to my room,' he said, his eyes glittering.

As soon as the doors shut Dante crossed quickly to the French windows. Cupping her hands around the sides of her face she peered into the darkness. 'Where can I hide?' she wondered. She looked at the enclosed courtyard. 'I have to get out of the front door to get away.' She moved to the dining room doors and eased one open. Peeping out she could see where the hallway branched off to the front door. She could see Paolo sitting in his chair near the corner. 'Damn!' she swore.

She returned to clearing up, hoping against hope that something would happen to prevent her wedding night. She jumped as the door opened and breathed out in relief when she saw it was Maria and Ana coming to collect the dishes. 'It's tonight,' she whispered wildly to them. 'Luis has got a marriage certificate and says I'm married to him. I have to go to his room tonight.' She stared wildly at the other women whose horrified faces mirrored her own. The door opened once more and Paolo returned. 'Come,' he beckoned to Dante. She clung to the table, unable and unwilling to move. 'Come,' he repeated impatiently, taking her arm and yanking her towards the door. Dante threw a last desperate look back over her shoulder at the other women as she was pulled from the room.

Paolo gripped her arm as he took her to her cupboard. 'Change to nightgown,' he ordered, waiting outside. Dante trembled as she changed her clothes. She sat on the mattress for a moment to gather her thoughts but Paolo entered the tiny room and roughly pulled her up.

As she was hustled along the dim hallway, she remembered the first time she had been taken on her night-time visit to the library and her fears about what would happen to her. 'This time it's real,' she thought frantically, her breath fast and shallow. 'What should I do?'

Paolo pushed open Luis' heavy bedroom door and shoved her forward. Luis sat in an armchair in a thick towelling robe, his hair wet and slicked back. 'Thank you Paolo,' he said smoothly. 'I won't need you again tonight.' Paolo closed the door quietly behind him as he left.

Dante's eyes darted around the room looking for any way out. The shutters were closed behind the windows. Luis heaved his heavy frame out of the armchair and moved towards her, stroking her cheek as he passed her. Dante flinched. He went to the door and calmly locked it then turned back to look at her, his hands on the belt of his robe. Dante trembled. 'You can't do this,' she said. 'It's not legal. I didn't marry you.'

Luis smirked at her. 'I have the papers that say you did,' he said, stepping forward towards her. She stumbled backwards away from him into the centre of the room.

'No!' she cried.

'Yes,' he disagreed, reaching her in one swift step. Dante felt the side of the bed behind her knees and knew that there was nowhere for her to go. She froze in horror as he pushed the straps of her nightgown aside and pulled it down to her waist, trapping her arms against her sides. He grabbed at her breasts, his face wolfish. The feel of his sweaty hands on her skin unfroze Dante. She struggled to get her arms free and tried to push him away as hard as she could. Luis grabbed her wrists, yanking both her arms behind her. He pushed one fat leg between hers and fondled her breasts roughly with his free hand. Dante tried to squirm away but couldn't escape. He pushed her nightgown over her hips and off her body completely. He ran his free hand over her naked buttocks, grasping at her flesh.

153

'Yes,' he said again, his voice thick with desire. He bit at her neck and shoved his hand between her legs. 'Stop, please stop,' sobbed Dante. 'You can't do this.'

'You will do as I say,' growled Luis. He flung her backwards onto the bed. Dante scrambled off the other side, but Luis strode round and was there instantly. He held her wrists together as he grabbed his leather belt from the floor one-handed, his eyes never leaving her face. Wrapping it tightly around her wrists in front of her body he pushed her back onto the large bed. The leather cut into her skin making her wince. She struggled to shake it loose before he could tie it properly.

Thinking quickly as Luis clambered up onto the bed Dante whipped the belt towards him. The large pewter buckle caught him in the face and he yelled in pain. Scrambling awkwardly away, Dante heard him roaring behind her. She grabbed with her constrained hands at the heavy lamp on the bedside table, feeling new strength in her desperation. She swung it wildly around behind her. It connected with the side of Luis' head and sent him sprawling onto the bed.

Silence. Dante's arms shook and she dropped the lamp onto the bed next to Luis. She slid the now loose belt from her wrists, too frightened to cry. Luis' fat form lay motionless on the bed. Blood seeped from his hair onto the sheets. 'Have I killed him?' she wondered, surprised by how little she cared that she might just have murdered someone. She edged away from his flabby body and off the bed, holding her breath in case he came to. She saw his chest rising and falling slowly and knew that he was still breathing. The sight propelled her to action. 'I have to leave. Now,' she decided. 'If he wakes up he'll kill me.'

She slipped her nightgown and flip-flops back on, grabbing at Luis' trousers and shirt as she passed the chair. She edged towards the door, keeping her eyes on Luis' unconscious form. She reached the door then stopped. 'I can't let him come after me,' she thought. She strode back to the bed, her heart pounding. She grabbed the belt and tied his hands tightly behind his back. She looked around and saw his discarded socks, shoving them roughly into his mouth. She lifted the lamp once more and held the heavy base over his head. 'I could crush his skull. One more smash should do it,' she thought. A wave of nausea rushed over her and she shook her head, recalling Maria's words about not wanting to be a murderer. 'I can't do it.' She dropped the lamp onto the bed and backed away. 'I have to get out. Right now.'

She headed back to the door and unlocked it as quietly as she could.

Easing open the heavy door she peered outside. Nobody was in the hallway. She removed the key from the lock and closed the bedroom door, locking Luis in the room from the outside. She noticed another large key on the chain. 'It must be the one for the front door,' she thought, her heart leaping. 'Maria said Luis has the only one.'

Gripping the keys tightly in her sweating hand and holding on to the stolen bundle of clothes, she tiptoed down the hallway towards the front door. Her heart was in her mouth. 'If Paolo or another staff member is guarding the front door then I'm lost,' she thought. She padded to a vantage point on the opposite wall from where she could see the front door and the guard's seat. Nobody was there. 'They must have taken Luis at his word that they wouldn't be needed anymore tonight,' she thought with relief.

'Keep moving, keep moving,' she urged herself, terrified that Luis would awaken at any moment. 'I just have to get out,' she thought as she urged her feet forward. 'This is my chance.' She flew across the hallway and over to the door, sliding the large iron key silently into the keyhole.

She paused for a moment to pull on Luis' trousers and shirt, tucking in her nightgown. Both items were enormous on her, and she had to clutch the huge amount of excess cloth on the trousers together with one hand. She hated his scent on the clothes. 'At least I might look like a man at a glance, rather than a girl in a nightie, and the dog might know his smell,' she thought, doubly glad now that her hair was short and no longer dyed blonde.

She turned the lock as quietly as possible and eased back the long iron security bar. It made a hollow, metallic clunk as it slid into place, sounding to Dante as loud as thunder. She held her breath but heard no-one. Deciding to repeat her trick with the keys, she slipped outside, closed the large door carefully behind her and relocked it. She was out.

Chapter 15

Turning round, she surveyed the landscape. Outside the front of the house was an imposing stone porch with columns either side of the door and three wide steps leading down to the gravel driveway. Large urns stood at the sides of the steps, filled with tumbling flowers.

The moon came out from behind a cloud and revealed the full length of the driveway with lawns stretching away on either side. 'Great,' thought Dante, her heart sinking. 'The second I step off this porch I'm going to be completely exposed.' She shoved her flip-flops into the trouser pocket and took a deep breath.

Her heart pounding, she waited until another cloud passed over the moon then ran, choosing the grass rather than the gravel. 'If there's a guard around I'll just have to hope he thinks I'm one of the guests,' she thought. 'I can do this.' She ran as quickly as she could without tripping over. The grass was wet under her feet, dampening the hems of the long trousers. At every second she expected to hear shouts from the house, or to see the lawns flooded with lights as they discovered her escape.

The moon came back out and she slowed to a casual pace, trying to walk like a man in case the guard was nearby.

Adrenaline kept her going, eyes forward, aiming for the large wrought-iron gates she could now make out at the end of the driveway. Suddenly, she heard a shout to her left. A dog started barking. 'A large dog by the sounds of it,' she thought in fear. She forced herself to look towards the shout and raise her arm in a casual wave, continuing to walk forward. The security guard moved towards her, the huge Alsatian at his side straining at his leash. 'I can't let him come right to me, he'll see I'm a woman,' Dante thought in terror. 'I'll call to him that I'm just taking a walk.' She raised her voice and called out in as manly a voice as she could muster, 'Hola! Quiero cambiar un poco.'

She gave him another wave and turned away from him as if she were just doing a circuit of the lawn and enjoying the night air. She strolled on, her heart beating frantically, until she heard the guard and the dog moving away in the other direction. She glanced back and saw them heading towards the house.

Wheeling round, she raced as fast as she could for the gates. A blaze of light made her head snap towards the house. Her stomach dropped. Lights were shining suddenly from several of the downstairs windows. 'Something's happened! They know!' she cried to herself. She broke into a run and hurled herself at the gates. She shook them but they were locked up with a chain.

'Climb! Climb!' she yelled at herself. Grateful for Luis' innate love of showy decoration, she used the elaborate swirling shapes of the iron as footholds to help her climb over, relieved to see that no second guard was waiting outside the gates.

The oversized trousers made it hard for her to stretch her legs, and her hands and feet were slippery on the cool ironwork. She forced herself upwards. A shout rang out behind her, back towards the house. She threw herself over the top of the gates, dropping with a painful thud on the other side.

Not even acknowledging the sudden pain in her knee and the deep grazes stinging her hands, she ran as fast as her legs would carry her. She was on a dark road and had no idea which way she was headed. She knew that Luis' men would be right behind her. 'I can't outrun them,' she thought, panicking, her breath rasping from her chest. 'They're going to kill me! What do I do now?'

She plunged off the road and into the woods on the other side. Her bare feet burned with cuts and scratches. Twigs snatched at her hair and whipped her face but she didn't slow down. Eventually she stopped, trying not to make any sound. Her laboured breathing sounded loud in her ears and she tried to hear any other noises. It was pitch black in the woods and she shivered, terrified of being discovered and almost as frightened of any possible lurking creatures. 'Are there wolves or bears in southern Spain?' she wondered, her skin prickling with fear.

Suddenly she heard men's voices shouting faintly back at the road and she froze, hidden behind a large tree. A few moments later she heard distant branches moving. Twigs and dry leaves on the ground crackled and snapped somewhere not far behind her. The trees off to her left were lit up faintly by a distant torch. Clutching her enormous clothes around her Dante stood like a statue. She felt faint with fear. The torch light was suddenly bright, sweeping around the trees behind her. A large cricket landed on her hair and she fought the urge to shriek and brush it off. The light turned and whoever was hunting her there started to move away.

Slowly the woods became completely silent other than the crickets and frogs chirruping in the bushes. 'I should keep moving,' she thought, flexing her cold, stiff limbs. 'I need to get as far away as I can while it's dark.' She moved cautiously out from behind her tree and started to pick her way silently through the woods, in case anyone had been left behind to listen for movements. 'I'll just stay in the woods but follow the direction the road was going as best I can,' she decided.

With her ears pricked for any sounds and staying barefoot to be as silent as possible, she picked her way slowly through the trees, limping now from the pain in her knee. She pushed to the back of her mind the thoughts of rabid wolves and hungry bears that tormented her. 'You've got enough real problems without imagining those as well,' she told herself crossly. She walked slowly on for hours, glad now that Luis had insisted on feeding her up over the last few weeks.

She realised that she was still clutching the two keys from the house, and she bent to shove them into the soft earth of the forest floor. She thought of Maria as she did so, a sob rising in her throat at having deserted her friend and at being alone once more.

She wiped her eyes. 'Maria would be glad that I'm out,' she told herself. 'I just hope she and the other girls won't be punished for my escape. I'll send the police for them as soon as I can. I can't tell the local police – I bet Luis bribes them. Damn it – I should have looked for Luis' cell phone! He must have one – I bet it was right there in the room with me.' Cursing quietly, she ploughed on through the forest. 'Let's hope it is an actual escape,' she thought, 'and not just a little night-time adventure before Luis' henchmen catch up with me.'

After several hours she saw lights twinkling ahead through the thinning trees and caught her breath, dipping behind a tree. The lights stayed put and Dante realised that she must have reached a town.

Approaching cautiously, she kept a sharp eye for any spies from Luis' house. She ran stealthily towards a low brick wall at the back of someone's house. No-one could be seen, and all the lights were off. 'It must be about 4am or so,' guessed Dante. 'Presumably everyone's asleep.'

Staying low against the wall she continued on to the next house. Peeping over their wall she saw a clothes line full of drying laundry that hadn't been taken inside overnight. Her eyes widened. 'Perfect! I can redo my disguise,' she thought. She eased herself gently over the wall and dropped into the garden. Reaching the clothes line she quickly unpegged a black skirt and pale cardigan.

She dashed back over the wall and back to the cover of the trees, noting that the dawn was approaching. Slipping out of Luis' enormous clothes she decided to keep her nightgown on. She slipped the black skirt over it, tucking in her nightgown once again, and slipped the cardigan on top of that, unbuttoned to make her nightgown look like a pretty vest top.

She decided to stay in the shadow of the trees until it was properly morning, in the hope that she could then blend in more easily with the people of the village if anyone was watching for her. 'If I head into town now, in the middle of the night, it will be deserted, and anyone watching for me will see me immediately. I'll stay here, hidden in the trees until morning.'

She felt suddenly exhausted and realised she had not had any sleep since the previous night. 'You can't go to sleep,' she warned herself. 'Someone could find you. You have to stay alert.'

She hunkered down between two large trees, wrapping herself in Luis' shirt and trousers for warmth, and waited for daylight.

She awoke to loud birdsong and didn't know where she was. Sitting upright from her slumped position, she saw the clearing in the woods and remembered the events of the night before. 'You fell asleep, you idiot!' she chided herself, looking anxiously around. She couldn't see anyone. The only sound was the birds in the trees above her. She stood and brushed herself off. She ran her hands through her hair, hoping that she wasn't too obviously homeless and on the run.

Stepping to the edge of the clearing she saw that the sun was already quite high in the sky. 'Let's do this,' she muttered to herself. She stashed Luis' clothes in a hollow log on the ground and strolled out of the woods as if she had been for a walk. Walking slowly and trying not to limp, she passed by the backs of several houses and found herself on a street bustling with stalls. 'Market day,' she thought, feeling overwhelmed by all the sights and sounds after so long imprisoned in the house. She tried not to stare at all the new faces and sights.

She stooped swiftly to pick up a basket she saw lying untended by a stall, and moved through the throng of women who were buying fresh fruit and vegetables. She kept her eyes on the ground looking for money but with her ears pricked for familiar voices. 'If anyone has dropped any coins I need to find them,' she thought. She kept her scraped hands gripped firmly around the handle of the basket and hoped nobody would notice her scratched and bloodied feet in her flip-flops. 'I'm so pale compared to everyone else I must stick out like a sore thumb,' she thought nervously.

Her persistent searching paid off and after about a quarter of an hour she had picked up a couple of silver coins. Her stomach rumbled at the smells emanating from the bread stalls, but she slipped the coins into her skirt pocket.

Making her way out of the market street she looked around for a bus stop. Across the street and to the right she saw her target but then her blood ran cold. Standing underneath the bus sign, smoking a cigarette and looking furious, was Paolo.

Dante whirled round and headed back into the safe anonymity of the jostling shoppers, her mind whirring. 'I have to get on a bus out of here, Maria said the next nearest town is miles away,' she thought. 'How can I get past Paolo?' She slipped down a side street and leant on a wall, considering her options. Back in the sunshine of the main street she could see stallholders replenishing their wares from large sacks.

She saw an elderly man unloading a sack full of pumpkins. 'They must be heavy,' she thought. 'I wonder where he brings them from? He must use a van.' She stood up straight. 'That's it!' she thought. 'I have to get out of here the same way I arrived – in the back of a van.'

Chapter 16

She headed purposefully back into the main shopping street, holding her breath in case a shout rang out to apprehend her. She followed the man with his empty pumpkin sack closely.

A couple of streets away from the centre of town they reached a playing field, converted for the day into a car park. She hung back in a doorway, watching. She saw the pumpkin farmer reach his small truck. She liked his friendly face. 'I've definitely never seen him at the house, so I hope he's nothing to do with Luis,' she thought, crossing her fingers superstitiously.

She noticed that the flat bed section of his truck was covered in saws and other farm machinery. 'I can't hide amongst that,' she thought with disappointment. The farmer got into the front and started the engine. 'He must have finished here already,' thought Dante. 'I'll have to find someone else's van to hide in.'

As the farmer pulled out of the car park and drew level with Dante he paused to let an elderly lady cross in front of him. On an impulse Dante stepped forward and knocked on his window, smiling politely.

'Good day sir,' she said in Spanish. 'Would you be so kind as to give me a lift out of town? I've missed my bus but have an appointment.'

'Si, si, con mucho gusto,' smiled the farmer, gesturing to his passenger seat. With a grin, Dante hurried round and hopped into the passenger seat, thanking the man profusely. She pulled the sun visor down to hide her face as much as possible and kept her basket on her knee to look like a local in case anyone glanced in.

She cursed inwardly as they got stuck in slow traffic moving through the stalls, with goats and people wandering freely alongside the vehicles. The farmer laughed and waved his hands in the air as if to say how chaotic it all was and Dante tried hard to look relaxed and laugh with him.

Her smile froze as she spotted one of Luis' men outside on the pavement, only a few feet from the van. He was scrutinising the market crowds, his face forbidding.

Dante broke out in a sweat. With mounting horror she watched him walk in the direction of her van. She forced herself to look elsewhere, scared that if she continued staring at him he would feel her gaze and look at her. She asked the farmer about himself and was glad when he started a long tale about his farm and how long he had lived in the area.

Eventually the van moved forward and suddenly they were barrelling down a side street and out into the country lanes. The farmer accelerated away. Dante breathed a sigh of relief, winding down her window to feel the wind in her hair. The farmer asked where Dante wanted to be dropped off.

'Well, I need to get to Madrid,' she said in Spanish. 'But I'm not sure how to get there. I'm quite new to Spain.'

'Madrid!' the farmer whistled. 'Well now, I'm not too sure myself but I think you'd need to get to Cadiz and then catch the bus or the train from there.' He glanced quizzically at her. 'What takes you to

Madrid? It's a long way for a young girl to go on her own.'

Dante forced an airy laugh. 'Oh I'm just sightseeing,' she said. 'I'm on holiday from...England, travelling around Spain for a while, but I got on the wrong bus yesterday and I had all my luggage stolen at the same time.' She shrugged, trying to look philosophical about her imagined loss. 'Now I'm here without any of my belongings, and so I'm meeting friends in Madrid to help me get home, so I just have to make it there somehow,' she gabbled, hoping her made up story was making sense.

The old man nodded. 'It sounds like you've had some bad luck,' he said. 'I'll drive you to Algeciras – you can catch a bus from there to Cadiz very easily.'

Dante's capable exterior wobbled when she saw the man smiling kindly at her and a tear leaked out. 'Thank you so much,' she sniffed.

They chatted easily in Spanish about the surrounding countryside and Geraldo's lifelong work as a farmer. Dante heard all about his five grandchildren. 'The proudest achievements of my life,' he admitted with a soppy grin.

After about twenty minutes they arrived in the outskirts of Algeciras, a larger town on the coast. Geraldo drove straight to the bus station and accompanied Dante to the ticket office. He spoke to the lady behind the counter and presented Dante with a ticket. 'Your bus leaves in five minutes from just here,' he said, smiling kindly at her. 'Muchas gracias Geraldo,' stammered Dante. 'You've been so kind- '

She broke off as Geraldo handed her some notes. 'Take this too,' he said gruffly. 'You have not had a good experience of my beautiful country so far, but now I hope that you will.'

'Geraldo, I can't possibly!' said Dante, touched.

'I insist,' he said, pushing the money into her hand. Tears sprang to her eyes at his generosity. She knew he couldn't really afford the gesture but she knew she needed the money more. Impulsively she threw her arms around his neck. 'Thank you Geraldo, you kind man,' she whispered. She drew back, looking solemnly into his eyes. 'I'll pay you back, I promise. I will find my money and I will send this back to you. Please at least take this for now to show I'm serious,' she added, pressing her basket into his hands, embarrassed that it was all that she had to give him.

He smiled and patted her hand. 'I hope you enjoy the rest of your time in Spain my dear. Get home safely,' he said, giving her a wave with the basket as he headed back to his van.

Dante was overwhelmed. 'This might be enough money to get me all the way to Madrid,' she thought, feeling much more positive about her escape plans. She turned to go to her bus and saw Jorge, Luis' gardener, guarding the entrance gate to the buses. Hatred rose in her at the memory of him spying on her in the bath. She felt sweat prickling her skin once again at the thought that she was about to be recaptured.

'Just brazen it out,' she told herself. 'The bus is going to leave in a minute, you have to get on it. Jorge hasn't seen you since you cut your hair off and you're not in uniform. He won't recognise you.'

Keeping her eyes down she walked briskly past him, giving her ticket to the guard. Her heart thumped as she waited what felt like forever for him to return her ticket and allow her to pass through. Eventually she was allowed through and she moved to the bus door. No-one called after her. She chose a seat on the far side of the bus and drummed her fingers on her knees until the engine started. 'Come on, come on!' she urged silently. 'Doesn't anything leave on time here?' Eventually the doors closed and the bus pulled away. She breathed out and tried to slow her beating heart.

She looked out of the window to see which direction they were taking and locked eyes with Jorge on the pavement below as he crossed to his car. She looked away at once, her heart pounding once more, willing the bus to go faster. 'Please don't let him recognise me,' she thought, waiting anxiously for a shout of recognition. No shout came, but Dante's head started to pound.

The bus accelerated smoothly out of the bus station and was soon speeding along the roads. It seemed to be a direct bus without frequent stops, for which Dante was extremely grateful. The wheels on the road made a soothing sound and she nodded off.

She awoke as the bus pulled into Cadiz. She looked cautiously around from her window but didn't see anyone she recognised. She made her way to the train station without incident and looked up at the departure board for the next train to Madrid. A different train caught her eye. 'Barcelona!' she whispered. 'That's even further away than Madrid. I'll go there instead. It's a night train too, so that takes care of

169

where I'm going to sleep tonight as well.' She felt better for having changed her plans in case Geraldo was somehow found and questioned by Luis' men. She laughed at herself. 'I'm acting like Luis rules half of Spain, but you never know, better to be safe than sorry.'

Two policemen strolled past and she turned away, trying to hear the crackling voice on their radio. 'Are they looking for me?' she wondered. 'Can I trust them to help if I report Luis and tell them about the other girls?' She felt a sense of foreboding. 'I can't trust anyone,' she thought. 'I'm still too close to Luis' house. I have to report this once I get to Barcelona. Is there a Spanish FBI?'

Saying a prayer for Maria, Ana and Sofia she limped over to the ticket office and acquired a seat on the sleeper train. Her heart went out gratefully once again to Geraldo when she saw that she had enough for the ticket and still had a small amount left over. Ravenous after the events of the last 24 hours, she bought herself a large ham, cheese and salad baguette and an orange juice then tucked herself away in a dark corner of the train station to eat.

Feeling much better for having eaten, she headed to the ladies toilets to make herself presentable. 'This outfit really doesn't look too bad,' she considered, surveying herself critically in the large mirror. She washed her hands and face and rinsed out her mouth, starting to feel human again. She slipped off her cardigan to wash and dry under her arms and then stretched to lift one foot at a time into the sink to wash them, ignoring the strange looks from the other patrons. Both feet were scratched and blistered, but felt much better for being clean. 'I'll have to get some proper shoes somehow,' she thought, looking at her thin flip-flops.

Back upstairs she had several hours to kill. She fingered the coins in her pocket, looking for a pay phone. 'I have to get in touch with Paige,' she thought urgently. Spotting a bank of phones she rushed over. She swore, seeing that they all needed a phone card of some sort. As she turned away she saw a solitary old-fashioned, coin-operated phone. Hurrying over, she lifted the receiver and then paused, her mind a sudden blank. 'I can't remember her number,' she thought, lost without her phone's address book. 'Damn. Think! Think! You remembered it the last time.' In the intervening months of drudgery and stress the number had completely slipped from her mind.

She thought for a moment and then dialled the number listed for Spain's telephone directory service on the phone. 'It's a number in the United States. Paige Osborne in New York City,' she directed the woman at the other end of the line. 'I'm sorry, we have no record for that name,' came the response. Dante felt a chill clutch her heart but tried to think rationally.

'Blake wouldn't do anything to harm Paige,' she told herself. 'It would look too suspicious for both his wife and her best friend to die. I'll try to remember her cell number and call her from Barcelona.' She returned to her seat and stared at the departures board, waiting impatiently for her train.

Eventually the time came to board and Dante found a seat by the window in the third carriage. It was a large, fabric-covered seat with comfortable headrest and plenty of leg room. It seemed like luxury to Dante after her months of confinement. She felt the usual flicker of excitement that she always experienced at the beginning of a train journey. It was dark outside and Dante watched the reflection of the bright carriage in the window as people boarded the train.

Dante tensed as a man in a suit sat down in the seat diagonally opposite her, then forced herself to relax as he nodded a hello at her. 'There are plenty of people in this country who aren't linked to Luis!' she reminded herself. The man pulled a sheaf of newspapers out of his briefcase and began to read, leaning on the table between them.   The train pulled slowly out of the platform and quickly picked up speed. Dante could feel her eyelids growing heavy. She leaned her head against the window and closed her eyes.

When she awoke it was daylight. Fields of crops flew past the windows, and the sun was warm through the glass. For the first time since her escape Dante felt she could believe that she was really free. She plotted her next move. 'When I get to Barcelona I'll go straight to the US embassy,' she decided. 'They'll help me and they'll contact police who can rescue the others. I'll probably be on a plane home by tomorrow at the latest.' She hugged her arms tightly to herself, excited but fearful at the thought. 'I wonder what I'll be going home to?' she thought.

The man opposite her was still asleep. She glanced down at his newspapers, spread across the table in a messy arc. She practised her Spanish and her upside down reading by deciphering headlines about

172

political machinations in Madrid and news about taxes. Her eyes roved to the next paper and she couldn't believe her eyes. 'The Times,' she whispered reverentially. Her Anglophile father had continually told her that of all the papers in the world, London's 'The Times' was the best. At that particular moment Dante would have read any newspaper at all as long as it was in English.

'Would you like to take it?' asked a heavily accented voice in English. Dante looked up with a start. Her neighbour was awake and smiling at her. 'I saw you looking at the newspaper – I have finished with it if you would like to take it.' He pushed it towards her. 'It is already two days old,' he apologised.

'Thank you very much,' smiled Dante. 'I haven't seen an English-language newspaper in a while.' She noticed his watch. 'Could you tell me the time? I'm wondering how long we have left?'

The man pulled back his cuff and glanced at his watch. 'It's seven o'clock. We should be arriving in Barcelona in about forty-five minutes.'

Dante thanked him and decided to keep the newspaper for later. She watched as the countryside gradually changed from pretty rural scenes to more industrial zones and then, unmistakably, to a large city. 'Barcelona,' she whispered to herself.

Chapter 17

Dante followed the crowd from the train and arrived in the main atrium of Sants station. She followed the signs for taxis and instructed the next available driver to take her to the US embassy. 'I hope I have enough money left for this, I have no idea how much it should be,' she worried, fingering her coins. She watched, fascinated, as Barcelona's beauty was revealed to her on the drive through the city. Even at that early hour of the morning tourists were already out in force, taking snaps of each other in front of statues and fountains.

The car drew up outside an imposing set of gates. '12 euros', said the cabbie. Dante's heart sank. 'I'm so sorry, I only have 8,' she said. The driver swore. 'You go to bank, señorita,' he said firmly. Dante wrung her hands. 'I can't, I'm so sorry, I've lost all my belongings, I don't have a bank card. It's why I'm here at my embassy,' she explained, embarrassed. 'Please, write down your name and cab number and I will come and find you with the rest of the money, I promise.'

'Yeah, of course lady,' shouted the driver. 'You think I'm stupid? You think I don't understand you rude Americans? Get out of my cab!'

Dante scrambled out, her face bright red, trying to commit to memory the man's name as she went from his licence picture hanging in the back. 'I'm sorry Manuel!' she called as he screeched away, giving her the finger. 'Nice!' she thought. 'Well, I probably deserved that.'

Shaken by her bad start to the city she turned to survey the embassy. A sign on the gate said that visitors' hours started at 10am. Dante sighed. 'Of course they do. Why would they want to start as early as the rest of the world when they have a cushy little embassy job? That would be too helpful.' She sat down on the kerb nearby, rubbing her arms briskly. 'I wish I had a coat,' she thought, shivering. 'It's a lot colder up here.'

Her mind turned to Luis and whether he had been informed of her escape. She looked up and down the street but could not see a public phone box. 'I'll call the police as soon as I finish here. The embassy staff will help me,' she said to herself. To keep her mind off Maria and the other girls she unfolded her newspaper and started to read. More political intrigue in the English parliament kept her entertained.

She was just enjoying a piece on newly released fiction when she heard a clock nearby strike ten. She jumped up and groaned when she saw a small queue had formed behind her outside the embassy while she hadn't been looking. She jogged a few steps to join the end of it. Glad of her paper, she continued reading as she waited to reach the front. On reaching the gates a security guard asked her name. 'Dante Kingsford,' she said, thrilled to be speaking to a fellow American in person at last. 'I need to speak to someone in the embassy. I'm an American citizen and I need urgent assistance.'

'Do you have an appointment?' the guard asked, skimming his finger down the list in his hand.

'No I don't. Do I need one?' asked Dante with concern.

'It speeds things up,' the guard explained. He buzzed her through the gates. 'Follow the signs up to the waiting room on the second floor,' he directed.

Thanking him, she strode into the building and up to the second floor, feeling relaxed for the first time in months now that she was practically back on US soil. A weight had lifted from her shoulders. 'It's just a matter of time before I'm home,' she thought, her mind empty of worries for once.

On entering the waiting room she saw at least a dozen chairs already occupied. She sighed in frustration. 'Take a ticket please miss,' said another guard, handing her a number.

'Please, I don't think you understand,' said Dante. 'I really need to speak urgently to someone who can help me. I'm a missing person and I need help.'

'Well, you're here now and you'll be seen just as soon as possible, but everyone thinks their problem is urgent,' said the guard.

'Really?' asked Dante. 'Do they all have lives at stake? It's crucial that I speak to someone immediately.'

'Everybody thinks the same miss. Please just take the ticket and wait your turn.'

'But I've been-'

'Take the ticket miss.'

Dante looked at the guard's impassive face and decided that arguing with someone trained in being obstructive would be a waste of time. Frustrated, she

177

chose a seat and continued with her newspaper to alleviate her irritation.

She turned to the society page and settled into her chair to enjoy some classy gossip. Suddenly she gripped the paper tightly, not believing her eyes. A picture of Blake with his arm round a laughing Paige stared out at her from the paper. She stared back at her, taking in the closeness of their pose and Paige's elegant new haircut. She scanned the attached piece frantically, her face pale.

'Blake Harrington, the charismatic New York entrepreneur and darling of the Arts scene, last week took delivery of his first wife's estate which was being held by the State pending the outcome of a coroner's report into her tragic death. Mrs Dante Harrington is believed to have committed suicide while on their honeymoon cruise in July last year. Dante Harrington was the sole heir of her father, William Kingsford, who also died last year. On Dante's death her entire inheritance passed to Mr Harrington. Payment of the inheritance last week makes Mr Harrington one of the richest men under 35 in New York and, were it not for his new wife, one of the city's most eligible bachelors. A few eyebrows were raised when Mr Harrington hastily mended his own heart, but no doubt broke a good many more, by marrying his close friend Paige Osborne three months ago in a small ceremony in Boston.'

Dante staggered to her feet, her face green. She couldn't breathe. She felt as though the room were suffocating her. 'Are you OK miss?' asked the guard, catching Dante's arm as she swayed.

Dante shook her head. 'Air,' she mumbled, stumbling out into the corridor. She stumbled down the stairs and across the courtyard, feeling as though she might faint.

'Done already?' asked the security guard in surprise.

'I'll come back,' Dante muttered, heading on auto pilot into the street. She didn't know where she was headed and she didn't care.

She walked for hours, trying to take it all in, the pain in her knee forgotten. Her head was spinning. 'Paige and Blake are married!' she kept repeating dully. She couldn't believe it. 'How could she leap into my shoes and try to replace me like this? And so soon?' she thought. She doubled over as a new thought occurred to her. 'This is what Paige wanted all along,' she thought, trying to take a breath. 'I didn't believe it before but it has to be true.'

Memories flashed through her mind of Paige never meeting her eye when she asked about Blake and frequently staring at him. 'She wasn't jealous of him, she was jealous of me!' Dante realised, remembering Paige's spiteful undertone a few times before the wedding. 'Maybe she really was in this with Blake all along so that she could marry him herself and they'd both be rich. The bitch.'

She slumped onto a bollard, feeling naive and increasingly faint. Looking up, she saw a restaurant across the street. She staggered over and asked the waitress for a glass of water. The waitress took pity on her seeing her shocked face and inappropriate clothing and pressed her into a chair inside. She brought her a large glass of water and a slim packet of breadsticks. 'Gracias,' muttered Dante. She took a long drink and stared at the table trying to fit together all the pieces.

'It all makes sense,' she thought. 'What an idiot I was. I knew Paige liked Blake too when we met him but I thought she was happy for me. In fact, she must have been jealous the whole time. Perhaps he was cheating on me with her all along,' she thought dully. 'They must have plotted together to get rid of me, and now they're rich. Blake will have inherited all my father's shares so he must now control The Kingsford Corporation.' Anger blazed through her at the thought of their betrayals. 'They will not get away with this,' she vowed.

She looked around the restaurant. Tables were being laid for lunch. A note by the door caught her eye and she stood to read it. 'Help wanted. Must have restaurant experience. Apply within.' Dante jumped as the waitress appeared behind her. 'Can I bring you anything to eat?' she asked. Dante made her decision in a flash.

'I'm looking for work,' she said in Spanish. 'I can cook well and I know how to wait on tables. May I apply for the position please?'

'Sure, I'll go and get my father,' smiled the girl. 'May I take your name?'

Dante thought of her old life lying in tatters and the chance for a new start. 'Aurelia,' she said. She thought of Maria and all her kindness. 'Aurelia Santa Maria.'

She watched as the girl headed to the kitchen to call her father. 'I can get this job,' she thought, 'and I'll be a completely new person.' She glanced at her reflection in the window. She looked like a totally different girl from the one who had happily set off on her honeymoon cruise. 'He really did kill me. Dante is dead. I don't want to be Dante anymore.'

She ran a hand through her hair and tucked her shoulders back with determination. 'I don't want my old life back,' she thought. Her eyes narrowed. 'I want revenge.'

Part II

10 years later...

Chapter 18

Reservations for dinner on the opening night of 'Milagro' were by invitation only.   The wealthy, rich and famous of New York arrived at the restaurant in chauffeur driven limousines, decked out in their glittering finery. A crowd waited eagerly outside, trying to snap pictures and ask for autographs before the guests were ushered inside and cocooned in the luxurious sanctuary of the restaurant.

A buzz of excitement electrified the waiting reporters. 'She's coming!' they whispered amongst themselves at last. A stretch limo drew up at the kerb. The waiting doorman stepped forward to open the rear door. The closest reporter, NBC's roving cub Kacey Errol, stepped in front of her partner's camera.

Lifting the microphone, she gestured behind her. 'The crowd is waiting impatiently to catch its first glimpse of Spanish celebrity chef Aurelia Santa Maria. Never has a chef inspired such interest in the general public and certainly not one so young. At only 33, and with her sultry European looks, she could easily pass for a movie star. Men and women alike seem to have fallen for her. She has just pulled up behind me and you can see, yes, there she is! You can hear the applause from the onlookers and I believe, yes, she's very kindly crossing over to the barriers to sign a few autographs. This is Ms Santa Maria's first visit to New York and she is here specifically to oversee the launch of her latest branch of 'Milagro.'

She waved eagerly at Aurelia. 'Aurelia! Over here! NBC News! May we ask you a couple of quick questions?'

Aurelia moved towards Kacey, effortlessly elegant in a long black evening gown and creamy cashmere pashmina. 'But of course,' she smiled, her thick Spanish accent evident immediately.

'Congratulations on the opening of your latest venture, you must be very proud of your 'Milagro' chain,' said Kacey, thrusting the mike towards Aurelia.

Aurelia smiled again, tossing her long, gleaming dark hair over her shoulder. 'I am of course very proud although I prefer not to think of 'Milagro' as a chain. My restaurants in Paris, London and of course, Barcelona, are all individual in their own ways, tailored to the needs of their city, and serving only the highest quality Spanish cuisine.' She waved at some squealing onlookers.

'We know that delicious Spanish cuisine well,' said Kacey. 'I believe almost every household in this country has at least one of your cookbooks. We're delighted that you've finally made it to the States. What took you so long?'

'Well, I am delighted to have so many wonderful fans in America,' smiled Aurelia. 'I wanted to be sure that my restaurants in Europe were complete and could maintain their high quality independently but now I feel that I can leave them for a while. I am so pleased to be here finally and to be spending some time in your wonderful country.'

The crowd behind her cheered.

'And will you be staying long?'

'Actually, I have decided to make New York City my home for some time. Thank you,' said Aurelia, to renewed cheers. She moved on and was caught instantly by another reporter.

'Aurelia, Susie Goldman, Fox News. You look stunning, as always. Who are you wearing?'

Aurelia glanced down at her slinky gown, its soft folds clinging to her slender but curvy frame in all the right places. 'This dress is a piece I had made for me by Dior in Paris, and my pashmina was a gift from a friend in London,' she smiled.

'Wow, I love that - so cosmopolitan! I love your chunky silver bracelet, and your hair is so beautiful and glossy,' gushed Susie. 'Our viewers will want to know, do you follow a strict beauty regime?'

Aurelia laughed huskily. 'Thank you Susie. Well, the best beauty regime for me is going to sleep with a clear conscience, drinking lots of water and eating a healthy Mediterranean diet.'

'Amen to that. Your latest cook book hit the shelves here in New York last week and is already topping the charts.'

'Well, I hope I can do my part to help people discover a love of cooking and the benefits of eating well.'

'Have a wonderful night. Congratulations!'

Aurelia smiled and waved to the crowd before being ushered inside, flashes popping all around her. In the foyer of her new restaurant she slipped off her pashmina and checked her appearance in the large gilded mirror. She looked dazzling, her heavy eye make-up dramatic yet classy. 'Good,' she thought. 'I need to impress tonight.' Her agent, Lucy, waited for her near the thick purple velvet curtain that shielded the foyer from the restaurant. 'Here we go,' she told herself. 'Make it count.' Motioning to Lucy to follow her, she slipped through a discreet doorway and followed the corridor to the kitchens.

Her chefs and staff broke off from the work at their busy stations to applaud her as she entered.

'Thank you everybody,' she called, raising her voice to be heard over the noisy clatter of the working kitchen. 'The guests have all arrived and are being served aperitifs as we speak. As you know, we have some restaurant critics in the crowd, as well as some of New York's wealthiest people – the people whom we hope will return to 'Milagro' again and again. Let us make this evening's the best meal they have ever tasted. Good luck everyone!'

Aurelia moved to the swing doors and peeped out into the dining room. She felt her usual burst of pride on seeing a new restaurant of hers beautifully laid out, stylishly decorated and full of eager diners. The subtle down-lighting blended beautifully with the soft candlelight on every table and an anticipatory hum of conversation filled the room. Glasses chinked as the first night's patrons enjoyed their complimentary cocktails and perused their stylish menus with excitement.

Aurelia's dark eyes scanned the room. There was Ian Anthony the notorious food critic inspecting the Champagne bubbles in his flute, and there too was Lucille Delgado, his fiercest competitor, calmly contemplating the room and jotting down notes.

Aurelia smiled to herself, confident that any reviews would be as glowing as always.

Her gaze continued around the room, scanning over the numerous captains of industry and their diamond-encrusted wives, several big movie stars and their dates, a best-selling author, a British pop group, and a huge rap star surrounded by heavy bodyguards. 'Why does he always wear sunglasses indoors?' Aurelia wondered in amusement. She continued to sweep her eyes over the guests. Eventually she found her prey. 'Mr and Mrs Harrington,' she purred under her breath, her heart beating faster at the sight of them.

She stepped away from the door, smoothing down her dress and checking her earrings. 'Let battle commence,' she whispered.

Once all of her customers had been served their desserts, Aurelia took her cue to step out of the kitchen. Appearing in the dining room, she was greeted with thunderous applause and the quick scraping of chairs on polished wooden floorboards as the diners rose to give her a standing ovation. Her maitre d' presented her with an elaborate bouquet of red roses, and she kissed him on both cheeks.

'Thank you Pierre,' she said, waving modestly to her guests to sit down and not make a fuss. 'Thank you all so much. I am delighted that you were able to come here this evening to be my first guests at 'Miraglo New York'. I am excited to be here at last in your wonderful city and I look forward to welcoming you here again on many occasions. Please, enjoy your desserts. Thank you.'

As the applause died down Aurelia circulated among the tables, greeting diners and receiving generous compliments. She worked her way around the room, ensuring that she spoke to everyone. Eventually she reached the far end of the room. 'Mr and Mrs Harrington, thank you for joining us this evening,' she said, smiling at the couple. Blake rose to greet her and she gave him her hand in such a way that left him no choice but to kiss it. She smiled warmly at him. 'I hope you both enjoyed your meal?'

'Oh, very much. It was truly delicious, thank you. Easily the best meal we've had in a long time,' said Blake.

'Outside of home you mean,' said Paige archly, looking annoyed.

Blake glanced impenetrably down at his wife before continuing. 'We were terribly flattered to be invited tonight alongside all these...' he waved his hand at the room, '...hugely important people.'

Aurelia laughed. 'Why, you are one of them!' she cried. 'Even in Spain we are aware of the brilliant business mind of Mr Blake Harrington. You are quite regularly in the business pages –you are one of the most impressive businessmen in New York today. And surely one of the most handsome,' she added, looking deeply into his eyes and touching his arm.

Blake looked flattered, then flustered, glancing once more at his wife. Aurelia smiled and winked at Paige. 'Of course you agree,' she stated.

'Of course,' said Paige with a thin smile. 'Women often try and make a play for my husband.'

190

'Then it is fortunate for you that he is devoted only to you, I am sure,' smiled Aurelia cat-like. She patted Blake's arm once more. 'Please, enjoy the rest of your meal.'

She glided away, thrilled by how the encounter had gone and enjoying the furious whispers left in her wake as Blake sat down. 'Oh good,' she thought. 'Paige still gets jealous. This is going to be easy.'

Chapter 19

The evening was a runaway success. Aurelia returned to her suite at 'The Mercer' just before 2am, sinking down into an armchair. She replayed the evening's events in her mind. 'Very satisfactory,' she decided. She crossed to the window and stared out at the city sky, reminded unavoidably of her wedding night on the cruise ship all those years before. 'The city doesn't change,' she murmured. 'Yet it feels completely different. No Daddy here anymore, no-one who even knows I'm alive.' She stared at her reflection. 'I have a whole host of admirers as the dazzling celebrity chef though.' She smiled and turned to look properly at herself in the mirror.

'It seems my disguise works like a dream,' she thought, taking in her tumbling waves of rich dark hair falling to halfway down her back, her tanned skin, and dramatic dark eyes. Her habitual four inch heels gave her a catwalk model's height and she understood why men always gave her a second glance. She kicked off her shoes, took off all of her expensive jewellery and removed her brown contact lenses. Tying back her hair, standing barefoot, she almost felt like her old self. 'Stay in character,' she commanded herself sternly, slipping into a silky nightdress and spritzing herself with expensive scent from Paris. 'You have a marriage to break up.'

She sat at the dressing table and pulled some of the hotel's headed paper towards her. She scrawled quickly in flamboyant writing, *'Blake, so wonderful to meet you at my restaurant last night. Thank you once again for coming. Perhaps we can meet up again soon – I would love to discuss business with you. I have some ideas which may interest you. Aurelia x.'* She spritzed the letter liberally with her heady perfume and sealed it up, addressing it to him at his home on East 87th. She placed it to one side, ready for hand delivery by courier the next day. Grinning to herself, she went to bed.

Blake contacted Aurelia at her restaurant the next afternoon. Smiling widely she took the phone receiver from her assistant. 'Hello?'

'Ms Santa Maria? This is Blake Harrington.'

'Aurelia, please,' laughed Aurelia huskily. 'How wonderful to hear from you.'

'Aurelia,' conceded Blake. 'I received your note and I would be delighted to talk about your business. When would be convenient for you?'

'Well, why don't you join me for dinner tomorrow night at 'Milagro'? Shall we say 8pm?'

Blake paused then said briskly. 'Sounds great. I'll see you then.' The phone clicked as he hung up. Aurelia stood for a moment, cradling the receiver thoughtfully. She returned to the main dining room where the tables were being cleared after lunch. After watching her staff at work for a minute she summoned two of her waitresses, motioning to them to accompany her to her office.

Sitting down opposite them she surveyed them. Both girls were stunningly beautiful, both aspiring actresses who were waiting tables until they received their big Broadway breaks. She leaned forward, clasping her hands together on her desk.

'Girls, I need to ask one of you a favour. I have a discreet piece of business that I must undertake and I hoped that one of you would be able to help me with it.' She looked at the girls frankly. 'A friend of mine is concerned that her husband is...fooling around. It has been suggested to her that she should test whether he is or not.'

'You want us to be a honey trap for him?' drawled Sienna, catching on at once. 'I saw that on a movie one time.'

'What's a honey trap?' asked Cherie. Sienna turned to her. 'It's where a sexy girl tries to sleep with a guy to see if he'd go through with it, and then lets his wife know that he's really a douche bag.' She turned back to Aurelia. 'Is he hot?'

Aurelia smiled. 'He is, as you would say, very hot, and also intelligent and powerful.' She noticed that both girls sat up a little straighter in their chairs.

'Is he like, 60 or something?' grimaced Sienna.

'Not at all,' laughed Aurelia. 'He has just turned 41. He is tall, dark, handsome and very, very rich.'

Cherie squirmed in her seat, looking regretful. 'I'm flattered that you asked me, with needing a sexy girl and all, but I've kind of just started seeing someone so I don't really think I should do this,' she said, sounding a little disappointed. Aurelia patted her hand across the desk. 'That is OK Cherie, I am sorry, I would not have asked you if I had known. Why don't you head back to work?'

Aurelia waited until Cherie had closed the door behind her, then looked Sienna straight in the eyes. 'Are you interested?' she asked.

Sienna toyed with her hair before answering. She looked up at Aurelia with a mischievous glint in her eye. 'You know what, I kind of am. It would be fantastic experience for my acting and I don't have a boyfriend right now. Who is he?'

Aurelia pushed a newspaper cutting across the desk and tapped the photo. Sienna gasped. 'Blake Harrington?' She sat back in her chair, gazing at the picture. 'Man, this will be easy. I'd sleep with him in a flash, what a hunk. ' She fanned herself with the picture, looking at Aurelia with sparkling eyes. 'This will be fun! I saw him at our opening night – was that his wife with him? Your friend?'

Aurelia pushed a pen around her desk. 'That was his wife – she is the one who needs to know about his naughtiness. So, you will do it?'

Sienna gave a casual shrug of her shoulders. 'Why not?' she smiled.

'Fantastic, thank you.' Aurelia lowered her voice. 'Please keep this totally to yourself, discretion is everything, we need to play this carefully.' Sienna nodded, eyes pinned to Aurelia's face. Aurelia continued. 'We will begin tonight. Blake will meet me here for dinner to discuss some business, you will be our waitress. I have observed you – I know that you know how to make your male diners fall in love with you.' Sienna grinned arrogantly. 'Do the same tonight please. We will start to lay our honey trail.'

'Sure thing boss,' grinned Sienna. 'This is not at all what I was expecting when I interviewed for this job, but it's a lot more interesting than clearing plates!'

Aurelia looked at her seriously. 'I would try my best to prevent it but there is a chance that your name could be mentioned. Would you be prepared for some bad publicity over this?'

Sienna's grin widened. 'There's no such thing.'

Aurelia smiled as Sienna sashayed out of the office. 'Step one,' she thought. She pulled a manila folder from her desk drawer and flipped once more through the various well-thumbed cuttings from gossip columns suggesting that the Harringtons' marriage was not always a totally happy one. 'Due to her jealousy or his murderous ambition?' she wondered.

She checked on the prep for the evening in the bustling kitchen then headed back to her hotel to change into a suitably glamorous dress.

She returned to 'Milagro' before 7pm, taking her place to greet her customers as they arrived. The restaurant was booked almost solidly for the following three months and Aurelia was pleased to see all her diners enjoying their food. She called one of her waiters over to her. 'Josh, your table was booked as a birthday treat for Senator Traven by his wife. Please make sure the cake with sparklers is brought out for dessert.'

'Yes ma'am.'

Aurelia surveyed the room, checking to make sure that everyone was having a perfect dinner. Just before 8 o'clock she moved to her private dining table in a discreet nook, hidden from view of the main restaurant by large potted ferns. She requested her usual sparkling mineral water with ice and a slice of lemon and waited calmly for Blake.

He did not keep her waiting. As the clock struck 8, Sienna sashayed over to the table, Blake following her. Aurelia leaned up to kiss him on both cheeks. 'Thank you so much for coming, won't you sit down?' She nodded at her glass. 'Can I interest you in a gin and tonic?'

'Wonderful, thanks,' smiled Blake, removing his suit jacket and sitting down. He accepted the glass from Sienna and looked quizzically at Aurelia. 'I was intrigued by your note,' he said, leaning forward. 'You're known as one of Europe's most successful businesswomen so I'm flattered that you wanted to talk to me.'

Aurelia's laugh tinkled musically. 'Straight down to business, so American!' Blake coloured slightly and she patted his hand. 'It is OK, we will do it your way and talk business first of all.' She beckoned to Sienna and ordered a spicy lamb dish for them both and a bottle of red wine, then settled back into her chair, looking intently at Blake.

'As you say, I am a successful woman in Europe. And, I hope too, to be successful here in New York. I love my restaurants, they are my passion, my vitality,' she said, running a hand through her long hair and pulling her heavy silky tresses forward over one shoulder. Blake nodded, his eyes fixed on her. 'Recently, however, I feel that I would like to widen my interests. I would like to... broaden my portfolio I think you would say?'

'That's right,' Blake confirmed, inclining his head. 'How can I help?'

'Well, I have been doing some research into the more interesting companies currently doing well on New York's markets, and I am very interested indeed in The Kingsford Corporation. I note that the company has been a strong performer for several decades now in fact and I like to align myself with success.' She looked at Blake. 'Is it possible for me to become a shareholder?'

Blake's smile reminded Aurelia irresistibly of a shark welcoming a baby seal into the water. 'Of course! We'd be delighted to have you on our list of members. You're choosing a very exciting time in the company's history.' He leaned back in his chair assuredly. 'I'm actually campaigning to restructure the shape of the company at present and I have big plans for it. As CEO and the largest shareholder it's really just a courtesy for me to get my other board members on side, but they do a great job and I like to have their backing.' He stopped, seemingly aware that he had become a bit sidetracked. 'We'd be excited to have your investment in our company. I can have some paperwork sent over to you in the morning if you'd like?'

'Well that would be wonderful, thank you! I would appreciate any help you can give me – I know so little about how business in New York works, but you seem to be the expert.'

'Oh, there's nothing to it,' said Blake airily, clearly flattered. They paused as Sienna brought their food and poured them both a large glass of plum-coloured Argentinean Malbec. 'I'll put you in touch with my broker in the morning and we'll put it all in motion.'

'Wonderful,' repeated Aurelia, raising her glass to chink against Blake's. She watched him as he tucked into his food. She felt icy hatred welling inside her at his easy command of her precious corporation and she fought to keep her voice calm, glad of her Spanish accent. 'What do you think of my lamb tagine?' she asked.

Blake wiped his mouth with the heavy linen napkin. 'Divine,' he said honestly. 'Really, I wish I could eat like this all the time.'

'Well of course you are welcome here as often as you would like,' smiled Aurelia. She leaned towards him, topping up his wine, flicking her eyes down demurely. 'I fear that I may have angered your wife by making you suggest that you do not eat well at home. I hope I did not cause any problems?' She smiled at him flirtatiously.

Blake shook his head, pressing some beans onto his fork. 'Not at all. Paige very much enjoyed her meal as well.' He paused. 'The truth is, she's pregnant with our first child and feeling somewhat hormonal right now. Nearly five months now.'

Aurelia suppressed the lurch of her heart at this news, recovering herself instantly. 'This can work for me even better,' she thought. 'Her hormones will drive her crazy.' She smiled at Blake. 'How wonderful, my congratulations,' she said. 'I hope you are ready to have your life changed forever and you no longer need to be the centre of attention in your house?' she laughed.

Blake smiled ruefully. 'Is any man ever ready for that?' he asked. 'Paige has wanted this for a long time, and it finally seemed like the right time to do it.'

'Your parents must be delighted at the thought of becoming grandparents?'

Blake looked away, shaking his head. 'Both my parents are dead,' he said. 'My father died when I was in my twenties and my mother died about four years ago now.'

'I am sorry,' said Aurelia. 'My parents also are no longer alive, it is a tragedy for me every day.' They were both silent for a moment.

Aurelia placed her knife and fork together and leaned back in her chair, contemplating Blake. 'I have to say I was a little surprised when I saw your wife. I pictured you with a blonde. Someone more curvaceous, more beautiful. You who are so handsome and wealthy, you could have your pick of beautiful women.' She leaned forward quickly, her hand out towards him, her eyes apologetic. 'Forgive me, I am rude – in Spain we say exactly what we think. I will need to learn to be more respectful in this country!' Blake smiled politely, although it didn't reach his eyes.

Aurelia beckoned Sienna over to clear their plates. The girl returned with dessert menus, leaning in towards Blake to clear a few crumbs from the tablecloth in front of him. Aurelia noted how Blake's eyes flicked to Sienna's generous breasts in her plunging top before promptly correcting his gaze. Aurelia smiled to herself. 'He's fighting it but he's still male,' she thought triumphantly.

'Can I tempt you to anything sir?' asked Sienna demurely. Blake cleared his throat. 'Just an espresso, thank you.'

'The same,' nodded Aurelia decisively. She waited until Sienna had left. 'I hope I have not offended you, I am sure you and your wife are blissfully happy together,' she said softly.

Blake sat back in his chair and eyed Aurelia. 'Tell me why you decided on New York,' he said, changing the subject abruptly. Aurelia obliged, smiling inwardly. She deftly charmed him back to good spirits over coffee and a cognac and left him in the hands of Sienna to see him out.

Sienna joined her shortly afterwards in the office. 'That man is a fox!' she said. 'When do I get to make a move?'

Aurelia smiled at the excited younger woman. 'Not yet. We must be subtle. You played it well tonight – I saw him looking at you.'

'You bet you did!' said Sienna, tossing back her tousled blonde hair, sure of her appeal. 'Men can't help it.' Aurelia shook her head, laughing.

The next day a sheaf of papers was couriered to Aurelia at 'Milagro', with a handwritten note from Blake. *'Thanks for a delicious dinner, please find attached the items we discussed. Blake.'* Aurelia flicked through the corporation's glossy brochure and skimmed through the paperwork she would need to fill in to become a shareholder. As promised, Blake had included details of a broker and Aurelia called him immediately, keen to put the transaction in motion.

After a successful call she sat back in her chair, satisfied.

Within a week she had received her certificate confirming her as shareholder of The Kingsford Corporation. She sent another note to Blake. *'Business update, keen to discuss. Dinner, usual place, 8pm tomorrow? Aurelia x'.* His PA called to confirm that Blake would be there. Once again Aurelia dressed glamorously, enveloping herself in expensive scent. Once again she asked Sienna to wait on their table. Blake was early, standing to greet Aurelia as she came to the table.

'Good evening.' His eyes told Aurelia how good she looked and she smiled.

'Hello Blake, please sit.' She shook out her napkin and ordered wine. 'Or perhaps Champagne?' she looked at Blake enquiringly. 'We are celebrating after all.' He nodded his agreement and she requested Sienna to bring them a bottle of vintage Krug alongside their baked Galician salmon. Blake raised an eyebrow at her. 'I'm not used to a woman ordering for me in a restaurant, but I confess I find myself in the unusual position of quite enjoying it. You know what's best here, after all.'

'Well, exactly. I hope I am not diminishing your manhood,' she teased him. 'I simply want you to experience the dishes that I am most proud of. So,' she said in a businesslike voice, clasping her hands together. 'I know how you like to do it – let us talk about our business first of all.'

Blake nodded. 'My broker confirmed that you've been sent your share certificate by now. I have

203

to say I was surprised – and pleased – at the amount of your share subscription. It was a huge amount to spend and it puts you in charge of almost 2% of the corporation's stock!'

Aurelia smiled. 'I was glad to be able to do it. I believe very strongly in your company, and in your leadership abilities and direction, so I wanted to – how you say – place my money where my mouth is.'

She toyed with the stem of her Champagne flute, watching the bubbles fizz their way up the glass. 'I have to tell you, I am hoping for more than just being a name on a share register. I would like to be more actively involved.' She looked Blake in the eye. 'I know that your corporation is currently looking to appoint two new non-executive directors. I would like to nominate myself for one of these positions.'

There was a pause. Blake sat back in his seat. 'Well, well,' he said. 'You certainly do go for what you want.'

'I do,' confirmed Aurelia quietly.

Blake considered. 'Well, you've definitely proven yourself to be a formidable force in the business world with your restaurants, your books, your endorsements.' He held up his hands. 'The unstoppable force of Aurelia Santa Maria has arrived in New York and I think it's better to be with you than against you!' He pulled out his Blackberry and considered his calendar for a moment. 'I'm next due to meet with the rest of the board a week on Friday. I'll propose you for one of the positions and let you know. I'd be excited to work with you.'

'Thank you,' said Aurelia graciously. 'And I with you. Does your wife work?' she asked, taking a bite of her salmon. Blake laughed shortly.

'Paige? No. She prefers the 'lady of leisure' tag.' He frowned, seeming to realise that he might have sounded disloyal. 'I'm very happy for her to do that,' he added quickly. 'It's not as if we need the money. And now that we'll be having a family, it's better that she can be at home.'

'She will not have a nanny like other rich women in New York?' asked Aurelia in surprise.

'Well, yes, there'll be a nanny but you know, there'll be...other things that she'll be doing, I'm sure.'

Aurelia raised her eyebrows, piercing a carrot with her fork. 'In Spain this seems unnatural to us. When we are mothers, we raise our children. We do not pay someone else to do so. In my family we also take pride in working until we are mothers. I could not just be somebody's wife. I have my own dreams, my own ambitions. I would want to have interesting conversation with my husband, not just talk to him about who I had lunch with, or what nail polish I chose.' She stopped abruptly, smiling kindly at Blake. 'I am sorry, I am doing it again, voicing my opinions and criticising your personal life, I apologise. I just mean that for me, I like to use my brain.'

'Paige has a good brain,' said Blake defensively.

'Certainly,' agreed Aurelia warmly. 'After all, she was wise enough to marry you.'

Blake flushed slightly at the compliment and his flush deepened as Sienna lent low towards him to collect his plate. 'You must watch her,' said Aurelia in amusement as they watched Sienna saunter away. 'She is a flirt and I think she likes you.' Blake coughed, not knowing what to say. Aurelia helped him out of his discomfort by reverting to other matters. 'So, you will go to your boardroom next week and I will wait anxiously on tenderhooks for your verdict,' she said.

'It's tenterhooks,' smiled Blake, 'and, yes, I will be in touch as soon as I can.'

On leaving the restaurant Blake hailed a cab and sat back in the seat restlessly. He felt a little aroused at the attention of two such alluring women and dissatisfied at the thought of his wife's mean temper waiting for him at home. 'Don't be so ridiculous,' he told himself. 'You can't have either of them.'

'Oh yes you can,' whispered a little voice in his ear, remembering the sultry looks Sienna had bestowed on him and her secret crush, revealed by her boss. He allowed himself to fantasise about alternative endings to the evening, feeling attractive and manly as he basked in the glow of imagined attention. He was feeling quite cheerful by the time he arrived home. He let himself into his brownstone townhouse, whistling under his breath.

Paige perched on the antique wooden church pew in the hallway, her eyes accusing.

'Where the hell have you been?' she spat at him.

Blake dropped his wallet and keys on the small table, loosening his tie, his good mood ruined instantly. He smoothed back his hair in the hall mirror and sighed.

'I was at a business meeting,' he said tiredly, heading towards the kitchen.

'Don't you dare walk away from me when I'm trying to talk to you,' cried Paige, following him. 'I know exactly where you were!'

'So why ask?' he replied, opening the fridge and cracking a beer. Paige ignored him.

'You were at that restaurant again with that Spanish slut!' she yelled. Blake took a swig of his beer, letting the ugly word hang in the air. He looked at his wife. 'If you mean Ms Santa Maria, then yes, I was meeting with her at her restaurant. To discuss business.'

'Really? Business? I found all her little notes to you,' she said as she flung Aurelia's couriered notes down onto the table in disgust. 'Why is she signing them with a kiss? Why do they stink of her perfume? Is there something going on between you?' she stared at him accusingly, hands on hips.

'We met to discuss business,' repeated Blake calmly. 'I don't know why she signs her letters like that, it must be a continental thing. When I meet her it's just to discuss business. She has just become a sizeable investor in the corporation.'

'I bet she has,' sneered Paige. 'She can throw money at you and thinks she can get into your pants that way.'

Blake didn't dignify that with a response. Paige continued her tirade. 'Who the hell does she think she is with her obvious hair extensions and her leathery skin?' Blake thought of Aurelia's long, naturally healthy hair and silky-looking light tan but said nothing.

'There is no way she is getting her claws into my husband! What 'business' did she need to discuss so urgently tonight with you?'

Blake decided that honesty was the best policy. 'She has asked to be nominated as a non-exec of the company.' He shrugged. 'She's a good businesswoman, and we need a more diverse board – she could be a good fit.'

Paige boiled over with rage. 'She what?' she yelled, nearly hysterical. 'She wants to be on the board now? My God, she is determined to spend all her time with you. This cannot happen! A good fit? A good fit for what exactly? This is totally fricking unacceptable! If anyone is going to be on the board it should be me! I have a business degree!' She burst into noisy tears.

Blake went to his wife and wrapped his arms around her, eager to defuse the situation so that he could go to bed. 'No-one is after me, and no-one will get me, I'm married to you and we're having a baby. You are clever, I know you are, but you've never had any interest in the corporation, and I like it that way. Don't upset yourself. You're the one I'm married to,' he said, hoping his often-repeated words didn't sound too mechanical. He kissed the top of her head. 'Let's go to bed.'

Mollified but still grumbling and sniffling angrily, Paige allowed herself to be led upstairs.

Chapter 20

Aurelia didn't contact Blake again but waited to hear from him. In the meantime she concentrated on making her latest restaurant as successful as its predecessors. She was interviewed on breakfast television and the evening news, and attended several book signings. Thanks to a steady stream of celebrity diners, 'Milagro' was an immediate staple in the gossip columns.

She spent a pleasant Friday afternoon selecting a new tan leather handbag in Bergdorf Goodman. She was strolling down Fifth Avenue when her phone rang. 'Hola?' she answered.

'Aurelia? Blake Harrington. I have some great news for you.'

'You do? Tell me at once!' she demanded excitedly.

'I've just come from my board meeting. The other board members are intrigued at the thought of your involvement in my corporation and we'd be very glad to welcome you as one of our new non-execs.'

Aurelia flinched at his arrogant use of 'my corporation' but forced herself to smile widely. 'Blake! How wonderful! I am so pleased! You must have handled the discussions brilliantly. Can we celebrate? Perhaps a small gathering of you and your board at 'Milagro' one evening next week, so that I can get to know everybody?'

'Great idea. My PA will be in touch to schedule something once I know everyone's availability. Congratulations, board member!'

Aurelia snapped her phone shut and smiled grimly.

The date was set for the following Wednesday. 'I am very excited to get to know everybody,' said Aurelia on the phone to Blake at his office a few days before. 'Will people be bringing their wives?'

'No,' said Blake. 'I think it changes the dynamic and it will be best if you can really have time to talk to your fellow board members. Plenty of time to meet everyone's partners another day.' Aurelia smiled into the phone. 'I think that is very wise of you,' she agreed smoothly.

At 8 o'clock on the Wednesday, Blake and his fellow board members drew up outside 'Milagro' in two cars. They headed inside, confused by the sound of music from the main dining room. 'It sounds like they're having a party!' exclaimed Donald Waterman to Blake. 'It does rather,' agreed Blake. He saw Aurelia approaching their group.

'Gentlemen! Thank you for coming!' She kissed Blake on both cheeks and shook hands with the other men, ushering Josh forward to take their coats.

Blake surveyed the room with a frown, taking in the chattering groups of young people and the dancing that had already kicked off. 'I thought we were keeping this as a small, intimate get to know you?' he said in Aurelia's ear, his voice cool.

Aurelia clutched his arm. 'I know that is what we said, do not be angry at the change of plans, I beg you. My staff heard about my news and wanted to celebrate my good luck with me – they have not yet had a chance properly to celebrate the successful opening of the restaurant, so I thought we could combine the two. I will spend my evening with you and your board of course, but if anybody wants to dance or party there is that option too!' She looked beseechingly at him and he laughed.

'OK, come and meet your board members,' he sighed resignedly. Sienna waved at him from the dance floor, and he gave her a brief wave in return.

Aurelia chatted informatively with the group of businessmen, seated in a large alcove to one side of the restaurant, as they ate paella and discussed business. The wine flowed freely and initial guards came down. Maurice Hillersbrand, the oldest member of the board, leant in towards Aurelia and patted her on the knee, slurring his words slightly. 'I have to say Aurelia, I was in two minds about letting a woman into our boardroom but I think you will grace it beautifully. If I were a younger man-'

'I hope I will be an asset and not just an ornament,' she smiled, cutting in quickly.

'Quite so, quite so,' he mumbled, slipping sideways towards her slightly. She stood up briskly. 'Would anybody like to dance?' she asked. Blake got to his feet, looking a bit the worse for wear after several large cognacs. 'I would like to dance,' he said decisively. He placed a hand lightly on Aurelia's back as he accompanied her to the impromptu dance floor, where the chefs, receptionists and waiting staff were partying. 'I haven't danced in a really long time,' he admitted.

Aurelia grabbed his hand, making him twirl her. 'Well that is a shame! A crime! Tonight, you will dance!' She was aware of his gaze on her body as she span around the dance floor. The song ended and as it segued into the next she whispered 'Excuse me for a moment, my head chef needs a word,' before slipping away. She nodded to Sienna as she left. Sienna instantly moved over to Blake. 'Now where do you think you're going?' she asked, slipping an arm around his waist and swaying her hair out in a golden sheen, laughing into his eyes. 'Won't you dance with a poor waitress?'

When Aurelia returned several minutes later Blake was no longer on the dance floor. She spotted him pinning Sienna against the wall in a dark corner, out of sight of his colleagues, his mouth on hers. Aurelia smiled. She headed back to the rest of the board members. 'Where's Blake?' asked Donald.

'Recovering from dancing I think,' Aurelia said. 'Can I interest anyone else?'

Murmurs of protest rose from the five men, all older than Blake. Donald spoke for them all. 'My dear, we've had a wonderful time in your delightful restaurant, and we're thrilled to have you on board.' He looked around, delighted by his own pun. 'Ahem, however I think it's time we left. It is only Wednesday after all.'

'Quite right,' smiled Aurelia. She accompanied them to the restaurant entrance and helped them on with their coats. 'Thank you so much for coming, all of you, I have really enjoyed meeting you – oh! Here is Blake now.' She eyed Blake carefully as he briskly rejoined the group.

'I'll head out with you guys,' he said. Not meeting anybody's eyes, he muttered a curt goodbye to Aurelia and strode out ahead of the group into the cool night air.

Aurelia waited until the door closed behind them, then sauntered back to her office. Sienna was waiting for her there, grinning like the cat that had eaten the cream.

'Good work,' congratulated Aurelia. 'It seems a pretty girl, strong alcohol and an unhappy home life will do wonders for testing a man's resolve.'

'That was fun,' said Sienna. 'He's a great kisser.' Aurelia felt a stab at her words but quenched it immediately. 'Why don't you rejoin the party?' she suggested. 'I'll be back out in a minute.' She waited until the door had closed then fished out her phone. Dialling *67 to ensure her number would be withheld, she placed a call.

Blake's car dropped him at home just before 1am. The house was in darkness. He eased open the front door and crept upstairs. When he was halfway up the stairs the light on the landing burst on, leaving him blinking like a naughty schoolboy.

'A quiet meeting of the board? Really?' demanded Paige. Blake sighed and straightened his tie. His wife ran her eyes over his tousled appearance. 'What happened Blake? Why are you creeping in like a burglar at one in the morning? You look like you've just come from a club!' She started down the stairs towards him, sniffing at him. 'You smell like a club!' she cried.

Blake sighed again and started back down the stairs. 'Don't start Paige, I'm not in the mood.'

'On really, why's that?' she enquired icily. 'Too tired from all your partying with Aurelia?' She sneered the name. 'Having too good a time there to come home to your pregnant wife?' she hissed.

Blake turned to face her at the bottom of the stairs, his voice icy in turn, the strong brandy making his head bang. 'That's right. I was having a good time. Like I never do at home.' Paige slapped him hard and burst into tears. Blake carried on into the kitchen and poured himself a glass of water.

Paige sobbed and gulped noisily but realised that Blake was not going to try and placate her. 'You'd better start treating me right,' she spat, before stalking from the room. Blake stared moodily out of the window into the darkness beyond.

The next morning he arrived at his office in a bad mood. The receptionists on the front desk giggled as he arrived. 'Good morning Mr Harrington,' they called in unison, smirking. Frowning, Blake entered the lift. Arriving on his floor he was met by his PA. 'Good morning Mr Harrington,' she said, looking anxious.

'Morning Lauren,' he replied, striding towards his corner office. 'Is everything OK?'

'Um, I was going to ask you the same thing, sir,' Lauren said. 'I take it you've seen the New York Times this morning?'

Blake stopped and looked at her. 'Of course, why?'

'Did you, ah, read all of it, or just the business pages?' Lauren asked nervously.

Blake sighed impatiently. 'Oh for goodness sake, whatever is the matter?' he asked. Lauren moved to her desk and handed him a copy of the gossip pages, tapping a piece in one of the columns. Blake read it, his eyes narrow. 'Shit,' he said.

'Is there anything I can do, sir?'

'No,' replied Blake shortly, heading into his office and shutting his door with a bang. 'Shit,' he repeated, as he sat at his desk and reread the snippet. *'Seen partying hard at celebrity favourite 'Milagro' and having a very good time indeed until the early hours of this morning, with someone who was very definitely not his wife: Blake Harrington, handsome CEO of The Kingsford Corporation.'*

He rubbed his temples. The banging in his head was back. 'Paige is going to lose it,' he thought. 'How the hell did the newspaper get hold of this?'

Donald entered Blake's office looking amused but trying to look concerned. 'Bad luck old chap,' he commiserated. 'It never does to get caught by the press. So that's where you disappeared off to after you went dancing!' His eyes twinkled.

'It's all rubbish,' snapped Blake. 'I don't know what they're talking about. You know I left with you guys, I just did a bit of dancing. Can't a man enjoy himself?'

Donald's eyes danced. 'Not in public it seems.' He clapped Blake on the shoulder. 'Don't worry, happens to us all. How's Paige taken it?'

'I don't think she will have read the paper yet, but it won't be good,' replied Blake grimly.

Later that morning Blake was on a conference call with potential clients in Japan. He spoke into his speaker phone authoritatively as he paced around behind his desk. 'Gentlemen, I think you'll appreciate that for the reasons I've outlined already-'. He broke off as his office door was flung open. Paige strode in, her face pale, a wild look in her eyes. Lauren ran in behind her. 'Mrs Harrington, he's on a call, you'll have to wait-'

Blake stood up. 'Paige, I'm in the middle of something right now,' he started.

'Oh I bet you are,' she said coldly. She raised her voice. 'I just bet you are! Like you were last night!' She flung a copy of the New York Times onto his desk, her hands shaking with fury. 'I know exactly what you were doing!' she yelled.

Blake could feel the shocked silence on the other end of the phone line. He spoke calmly into the handset. 'Gentlemen, as you can hear, I'm afraid you will need to excuse me. I will have my PA set up a convenient time to call you back, I do sincerely apologise.' He pressed the button to end the call and turned angrily to his wife. 'What the hell do you think you're doing?' he asked furiously.

'Ha! What do I think I'm doing? Me?' shrieked Paige. 'I'm here to tell you I know that you're having an affair with that Spanish slut. Argh!' she

216

yelled in fury, sweeping two large glass ornaments off their shelf. They smashed on the floor. A crowd was gathering outside Blake's office. He shot a fierce look at Lauren who headed out to try and disperse them. Blake saw Maurice outside his own office, frowning at the commotion and shaking his head disapprovingly.

Blake grasped Paige's arm and spoke quietly and firmly to her, his tone threatening. 'Paige, stop it immediately. I am not having an affair with anyone, but this is hardly the right time or place to discuss this.'

Paige fought to free her arm and made as if to slap him again. He gripped her wrist roughly. 'You have to calm down. This is not good for you, or for the baby.'

'I don't care!' yelled Paige, her voice shrill. 'Your baby can go to hell!'

Blake stepped back, shaken. 'You don't mean that,' he said quietly. Lauren looked on quietly from the doorway, her eyes round with shock, her hand over her mouth. Paige span on her heel and barged past Lauren, making for the lifts.

'Let her go,' said Blake, at Lauren's enquiring look. 'I can't talk to her when she's like this. She'll probably go and moan to her girlfriends now about what a vile pig I am and then I'll have to face the music when I get home.' He sat down at his desk. 'Please try and reconnect me to Mr Harushi.'

Lauren smiled sympathetically and headed back to her desk, her face still shocked.

Chapter 21

Across town, Aurelia was starting to oversee the lunchtime rush. Her lunch bookings were predominantly for businessmen most days, and every table was full as usual. She was advising a young, brash group of traders on a wine to accompany their garlic prawns when she heard a commotion at the front door. 'Where is she?' yelled a voice. 'Let me through!'

The chatter in the dining room ceased and all eyes turned towards the velvet curtain, as Paige burst through it. Spotting Aurelia immediately she charged towards her, her eyes furious, her fists clenched. 'You bitch!' she screamed. 'Keep your hands off my husband!'

Aurelia stood her ground, looking calm and stately. She shook her head at her security guard and he hung back. She spoke quietly but made sure her voice carried.

'Mrs Harrington, please calm down. I do not have my hands on your husband. We are business colleagues only. It is offensive to me that you would suggest that I would have a relationship with a married man.'

'I don't believe you!' hissed Paige. She slapped Aurelia hard across the face. The gaping diners gasped at the loud crack.

'Mrs Harrington,' said Aurelia haughtily. 'If you lay another finger on me I will have you arrested. I repeat that I am not involved with your husband. How dare you barge into my restaurant in this way?'

Paige brandished her newspaper in Aurelia's face. 'I've seen this,' she hissed. 'I know he was here last night and I know what he was doing.'

Aurelia spoke more quietly. 'He was not doing anything with me.' She flicked a glance at Sienna. Paige followed her glance. She took in Sienna's voluptuous body, provocatively open-necked shirt and luxuriant blonde hair. With a yell of rage she launched herself across the restaurant and grabbed a shocked Sienna by the hair, clawing at her face.

'Somebody call the police!' cried Aurelia. Her security guard charged in and pulled the furious Paige off Sienna. The waitress sobbed, clutching her shirt closed where a button had been pulled off. Aurelia dashed over and wrapped her arms around Sienna. 'Shhh, it is OK,' she soothed. 'Please, go to my office and wait for me there.' Sienna hurried away.

Aurelia turned frosty eyes on Paige who was struggling in the strong grip of the security guard. 'You will come with me,' she directed her, motioning to the guard to bring Paige out to the foyer. 'Stay here,' she snapped at Paige in the foyer, before returning to her restaurant, where an excited clamour had now broken out.

She raised her voice to be heard. 'Ladies and gentlemen, I must apologise for the disruption to your lunch. I can assure you that this will not happen again. Please accept your drinks bill on the house for this meal, and I apologise again for the inconvenience. The waiting staff will come round momentarily to help you with more wine.' She smiled ruefully, rolling her eyes at the sky and gesturing with her hands despairingly in a very Mediterranean fashion, which raised a polite laugh.

She slipped back behind the heavy curtain. Paige was still seething, her chest heaving as she sat on the velvet banquette, her wrist gripped by the security guard. Aurelia contemplated her. 'Finally you're getting your comeuppance for trying to replace me,' she thought to herself. 'How dare you step into my shoes like that? I bet you couldn't believe your luck.'

She didn't speak to Paige, but waited until she saw the police lights appearing outside. She nodded to her guard and he stepped forward to open the door for the two burly officers. Aurelia glided forward and placed her mouth next to Paige's ear. 'You were right,' she drawled quietly. 'I have slept with Blake.' She leaped back as Paige lunged for her, just as the policemen came through the door.

They rushed forward to restrain Paige, and Aurelia wiped a shaking hand across her brow, smoothing back her hair. 'Thank you officers,' she said, clutching at her chest. She pointed at Paige. 'She is a madwoman. She burst in here, accusing me of all sorts of lies, and attacked me and one of my waitresses. The poor girl is in my office, in shock.' She held onto the booking counter, looking frail. Her receptionist put an arm around her shoulders. Aurelia smiled weakly at her.

One of the officers was cuffing Paige and reading her rights to her. The other officer approached Aurelia. 'We'll need to take a statement from you and from the waitress you said she attacked,' he said.

'Would you be able to come down to the precinct later today?'

'Of course Officer,' said Aurelia faintly.

'She slept with my husband!' cried Paige, struggling wildly.

'Yeah, yeah. That's not a crime honey,' said the officer, 'but assault and battery is. Let's go.' They pulled Paige from the restaurant and suddenly the foyer was peaceful again. Aurelia watched the flashing lights as the car pulled away then patted the guard's arm. 'Thank you Simon,' she said huskily.

She took the staff corridor down to the kitchen and walked quickly through to her office. Sienna sat in a chair, wiping her eyes, vicious scratch marks evident on her face and neck. She raised red eyes to Aurelia. 'What the hell was that?' she asked.

Aurelia sighed, sitting down. 'I am sorry, she is unstable. She handled the news badly. I am so sorry you were hurt. We will have to file a police report against her later on – we will not bother the police with details of our honey trap. The only relevant part is that she attacked us.'

She smiled slightly, opening her drawer. She pulled out an envelope. 'I have something that I hope will make it up to you for your involvement.' She tapped the envelope on the table in front of her. 'I have some very interesting friends, including some very famous people. I happen to know that my friend Victoria Fursley is looking for people to audition to play her sister in her new movie.'

Sienna's eyes grew round. 'You know Victoria Fursley?' she asked in wonder.

Aurelia shrugged. 'She is a fan of my restaurants. We met in London.' She held out the envelope. 'Here is a plane ticket for you to Los Angeles in two days time. The studio will send a car for you there and set you up with accommodation. I think you will find that, unless you do something very bad at the audition, the part will be yours.'

Sienna shrieked and threw her arms around Aurelia. 'Thank you so much!' she cried. 'I can't believe it!'

'I will be sorry to lose a good waitress, and one who is so discreet, but I look forward to seeing you in the movies. Perhaps you will return as a dinner guest when you are famous.'

'Thank you, thank you!' Still shrieking, Sienna flew back to her duties in the kitchen.

Aurelia picked up her phone and dialled Blake. When he answered she spoke coolly. 'I think you should know that your wife has just been at my restaurant where she attacked me and Sienna. She is now being taken away by the police.'

'Oh God,' groaned Blake. 'I'm so sorry Aurelia. She's...difficult.'

'She is mentally unstable,' corrected Aurelia bluntly. 'She should not be allowed out of the house. Am I to be attacked now that I am going into business with you?' she demanded haughtily.

'Of course not, I'm so sorry.'

'If you cannot control your wife then you are not the man I thought you were. She attacked me in front of a room full of diners at my restaurant – I am afraid this will not be easily kept from the press. It was

223

clear to everybody who she was.' She softened her tone. 'She is an embarrassment to you Blake. A liability. She will start to affect your business.'

Blake was silent on the other end of the line, remembering the encounter earlier that day at his office. Aurelia continued.

'I am sorry, I know that she is your wife, but I begin to believe that she really is mentally ill. You should have heard the things she accused me of. She should be locked up somewhere, for everyone's sake.' She heard Blake sigh heavily. She continued in a softer tone. 'Both Sienna and I have to go to the police station later this afternoon to make statements. Out of respect for your privacy I would not choose to press charges but I am sure that Sienna will want to.'

'No,' said Blake quickly. 'Surely it needn't come to that. What can I do to stop that?'

'I will speak to Sienna but what assurances can I give her that she will be safe? The poor girl is terrified. If she thinks she could be attacked again at any point she will be traumatised.'

'I know. I feel awful that she was involved.' Blake paused. 'Paige is very jealous and has become convinced that in fact you and I are having an affair. I should have seen something like this coming.'

Aurelia spoke gently. 'Do not blame yourself Blake, this is not your fault. I have seen it before. I had an aunt who was...difficult,' she said delicately. 'She made my uncle's life hell with her jealous rages over nothing. In the end he had to have her admitted to a private home for disturbed people. Everyone felt extremely sorry for him.' She sighed. 'Your wife reminds me very much of my aunt, and I feel sorry for you.'

Blake laughed. 'I don't think I need to send Paige to a loony bin just yet!'

Aurelia didn't laugh. 'Of course, you must do as you think best. In Spain she would not be allowed to disgrace her husband,' she said solemnly. 'A man of your standing cannot have a crazy wife. She will ruin you.' She let that sink in before continuing in a brisker tone. 'Anyway, I will speak to Sienna and try to stop her pressing charges. I urge you not to let your wife come near me or my staff again or I shall be most displeased.' She hung up.

Blake strode out of his office to deliver some papers to Lauren for filing. He noticed that conversation on the floor ceased abruptly when he appeared and he scowled, Aurelia's words about his reputation ringing in his ears. He retreated to his office and slammed his door.

His phone rang and he yanked it off its receiver. 'Yes?' he snapped.

'Hello Mr Harrington, this is Lawrence Kessler.'

Blake recognised his lawyer's voice and sat down. 'Hello Lawrence. Did my wife call you?'

'Mrs Harrington is being detained by the police and did indeed use her statutory telephone call to contact me. I informed her that I would let you know where she is being held. I assume that you will meet me there? I'm on my way now.'

Blake rubbed his eyes. 'Actually Lawrence, I can't do this right now. Would you please take care of

225

this, and make sure that she gets home safely? I'll try and get home early to meet her there. I'm hopeful that the people she attacked won't be pressing charges, so this might all go away pretty easily.'

'Of course,' replied his lawyer smoothly, used to rich clients and their odd behaviour. 'Leave it to me.'

Blake thanked him and hung up, staring at the photo on his desk of the 20 week ultrasound scan of his unborn son. 'She said he could go to hell,' he thought. 'Maybe she really is mad.'

He reached home by 5pm. He had been relieved to receive a further message from Lawrence that charges had been dropped and that Paige had been released with only a caution. He sent up a grateful thank you that Aurelia had been able to persuade Sienna not to proceed with the matter.

He entered his house, unsure of what mood he would find within. Paige was in the sitting room, staring into the empty fireplace, her hands around a cold mug of tea. Blake sat down opposite her, at a loss as to what to say to her. 'Paige-', he started.

'You slept with her,' his wife said coldly.

'Who?' asked Blake in confusion.

'Who? Was there more than one?' cried Paige, instantly in a fury. 'Aurelia. You slept with Aurelia. She told me.'

'I have never slept with Aurelia, or anyone else since I married you,' said Blake firmly, his voice rising too. 'This is ridiculous. I don't believe that Aurelia said any such thing to you. It would be a lie.'

226

'Oh? You'll call me a liar?' yelled Paige. 'But not precious Aurelia? Or was it that other slut at the restaurant with the big breasts? I know that's what you really like. Tell me the truth!' she yelled.

'I am telling you the truth!' cried Blake, exasperated. 'I haven't slept with anyone.'

'SHE TOLD ME!' Paige yelled furiously. She hurled her mug into the fireplace and watched with glittering eyes as it smashed against the stone. Blake strode to her and grasped her by the arms. He shook her. 'Paige, stop this. You need to calm down right now. You can't act like this.'

Paige's eyes glittered. 'Oh really? Yet you can act exactly as you please? You're the person who should be in disgrace here. One wife who died in suspicious circumstances and now here you are cheating on your second wife.' She laughed sarcastically. 'I'd be very careful if I were you Blake. People might start to talk about how you treat your wives. I could tell them some stories,' she taunted.

Blake face grew cold with fury. He stared at her for a long minute, his hands gripping her arms fiercely. 'You're mad,' he said quietly. 'You really are.' His eyes dared her to continue

'Well you're stuck with me,' spat Paige, wrenching herself from his grip. 'And you'd better start treating me properly or your life is going to become pretty unpleasant.' She stormed from the room and stamped upstairs, slamming the bedroom door.

Blake rubbed his chin as he sank down into a chair. 'Aurelia was right,' he thought. 'Paige is losing it. I can't live like this.' He thought of his company and his hard-won reputation. 'I can't have her telling stories to people,' he whispered. 'I can't have it. This has to stop.' He stood decisively and made a phone call.

A week later Blake met Aurelia for lunch. 'You look stressed,' she said, noting the dark circles under his eyes and his haggard look.

He barked a harsh laugh. 'Stressed would just about cover it,' he admitted. He took a long gulp of his gin and tonic. 'I've sent Paige away,' he stated baldly.

Aurelia's heart leaped but her face showed only concern. 'You have? Where to?' she asked, marvelling inside at how quickly his loyalty to his wife had eroded. 'That shouldn't really be a surprise to me though,' she reminded herself.

'There's a place called 'Oakingham',' Blake explained. 'It's not a mental hospital or anything like that – more of a stately home where stressed out people can relax for a while and be looked after properly. And securely.' He smiled grimly. 'Maybe I should be checking myself in there too. It's nice – horrifically expensive of course - but beautiful grounds, discreet nurses, good food, plenty of activities, even a spa. I'm hoping Paige will relax and see it as a sort of retreat.' He grimaced, recalling the hysterical scenes at 'Oakingham' four days earlier when he had left his wife there, and the vicious threats she had hurled as he retreated. 'It's for the best,' he added, fingering a cut on his hand gained by picking up Paige's smashed crockery.

Aurelia put her hand on his. 'It will be hard Blake, but you are doing the right thing. She seemed very unhappy in New York – maybe a change of scene will be what she needs. And now you can focus on your business, which is your true destiny, like all great minds.'

Blake smiled briefly at her, glad of a fresh topic. 'Well, on that note, as you know, it's the annual general meeting of the shareholders next month. I think that's the perfect time to announce my plans for restructuring the company.' Aurelia clenched her fist under the table but nodded encouragingly and he continued. 'We'll also announce your and Tom's appointments as non-execs.'

'How exciting!' exclaimed Aurelia, her eyes gleaming. 'Will I need to make a speech?'

Blake laughed. 'That won't be necessary, but we will have you sitting up on the stage with us for the meeting, so that everyone can see you. I suspect you might need to be prepared to sign some autographs.'

'No problem,' laughed Aurelia, taking a sip of wine. Blake looked around the restaurant.

'Where's Sienna today?' he asked casually.

'She does not work for me anymore,' Aurelia told him. 'I sent her to LA to audition for a movie role I am sure she is going to get.'

Blake looked at her, speechless for a second. 'Thank you Aurelia – I know you only did that so that she wouldn't press charges, and I'm grateful.'

Aurelia smiled slyly at him. 'Well, you can make it up to me. I have no date for a gala at the Metropolitan Museum this weekend. Take me,' she challenged him. 'You can brief me on likely proceedings at the AGM.'

'As it happens I'm already going to the Met gala myself, but I would be delighted to accompany you,' said Blake gallantly.

'It is a date then,' smiled Aurelia.

Chapter 22

'Mr Harrington is here to collect you Ms Santa Maria.'

'Thank you, please tell him I will be right down.' Aurelia hung up the phone and surveyed herself in the mirror. Her daring backless emerald gown fell in soft folds to the floor, setting off her glowing Mediterranean tan perfectly. Her deep brown eyes were darkened still further by generous lashings of eyeliner and dense smoky eye shadow. The diamond cuff on her wrist echoed the simple yet dazzling gems in her ears. She wore no other jewellery and her hair fell loosely down her back and around her shoulders. She nodded in approval and spritzed a final mist of perfume over her hair, before slipping on her strappy heels. Tucking her jewelled clutch under her arm she strode out of her suite.

Stepping out of the lift into the elegant lobby she saw the open approval on Blake's face. He seemed lost for words as she approached. 'You look amazing,' he managed as she reached him. She acknowledged his compliment gracefully and took his arm, trying to suppress her awareness of how overwhelmingly good-looking he was in his tuxedo. She noted the admiring gaze of all the men and several of the women in the lobby as they passed through. 'Focus!' she reminded herself sharply. 'This is not a date! There'll be time to start dating people when all this is finished.'

They were bombarded by requests from the jostling paparazzi as they made their way up the red carpet outside the museum. Aurelia posed happily, glad to be in as many newspapers and as many television segments as possible, her hand resting proprietorially on Blake's arm. She dazzled the waiting crowds, posing generously for snaps with fans, before heading inside.

Leaving Blake to his own devices before the dinner she circulated inside the gala, mingling with the other important and wealthy people of the city. Over dinner she flirted gently with a retired US Army colonel on her left, leaving Blake to battle through an aggressive conversation about charities with an argumentative corporate wife on his other side.

Aurelia enjoyed bidding in the charity auction after dinner, winning a luxury weekend in Vermont. She looked modestly shocked as bidding reached flatteringly high levels to acquire a private dinner for two at 'Milagro', personally cooked by Aurelia herself. 'It seems New York has really taken to you,' Blake murmured in her ear as the crowd applauded the persistent winner. Aurelia smiled as one of the official photographers snapped them with their heads close together.

'I hope so,' she replied. 'I love it here. I think it could become my home permanently.'

Blake's surprise showed on his face. 'Really? You don't miss Spain?'

The briefest of shadows flickered across Aurelia's face before she shrugged. 'I was there for a long time,' she said. 'I tried Paris and also London, all wonderful places of course, but New York, well, this really feels like home.'

'What about your other restaurants?' asked Blake. 'Who looks after them while you're away?'

'Now there I have been extremely fortunate,' smiled Aurelia. 'In Barcelona I was lucky enough to convince my mentor, Maria, the lady to whom I owe all my success in cooking, to manage 'Milagro' for me.' She laughed. 'She makes more of a success of it than I ever could! In Paris, I brought in a colleague who trained with me in Spain, Ana. In London I ran the restaurant myself for two years, experiencing the city and improving my English, then appointed a wonderful woman called Carolyn to manage it for me while I am here. Her cakes are divine.'

'All women,' noted Blake with interest. 'Was that deliberate?'

'I find them easier to trust. Some of them at least,' she added, looking away. She smiled brightly, her eyes glittering. 'And now, 'Milagro New York', my jewel in the crown.' The swing band began to play its next set and she jumped up, pulling Blake with her. 'Come, we will dance!'

The next morning Aurelia took breakfast in her suite, requesting a copy of all of the Sunday newspapers. She trawled through them carefully, inspecting the society sections. She noted with pleasure that she was either pictured or mentioned in every column, her name regularly intertwined with Blake's. Her favourite was The Observer's snippet. *'Blake Harrington, dashing CEO of The Kingsford Corporation, appears to have met his match in beautiful celebrity chef Aurelia Santa Maria. The exotic and stunning chef was Blake's date at the Met gala last night, and all eyes were on them as best-looking couple of the evening.'*

'Oh, wonderful!' she breathed on seeing the double-page spread in the Sunday supplement of the New York Times. A large photo of her arriving at the gala with Blake was in the centre of the segment. She carefully folded her chosen papers and placed them to one side for keeping. She placed a phone call to Barcelona, smiling as the receiver was picked up. 'Hola Maria, es Aurelia.'

The next day on her way to the restaurant she stopped at a newsstand and bought copies of 'People', 'US Weekly' and 'Manhattan Life'. Once in her office she perused the magazines eagerly, laughing triumphantly at the several glossy photos of her and Blake at dinner, on the dance floor, chatting conspiratorially and laughing together. She placed them neatly together along with the Sunday newspapers she had brought from her hotel, and slid them all into a large brown envelope.

Disguising her handwriting, she wrote a note: *'Paige, we all miss you in New York but get well soon. Enclosed some holiday reading material for you, enjoy! xxx'.* She slipped the note into the envelope and sealed it up. She asked her assistant to make sure it went into the post that day. Chuckling to herself, she headed for the kitchens.

Three weeks later Aurelia set off to the imposing head office of The Kingsford Corporation in Midtown. She had driven past it numerous times during her stay but this time was different. 'This is the first time I've been back inside since I was here with Daddy,' she thought sadly. She stood on the pavement and tipped her head back to take in the full height of the tall skyscraper, remembering all of her childhood visits to her father's office.

She took a deep breath and pulled her shoulders back before striding to the large revolving glass doors. She knew she looked sharp underneath her heavy winter coat, in her soft grey suit and elegant heels, hair cascading glossily as usual around her shoulders. 'Let's do it,' she said to herself with determination.

She joined the flow of people swarming into the building and following the signs to the in-house conference suites. She saw Blake striding towards the room frowning deeply. She hurried to catch up and fell into step alongside him, her coat over her arm. 'Hi,' she said. 'Is everything OK?'

Blake looked weary. He glanced around at the crowds of shareholders. 'Come in here,' he said, motioning to a smaller meeting room off the hallway. He closed the door, muffling the sound of the other people flowing past outside. 'Is everything OK?' Aurelia asked again.

'It's been a difficult few weeks,' admitted Blake. He slumped into a chair. 'Paige is going off the deep end,' he said. 'She got hold of a load of pictures showing me at that gala the other week.' He looked uncomfortable. 'You were in some of the shots with me, and now she's absolutely convinced that we're having an affair.'

'I see,' said Aurelia quietly, sitting down opposite him. He looked at her, his face a picture of misery. 'It was awful Aurelia. She was like a mad woman – throwing things, screaming, red in the face, spitting at me.' He looked down at the floor. 'I tried to tell her that you and I were just friends, that we haven't... that we're not having an affair, but she wouldn't listen to me. The nurses had to sedate her in the end.'

'I'm sorry,' said Aurelia sympathetically. 'It must have been awful for you.'

'It's worse,' said Blake, rubbing his eyes. 'She's been furious and vicious ever since. The head doctor at 'Oakingham' called me yesterday.' He stared at Aurelia. 'They're worried about the safety of the baby. They said they can't allow him to stay with Paige after he's born. I'm going to have to raise the baby by myself until she's better, if she ever is. That was never my plan.' He rubbed at his temples. 'If they take the baby away it's going to kill her.'

He dropped his head into his hands. Aurelia let this latest news sink in. 'Blake, I feel for you, I really do but we will have to discuss this later.' She stood up. 'Out there is a conference hall full of people waiting to hear from the CEO of the corporation. You have a job to do. You need to be a big hit today when you talk about your plans for the restructuring so that the shareholders will view it positively. Focus on that for now.'

Blake nodded, trying to compose himself. Aurelia patted him on the shoulder. 'I'll see you in

236

there,' she said. She slipped out of the room and across the hallway, humming lightly to herself.

Arriving in the large hall she saw Donald and the rest of the board up on the stage checking the running order of events and accepting cups of coffee. She headed over to the stage and was greeted warmly by everyone. 'Hi, it is wonderful to see you all,' she said. 'I just wanted to come up and say hello.' She pointed down to the front row of seats in the audience with their reserved signs guarding them. 'I will go and take my seat, am I down here?'

Donald caught her arm. 'No, you're a member of our board and you belong up here with us now,' he said kindly. 'Won't you please have a seat over here?' He led her to a seat near the end of the table and Aurelia saw a place card with her name on it. She sat down and surveyed the two thousand or so shareholders who had made the journey in for the AGM as they chatted and settled down in their seats.

She watched Blake intently as he strode down the aisle and made his way to the front of the room. 'What a great actor,' she thought bitterly, seeing no visible signs of worry or distress. 'But then, I already knew that.'

Blake shook hands with audience members on his way through the hall, smiling and waving like a campaigning president. 'Maybe that's next on his ambitious list of targets,' thought Aurelia.

As he reached the stage Blake nodded at his PA and upbeat rock music flooded the room. The screen behind the board members on stage sprang into life showing a montage of headlines from the previous year, all praising The Kingsford Corporation. As the last picture faded away the shareholders burst into applause.

'Ladies and gentlemen, welcome to the annual general meeting of The Kingsford Corporation,' said Blake, standing at the lectern at the front left-hand of the stage. 'Thank you for being here with us today. Thank you also to those of you who have been able to dial in via conference call, we appreciate your effort,' he said into the ether. 'On behalf of the board of directors, I declare this meeting open. This has been another very successful year for the corporation and I'm sure you're eager to hear the specifics.'

He brandished a slim folder of documents. 'On your chairs you will have seen that you had a packet of information.' There was a rustle as the audience flipped open their folders. 'The first document in there is today's meeting agenda and we'll proceed in the order listed. Without further ado, I'd like to hand over to Donald Waterman, our Chief Financial Officer, to update you on this year's figures.'

Aurelia listened carefully to all of the presentations, making notes on her pad. She flipped her pad shut as Blake stood once more.   'We'll break for coffee in a moment ladies and gentlemen but before we do that it gives me great pleasure to announce to you the appointment of two new non-executive directors to our board. Our first new director is Mr Thomas Marshall, former CEO of Synergista, director of Britt Electronics and advisor to the current administration on environmental policy. A most distinguished addition to our board.' He waved a hand in Tom's direction as

Tom rose from his seat and raised a hand to the audience. They clapped politely.

Blake smiled and continued. 'Thank you Tom. Our next new board member is a highly successful businesswoman in her own right and brings exciting fresh ideas and new perspective to our team. Ms Aurelia Santa Maria.' The room erupted into eager applause and Aurelia rose, waving briefly as Tom had done. 'Well,' said Tom sardonically as Aurelia sat back down beside him. 'I think we know which of us is the more popular choice!' He winked at her and she laughed. Front of stage, Blake continued.

'I suggest we break here for refreshments. Coffee and tea will be served in the lounge behind this room, and you'll have a chance to mingle with our new board members. We'll reconvene in here in 30 minutes' time for a final presentation of the day that is particularly dear to my heart.'

Aurelia and Tom moved slowly into the next room, greeting shareholders as they went and fielding questions. The break flew by and a bell rang to announce the imminent restart of the meeting. Aurelia saw Blake preparing to head back into the main hall. 'Would you please excuse me?' she asked the elderly couple she was talking to. She moved swiftly to the side of the room and stood behind a group of portly businessmen, pulling out her phone. Disguising her number she dialled Blake's cell phone. She watched him across the room as he pulled his phone out of his pocket and pressed the button to answer it. 'Hello?' came his voice in her ear, as she watched his mouth speak the same word.

Aurelia resumed her normal voice. 'Hello darling, it's Dante.'

Chapter 23

Aurelia watched as Blake's face registered shock, then panic. The colour drained from him and he stared at his phone aghast. She hung up. She slid her phone back into her handbag and walked briskly back to her seat. She smiled as the other board members resumed their seats next to her on stage. The last audience stragglers filed in. Blake looked ashen. 'Like he's seen a ghost,' thought Aurelia with satisfaction.

Blake stumbled his way through his restructuring presentation, leaving his fellow directors looking uncomfortable and confused. Aurelia knew that this was the part of the programme that Blake had been most looking forward to. 'His precious plans for reshaping my company,' she thought. 'Well they're not going down too well.'

Blake's usual confident presentation style was gone, replaced by long pauses and hesitation as he seemed to forget what he wanted to say. His speech was disjointed and confusing. The audience began to fidget. Blake drew his speech to a clumsy end and sat back down, visibly sweating. Donald looked at him uncertainly and got to his feet.

'Ah, ladies and gentlemen, I think that brings us to the end of our presentations for this year so thank you for your attendance today. It's always a long meeting, but we do appreciate your attention.' He motioned towards the back of the room. 'A hot buffet lunch will be served back in the lounge where you took coffee break, please help yourselves, and thank you once again.'

A smattering of applause broke out and the audience trickled out in search of food. Donald sat down next to Blake, his face concerned. 'Blake, are you all right?' he asked. Blake shook his head slightly. 'I'm fine,' he muttered in a low voice. 'I'm just not feeling too well all of a sudden.' He stood abruptly. 'I need a drink.' He walked off the stage without talking to anyone else and headed towards the lunch room.

Donald looked over and caught Aurelia's eye. He shrugged, puzzled. Aurelia shook her head and also headed for the lunch room. She saw Blake take a glass of red wine at the drinks table and knock back almost the whole glass in one go. Smiling, she turned to greet the clutch of shareholders at her elbow.

When the guests began to drift off home and the room started to thin out Aurelia found Donald. 'I have to leave,' she said. 'I left the restaurant in capable hands for the lunch shift but I need to be back for the evening.'

'Of course,' said Donald, shaking her hand. 'We'll see you next week at our first board meeting together.'

'I am looking forward to it already.' Aurelia's smile turned to a concerned frown as she glanced over at Blake, sitting to one side with his tie askew, staring into space. 'Look after him, won't you?'

'I will,' said Donald firmly. 'I don't think he's well. He's been under a lot of strain at home.'

'Of course, poor thing. Well, good luck!' Aurelia took her leave of the room. She wandered slowly along the corridors of the building, loathe to rush out of her father's premises. The ostentatious art deco lobby still looked exactly the same, only the receptionists had changed.

She stared up at the enormous sun burst-shaped clock, remembering how she had loved it as a child. She turned as footsteps hastened towards her.

She blinked as she recognised her father's secretary Sherry, the woman who had looked after her when her father was in meetings, who had explained the clock's detailed workings to her, who had taken her for ice cream and ridden with her in the lifts right up to the observation deck and back down, and who had shown her how the offices worked on her work experience placements. 'Excuse me!' called Sherry.

Aurelia started to back away, suddenly convinced that she had been recognised. Sherry bore down on her, a small but brisk lady, now in her fifties. 'Excuse me,' she said. 'I'm sorry to bother you, but could I trouble you for your autograph please Ms Santa Maria? I'm a huge fan.'

Aurelia's eyes filled with sudden tears and she bent low over the proffered paper. 'Of course,' she said huskily, remembering Sherry's many kindnesses to her. 'What name should I write?'

'Please make it out to Sherry   Sherry Higham.'

Aurelia looked up in surprise at the strange surname. She glanced at Sherry's hand and saw a wedding band and sparkling diamond. She smiled as she wrote out her usual message and handed it back to Sherry. 'How lovely to meet you,' she said, returning Sherry's pen. 'You seem like a very nice lady. I hope you are very happy in your life.'

243

'I am, thank you,' replied Sherry, puzzled by the intensity of Aurelia's tone.

Aurelia rushed away, jumping into the first taxi she could find. She breathed out heavily as the cab drew away. 'That was weird,' she thought. 'I really thought Sherry would know me, but then, why would she? Does anyone? Do I?' She glanced at herself in the rear view mirror but glanced away again immediately, feeling unsettled.

Chapter 24

Aurelia phoned Blake at home that evening. 'I wanted to check on you. You seemed...distracted after the meeting today,' she said. Blake sighed heavily. Aurelia could hear ice cubes clinking in a glass. 'I just have a lot on my mind,' he said, his voice sounding slurred.

'Have you been drinking? Do you want to talk about it?' asked Aurelia.

'No,' said Blake bluntly. There was a pause.

'Well, you know where I am if you do want to talk at all,' said Aurelia gently. 'Why don't you stop drinking and go and get some sleep?'

Blake laughed harshly. 'Sleep? I wish. Whisky is my only pleasure at the moment, so that's what I'm doing. Good night.' He hung up. Aurelia replaced her receiver gently. 'Enough,' she said to herself. 'For now.' She checked her watch and placed another call to Barcelona.

The following week Aurelia returned to the offices of The Kingsford Corporation. 'Good morning, I'm here for the board meeting,' she informed the sleek receptionist. She pretended to listen to the directions to the 52nd floor and then entered the lift. Memories came rushing back at the familiar smell in the lifts. Her sense of déjà vu was almost overwhelming as she stepped out onto the executive floor to find that, other than a subtle refit to keep the decor up to date, almost nothing had changed in over 11 years. 'Last time I was here I was in love and about to be married and now, here I am, still as single as I ever was, with only my plans to keep me warm at night.'

'Aurelia!' cried Donald, advancing on her, his hand out to shake hers. He noted her subdued face. 'Is everything all right?'

Aurelia shook herself. 'Oh, yes, I suppose I am just feeling a little overwhelmed at attending my first board meeting, that is all,' she said, smiling at Donald.

'Now there's nothing to it, you'll be wonderful,' promised Donald. 'Let me show you to the board room.'

The other board members were already in the room, mingling at the far end of the highly-polished table over coffee. She joined them and they chatted easily until Blake entered the room promptly at 10am. His PA sat down at the far end of the table and prepared to take the meeting notes.

'Good morning everyone,' Blake called. 'Let's get this started.' He waited until everybody had taken their seats. 'Thank you all for another successful AGM last week.' He coughed, looking down to rifle through his papers. 'I apologise for lack of clarity in my final presentation of the day. I'd like to run through the main points now of what I was trying to get across.' He paused as his phone rang. 'Excuse me, let me just get rid of this,' he apologised to his colleagues. 'Hello, Blake Harrington,' he said crisply.

Aurelia smiled as she glanced at her watch. 'Good old Maria, perfectly on time,' she thought, imagining her friend playing the pre-recorded message as directed. She watched in satisfaction as Blake's face registered terror, turning a sickly shade of green. He smashed his phone down onto the table, making his colleagues jump.

Blake backed away towards the door, pulling at his tie as if it were choking him. 'I have to go,' he mumbled. He fumbled for the door handle and dashed from the room. A shocked silence reigned.

Tom Marshall broke the silence. 'Is he always like that?' he asked in surprise, his face disapproving. 'What the hell is this circus I've joined?'

Donald strode to Blake's place at the head of the table. 'Tom, Aurelia, everyone, I must apologise for Blake's behaviour.' He nodded at Lauren who was motioning that she would like to be excused to follow Blake. 'As most of you know, he is under extreme personal pressure at present with his heavily pregnant wife being...unwell.'

Understanding nods and murmurs sounded around the table. Aurelia cleared her throat.

'Donald, if I may? I do of course sympathise with Mr Harrington's situation and I hope and pray that his wife – and he – will return to full health very soon.' She paused delicately. 'However, in my position as shareholder I confess to being concerned about his current abilities to do his best for the corporation. I must protect my own financial interests,' she added with a steely tone to her voice. 'As I am sure you all appreciate.'

'Hear, hear,' said Tom robustly. 'I've aligned my name with this corporation and I won't have my reputation dragged through the mud by his personal life upsetting him.'

247

Donald felt the board meeting slipping out of his control and tried to placate his new board members. 'Tom, Aurelia, I do of course understand your concerns but I feel sure you have nothing to worry about. Those of us who have worked with him for many years know him to be a real asset to the company, don't we?'

He looked around the table at his colleagues. Maurice started as if waking from snoozing. 'The man's becoming a problem. Bringing his private life into the office. His wife was here the other day, shouting and screaming, smashing up his office. Would never have happened in William's day.'

Silence ruled once again. Donald seemed at a loss to know what to say. Aurelia leaned forward. 'Donald, sometimes new colleagues have fresh eyes. I am sure nobody is actually suggesting a vote of no confidence in Blake, but it seems that several of us do have concerns. Perhaps we could simply keep an eye on him, as friends, and ensure that he is stable enough to continue without damaging his own health, which is the most important thing.'

Donald nodded slowly. 'Yes, yes, I think that might be best.' He looked sadly around the table. 'We'll reconvene in a month as usual. If you still have concerns at that point then we will have to discuss what needs to happen.' He stood up. 'Let's move on to a discussion of this year's marketing strategy, agenda item number three.'

Aurelia settled back in her chair, satisfied. After the meeting she hung back to speak to Donald. 'Why don't I go and speak to Blake, to check he is OK?' she suggested. 'I am concerned for him with his wife being away – perhaps he finds it easier to speak about his feelings with a woman.'

Donald patted her arm. 'Thank you, that's kind. I'll show you to his office.'

They walked together through the open plan centre of the floor where accountants and tax consultants worked diligently. Donald leaned in towards Aurelia conspiratorially. 'I always feel rather sorry for this lot,' he said in a low voice. 'I can't say I'd enjoy working in open plan. It saps a man's dignity.'

'And a woman's,' smiled Aurelia. 'I agree, I would not like it myself.' Donald pointed out Blake's door and spoke to his assistant. 'Lauren, have you met Aurelia Santa Maria? Our new board recruit. She'd like a word with Blake.'

Lauren smiled but looked worried. 'Go right in, he's not on the phone. He's not doing anything – just sitting there,' she said quietly. Aurelia gave her a reassuring smile and entered Blake's office, shutting the door quietly behind her.

'Hello Blake,' she said softly. Blake turned hunted eyes on her.

'Aurelia-' he started before being unable to continue. She quickly crossed the room and perched on his desk, taking his cold hands between hers and chafing them.

'Blake, what is it?' she asked. 'What is the matter? You must tell me, we are worried about you.'

'I think I'm losing my mind,' said Blake in a low voice.

249

'I am sure that is not the case. Why do you say that?' asked Aurelia.

Blake was silent for a long time. Eventually he raised red eyes to Aurelia. 'I've been receiving calls from beyond the grave,' he whispered.

Aurelia widened her eyes. 'What do you mean?' she asked quietly.

A sob broke from Blake's throat and he coughed to hide it. He raked his hands through his hair, looking desperate. 'Twice now, I've had calls from Dante, my first wife,' he explained.

'You were married before Paige?'

'Yes, to Dante Kingsford, the daughter of the founder of this company.' He looked away. 'I don't like to talk about it. She disappeared on our honeymoon – suicide they decided in the end,' he said quietly.

Anger flared in Aurelia at the ease with which he told his lie but she kept her voice calm. 'How terrible for you,' she said with feeling. 'But then, as she is dead this must be an imposter.'

Blake shook his head slowly. 'It's not,' he whispered, looking ill. 'I'd recognise her voice anywhere. It's Dante. She's haunting me.' He stood and walked over to his drinks cabinet. He poured himself a large Scotch, his hands shaking.

Aurelia watched as he downed the amber liquid, clutching the cabinet for support. She crossed to him and took his arm, pressing him into an armchair. She sat opposite him and spoke seriously. 'Blake, I think you are very stressed at the moment and I understand why. You have a lot on your mind, all of it difficult and complex. Why don't you take a break?' she soothed.

'Take some time off, relax on a beach. Let someone look after you.'

Blake rested his head on the back of the chair. 'I can't let the company down. I didn't really deserve the start I got here,' he confessed. 'I need to continue to prove that I do deserve to run it and that I can do it better than anyone alive. If I'm not here-'

'The company needs you strong and well,' interrupted Aurelia smoothly, biting back angry words at his near-admission of guilt. 'You are not helping yourself or The Kingsford Corporation in this state. When you start hearing ghostly voices your mind is telling you that something has to give. Logically we know it cannot be your dead wife. You need a break.'

Blake sighed heavily, before nodding. Aurelia continued. 'You will need to be strong for your little boy when he is born too, so why do you not ask the board for some extended leave? We can keep the company going for you, and you will return strong and healthy with new energy.'

Blake nodded again, looking calmer but deflated. 'You're right,' he confessed. 'It's all getting to me – this mess with Paige, trying to restructure the corporation, worrying about my baby and how I'm going to manage that. Maybe I need some time to sort out all of that.' He looked at Aurelia as if wanting to be told what to do. She felt repulsed by his weakness.

'I think that is a great idea,' she said firmly. 'Why don't you ask Donald and the others about taking a few months off? We will all help you in the meantime and you will feel like a new man.'

Blake's phone rang and he looked at it in terror, relaxing when he recognised the number. He rejected the call and sat for a moment in silence. 'I have to do this,' he decided. 'I can't live in terror of crazy phone calls. I have to sort my head out before I go totally mad.' He stood up. 'Thank you Aurelia, I don't know what I'd do without your support at the moment. I'm going to speak to Donald right now. I have to get out of here.'

Aurelia hugged him briefly and left his office. She headed for the lifts, trying hard not to whistle.

Aurelia waited for news of Blake's extended leave of absence to hit the business press a few days later then anonymously released a few details of her own over a couple of days. She watched with glee as the papers picked up on her spin. *'Harrington loses confidence of his board,'* read one headline. *'Fights and disagreements in The Kingsford Corporation boardroom'* cried another and *'Harrington flees the country as Kingsford Corporation shows signs of collapse'* ran a third.

She placed a call to Donald, her voice angry. 'Donald, what on earth is going on? Why are the papers saying such terrible things that are not true? Have I made a bad investment? I see the share price is plummeting.' She smiled to herself as she spoke, noting the day's final stock figure was down even further.

Donald sounded flustered. 'Aurelia, what can I tell you? I don't know where these vicious lies are coming from but I'm trying to find out.'

'Signs of collapse?' said Aurelia, reading from one of the headlines, her tone full of panic. 'Have I wasted my money?'

'No, no,' soothed Donald hastily. 'I vouch for the company. This is just a tough storm that we need to weather, but then we'll be back on firm ground.'

'So you are saying I should continue to invest in the corporation?'

'Of course. Please have faith,' begged Donald.

Aurelia finished the call and immediately placed another call to her broker. 'When Kingsford stock hits 95 cents, start buying,' she directed. 'I am transferring $30 million to my account right away.'

Chapter 25

Aurelia strode confidently into the board room at the following month's meeting. 'Good morning gentlemen and a happy new year to you all,' she called. She surveyed the sombre faces as she unwound the thick red scarf from around her neck and took her seat. 'I see you are all feeling about as happy as I am with the state of the company,' she said with a rueful smile.

'It's a disgrace,' said Maurice angrily. 'My shares are virtually worthless. They're supposed to be my pension. I didn't spend 30 years at this company for this.'

Donald entered the room and heard Maurice's words. He closed the door and took his place at the head of the table. 'Let's get this started,' he said. 'Things can't go on as they are. Our sole agenda item for today is to discuss how to turn around the corporation's fortunes. Never in the company's history has anything like this happened.'

'William would be disgusted,' grumbled Maurice. Donald ignored him and continued. 'It seems to me that our troubles stem primarily from Blake having stepped down as CEO, albeit temporarily.'

'With respect,' said Aurelia. 'I think your troubles were starting before Blake left, when he became incapable of focusing properly on the company. His standing aside was the right thing to happen, the issue now is how we move forward. As a representative of the shareholders, I am not convinced that reinstating Blake is the right move.'

Tom and Maurice nodded but the rest of the board members gaped at her authoritative tone. Donald frowned at her, his eyes steely. 'Aurelia, I appreciate your enthusiasm for solving the problem but might I remind you that you have not been with us for long and as such your input is not really appropriate. I don't think it's quite fair to say that you represent the views of the shareholders.'

'On the contrary Donald,' said Aurelia. 'I took your advice to continue investing in the corporation and I now hold 25% of the stock.' She took in the shocked faces of her colleagues. 'I am sad that this once great institution has fallen so far, but I am glad in that it has enabled me to purchase such a significant share of the stock.' She stood, looking at each of her colleagues in turn. 'I want to be a part of making this corporation great again,' she said, her voice strong and imposing. 'I know we can do this. Let us focus on making the company great, rather than needing to rely on the reputation of one man.' She sat back down to applause from Maurice and Tom. A couple of the other board members joined in.

Donald looked astounded. '25 percent?' he repeated. 'I feel quite steamrollered by this I must say. All these changes, happening so fast,' he said uncertainly.

'Today's world is fast,' insisted Aurelia. 'We must keep up with it. I have not become so successful within just ten years by working slowly.' She saw heads nodding around the table. 'This is for Blake's sake as much as anyone else's,' she said solemnly. 'We all know how hard he has worked, but at present his shares are worth as little as the rest of ours.' She lowered her eyes sadly. 'I don't feel secure in his leadership but I want to do the best I can for him, as a dear friend.'

Donald stared at his papers. 'I don't feel we can just write Blake off,' he said slowly. 'We have to give him another chance to show he's back to his old self.'

'Of course,' agreed Aurelia. 'I was going to suggest it myself. Let us hope that he can restore our faith in him. That would be the best solution of all.'

'Let's have him back in to meet with us at next month's meeting,' suggested David Ross. 'He'll have had two of his three months off, and we can see if he's back to normal.'

'Done,' said Donald, looking relieved. 'I'm sure he will be. Let's turn to look at interim management processes for the time being. What can we do to lift this share price? I'd like to hear ideas from all of you. Aurelia, why don't you start?' he challenged, looking at her without smiling.

'I would be delighted,' she said, meeting his gaze levelly. 'I happen to have several very good ideas.'

She was tired when she returned to her hotel that evening. She ran a bubble bath and stepped into it wearily, feeling the welcome warmth soothing her muscles. She rested her head back and ran over in her mind the day's events. 'The board members were impressed with my strategies,' she smiled to herself. 'And so they should be. I was taught by the best, using this exact company as my textbook.' She remembered the countless hours of discussing business with her father in his study as she grew up, longing for the day when she could work alongside him.

Her heart filled with ice as she thought about Blake. 'He robbed me of my father when he tried to murder me,' she thought. 'He deserves exactly what's coming to him.'

She stepped out of the bath and dried off before wrapping herself in a thick, soft robe. She checked her phone and saw a text message from Donald. 'Tried to speak to Blake, but Paige in labour, three weeks early. Will keep you all informed, D.'

Aurelia sank into a chair, picturing Paige's pain. 'Good,' she thought viciously. 'I hope it takes hours.'

She awoke the next morning to another text flashing on her phone. 'Edward Martin Osborne Harrington born this morning, 5:13, being kept in hospital for time being.'

She texted back. 'Thanks Donald, wonderful news for Blake, let us hope it is a fantastic new beginning.'

She waited impatiently for two days to pass, then called Blake. 'I heard your lovely news,' she congratulated him. 'I am so pleased for you, you are a father!'

'Thanks Aurelia.' Blake sounded tired. 'They're not letting him home yet as he was slightly premature, but he should be home by the weekend.'

'May I come and see him?' Aurelia asked.

Blake paused. 'Donald told me about your campaign to remove me from the board,' he said, his tone accusing.

'Oh Blake, it is not a campaign. I am looking out for your interests as a friend. Which I hope I am by now,' she added quietly. 'Please let me come and see you and explain myself properly. I long to see your baby and to see how you are too,' she said, her voice soft.

Blake agreed that she could visit on Sunday and hung up, still sounding angry. Aurelia sent her assistant out to buy an elaborate selection of baby presents.

She counted the days until Sunday but at last it arrived. Her chauffeur dropped her off mid-afternoon and helped her to carry the large gift basket up the steps to Blake's townhouse. Blake came to the door to let her in and she gasped.

He smiled mockingly, wincing as his smile crinkled the large bruise around his left eye. He had not shaved and his clothes were crumpled, as if he had slept in them.

'What happened to you?' asked Aurelia as she followed him into the house. Blake showed her into the drawing room, where a Moses basket lay on the floor. Aurelia peeked over the edge and saw a tiny, dark-haired baby sleeping peacefully. She placed the large, cellophane-wrapped basket on the floor next to it carefully. She tiptoed over to the sofa and sat down.

'Blake?'

He stood at the fireplace staring down at his son. 'I made the mistake of trying to be present at his birth,' he said quietly. 'Paige went mad and punched me. I had to leave the room.' He sighed tiredly, moving to a chair. 'She did herself no favours. As soon as Edward was born they took him away. They didn't even let her hold him.' He closed his eyes. 'I could hear her screams down the hall in the waiting room, crying for her baby,' he said. He looked at Aurelia with tears in his eyes. 'It was the worst thing I've ever heard,' he said. Aurelia's eyes flashed as her thoughts leaped to their honeymoon. 'Really?' she thought. 'Worse than me begging you not to throw me overboard?' She swallowed and tried to act sympathetically.

'I am so sorry,' said Aurelia quietly, stretching out a hand to Blake. He gripped it, taking a deep breath.

'It's the right thing though,' he said. 'She was like a crazy woman, lashing out at me, yelling. Apparently she's regularly like that with the staff at 'Oakingham' too, so how could they trust a tiny baby to her?'

Aurelia shook her head sadly. 'I cannot believe it has come to this,' she said. 'You must be heart-broken.'

Blake's face hardened and he dropped her hand. 'Let's ditch the small talk, shall we?' He looked at her. 'Why are you trying to discredit me at work?'

Aurelia shook her head sadly. 'Blake, I am not at all. I suspect rather it is Donald who is trying to discredit me. I do not think he is too keen on a young woman being in the board room.' She shrugged. 'I have made it very clear to the board that my concerns for you are as a friend. I am worried about you. Look at yourself!' She gestured at his bruised face and crumpled clothes. 'All I said was that I did not want you to come back before you are ready. I want you back at full strength. Ask the other board members – I specifically said that I wanted to make sure the share price picks back up to protect you as the largest shareholder. Ask them!'

She looked earnestly at him. 'I am on your side Blake. Donald wants you to come in next month and show us that you are ready to come back and I totally supported that, you can ask anyone. Ask Donald!'

She sat back in her chair, looking annoyed. 'To be honest Blake, I am surprised to be treated with such suspicion when all I am doing is trying to protect my investment and also take care of a friend at the same time. I am a little insulted.' She pouted slightly, inspecting her finger nails.

Blake sighed. 'I'm sorry Aurelia. My head's all over the place at the moment.'

'I understand,' she said softly. She looked at Edward as he stirred in his basket. 'How are you going to cope with him?' she asked. Blake shrugged. 'A nanny starts tomorrow, so I'll be relying on her until Paige gets better again.' He looked at the gift basket next to Edward as if seeing it for the first time. 'I'm sorry, I haven't thanked you for the present!' he exclaimed.

Aurelia waved away his thanks. 'It is my pleasure. There is a little something in there for you too,' she said, smiling wickedly at him as he drew out a large bottle of Scotch. 'From the tales I hear from other parents, you might need a stiff drink or two!'

Blake kissed her on the cheek. 'Thank you Aurelia, you're very kind.'

'Not at all.' She stood up. 'I must go. Remember, I am your friend and I am here if you need me. We are all on your side and we will see you at the meeting next month. Take care of yourself.' She waggled her fingers at the baby and swept out of the house.

She amused herself over the next few weeks by making regular calls to both of Blake's phones as the ghost. 'I'm getting to him,' she thought in delight on hearing the nanny pick up the house phone several times in a row. 'He's too scared to answer his own phone.' She pictured him terrified to answer his cell phone and laughed. 'That won't go down too well in the business world,' she thought.

She called him as Aurelia late one evening and heard the tell-tale chink of ice in a glass in the background. 'How are you Blake?' she asked.

'I'm fine,' he said quickly. 'Everything's fine. I'm managing fine. I need to come back to work.'

'You sound very jumpy.'

'No, I'm not, everything's fine. I'll see you next week at the office, you'll see I'm fine.'

Aurelia hung up, amused. 'Fine,' she said to herself, echoing Blake's new favourite word. 'I'll see you there.'

She called Donald. 'I am worried about Blake,' she confessed. 'I do not think we should put him through this visit to the board next week.'

'I'm sure you don't,' said Donald, his tone wintry, 'but why don't you leave that up to us? I'll see you next week.' He hung up.

262

Aurelia shrugged into the disconnected call. 'I tried,' she said with a smile.

Chapter 26

The board members were all assembled.
Nobody spoke. The tension was thick in the air and the
wall clock's ticking seemed louder than usual. Donald
started to tap his pencil on the table irritably, but broke
off when he heard footsteps approaching. 'Aha!' he
cried, leaping to his feet. 'Here he is!'

The door was pushed open and Lauren entered,
followed by Blake. Donald's smile slipped as he took
in Blake's thin frame and haggard appearance.
Correcting his smile he reached out to shake Blake's
hand, clapping him on the shoulder. 'The wanderer
returns,' he cried jovially. 'Look everyone, here he is!'
Blake raised bloodshot eyes to his colleagues. 'Hello
everyone,' he said, trying to smile.

The board members gathered round him,
shaking his hand, then retook their seats. Donald
ostentatiously removed himself from the head of the
table and offered the seat to Blake, glancing
triumphantly at Aurelia. She met his gaze levelly.

Blake sat down, all eyes on him. Aurelia
surreptitiously pressed a button on her phone under the
table and Blake's cell phone started to ring. He jumped
and drew the phone slowly out of his pocket, sheer
dread on his face. Seeing a withheld number he
dropped his phone onto the table and backed away. The
ringing stopped.

Blake looked up to see eight faces staring at
him open-mouthed. He started to speak but couldn't.
He turned and fled from the room.

Aurelia coughed delicately. 'I was hoping you would not have to see that,' she said. 'I did feel that Blake was not up to coming in today but I was overruled.' She glanced at Donald, before looking away. When she spoke her voice was very low. 'Blake believes he is being haunted by the ghost of his first wife. He believes hers is the voice he hears on his phone whenever he answers a call.' She shook her head sadly. 'I am terribly worried about him.'

'The man's mad!' said Maurice. 'He should be locked away in that loony bin with his crazy wife!'

'Maurice!' said Donald sharply, his face pale. 'There is no call for that.'

Tom leaned forward. 'I think what there is call for, and what is long overdue, is a vote of no confidence in Mr Harrington. Either he leaves the board or I do.'

A murmur of agreement ran round the room. Donald sighed. 'Very well.'

The motion was put to a vote and passed unanimously, even Donald raising his hand wearily. He addressed the room. 'As Chief Financial Officer I should like to propose myself as interim CEO,' he said. 'Are there any objections?'

Aurelia raised her hand. 'I should also like to propose myself as interim CEO,' she said. She surveyed the room regally. 'You have heard some of my ideas for the corporation and you all agreed at the last meeting that they were sound. I have proven myself to be a success in business and I know that I can turn this company around. I ask you to place your trust in me, on an interim basis only. We can revisit the issue in three months and if you do not think that I am right for

266

the job then I will step aside.' She looked each of the board members in the eyes in turn. 'Let me show you how great this corporation can be,' she said earnestly.

Donald laughed. 'My dear, your enthusiasm is, as always, more than admirable but I really don't think - '

'Why not?' broke in Tom. 'I liked her ideas last time, and she was right about Blake. We've got nothing to lose over three months – the share price can't really go much lower.'

'What about your restaurant?' asked David.

'I have a wonderful team at the restaurant – they know how to run it according to my wishes,' Aurelia said. 'I would like to look in there every day, but other than that I would spend full working hours here, focused 100% on the corporation.'

'All right,' sighed Donald. 'We'll put it to the vote. Raise your hand if you vote for Aurelia.' All hands except his own went up. 'Congratulations,' he said to Aurelia, trying to smile but looking constipated. 'It seems you are the new acting CEO of The Kingsford Corporation.'

Aurelia nodded her thanks and stood up, moving to the head of the table. 'Let's make some money,' she said.

Three nights later, Aurelia was just leaving 'Milagro' when her phone rang. She saw that it was Blake's home number. 'Hello?' she said.

Blake's voice was hollow. 'Paige is dead.'

Aurelia leaned heavily against the door frame, speechless for a moment. She took a deep breath. 'I will be right there, hold on,' she said, summoning a taxi.

'As fast as you can, please,' she urged the driver. As the taxi raced through town she fought down an unexpected wave of sadness, remembering happy times she and Paige had shared in college. 'Oh stop it,' she muttered angrily to herself, dashing away a tear. She dug her fingernails into her palms. 'So she's dead. You wanted to split them up and they're certainly over for good now. She didn't care that you were dead, she was delighted to take over your life, so don't you dare cry over her! Focus on Blake and what you need to do next.' She checked her make up in her compact mirror as the taxi drew up in Blake's street.

She hurried up the steps of Blake's home and was ushered in by the nanny. 'How is he?' Aurelia asked anxiously. Jenny grimaced. 'Drunk. He's in the drawing room not looking too good.'

'Thank you Jenny,' said Aurelia. 'I have been worried about his drinking, and this terrible news is only going to make things worse. Would you please do me a favour? Please note down how much he is drinking each day, so that we can keep an eye on it?' She smiled gratefully at the younger woman and moved into the drawing room.

Blake sat on the floor, his back against an armchair, staring into the fire. He was clutching an empty glass. He didn't seem to notice Aurelia's arrival. She crouched down next to him and touched his arm. 'Blake?' she said gently. 'I am here, let me help you.'

She removed the glass from his grip and set it on the coffee table.

'What happened?' she asked. Blake turned to stare at her.

'She's dead,' he said. 'I said it would kill her if they took the baby off her, and it has.' He stared at his hand, realising that he no longer held a glass. He lumbered to his feet and staggered to the drinks cabinet, sloshing Scotch into two glasses. He handed one to Aurelia who put it to one side. He took a big swig of his and slumped back down onto the sofa.

'They've killed her,' he said. 'They should have let her see the baby. She was hiding her medication, pretending to take it. She saved it all up until she had enough to overdose on. They found her and pumped her stomach but it was too late.' He gave a sob. 'I should have been a better husband,' he said. 'I killed her,' he wept.

'Well this is progress,' thought Aurelia. 'At least he's started admitting his role in his wives' deaths.'

'There is nothing that you did wrong,' she soothed, stroking his hair. 'Paige was ill.'

'She was ill and I failed her,' he wept. 'I was cold and distant to her. I was a bad husband. I'm a bad man,' he confessed.

'No,' murmured Aurelia. Blake drew in a breath. 'All I have left in the world is Edward.' He looked wildly around for his son.

Not seeing him, he clambered to his feet and set off determinedly upstairs. Aurelia followed him. He burst into his son's nursery where Jenny was rocking the baby to sleep in his crib. 'Give me my son!' cried Blake, pulling him from his crib. He clutched him to his face and crooned at him. Edward began to cry lustily, hating the prickly unshaven face and whisky fumes. 'Don't cry, don't cry, I'm your daddy,' said Blake, anguished. He thrust the baby at Jenny. 'Make him stop crying!' he yelled in frustration.

Jenny looked aghast at Aurelia, who pulled Blake from the room. 'Be quiet,' she ordered sternly. 'You need to let Edward sleep.' Blake fell to his knees on the carpet. 'He's all I have,' he moaned.

'I know he is, and he is your son and he loves you, but now he needs to go to bed, and so do you.' She heaved him up off the floor and along the corridor. 'Which is your room?' she asked.

She held his arm as he stumbled along to the last door on the right. She was struck by how much the colour scheme in his bedroom reminded her of the honeymoon suite on the cruise ship. He fell onto the bed, grabbing at Aurelia's wrist. He tried to focus his eyes on her. 'He's all I have,' he repeated. 'I'm losing everything – my wife, my career, my money. It's all going wrong.'

Aurelia detached his fingers from her wrist. 'Try and sleep now,' she said, switching off the lamp. She stood at the door listening to him feverishly muttering 'It's all going wrong,' and smiled grimly as she left the room.

'Yes it is,' she said quietly as she walked away. 'Not nice, is it?'

She waved at Jenny as she passed the nursery and motioned that she would let herself out. She decided to walk part of the way back to her hotel as it was a clear night. She revelled in the night air, her sadness about Paige forgotten.

'I need to discuss this latest development,' she thought excitedly. Pulling her phone out of her handbag she dialled the familiar number in Barcelona.

'Hola?'

'Maria it's me. I have news.'

'Querida!' replied Maria warmly. 'Como esta? Is everything well?'

'Oh yes, things are all coming together perfectly,' crowed Aurelia. 'Paige is dead and Blake is playing right into my hands.'

There was silence on the other end of the phone. 'Paige is dead?' repeated Maria slowly, her tone horrified. 'What on Earth has happened? This is tragic for a young mother – for anyone – and yet you sound...excited? Am I misunderstanding?'

Aurelia sighed impatiently. 'Yes, I know, it's terrible news – for her at least – but it makes my plans even easier, and I didn't even really have to do anything!'

Maria drew in a breath. 'Have you heard yourself?' she asked sharply, 'Have you heard what you are saying? You sound like a monster. What is happening to you?' Aurelia was silent and Maria's tone grew more gentle. 'Querida, you are like a daughter to me, and you know how much I love you, but it breaks my heart to hear you so spiteful and so intent on revenge. If people are dying because of your plans then this has gone too far, surely! I know they hurt you but it was such a long time ago now. Look at you – you are wasting the best and most precious years of your life in this vendetta. You have not married, you have not a family of your own, you refuse to let anyone be close to you – this is no life! Please, for your own sake, stop this now, I beg of you!'

'I thank you for your concern,' began Aurelia frostily.

'You thank me for my concern?' cried Maria, tears in her voice. 'Are we polite strangers now? Can I not say what is in my heart when I am so worried and frightened for you? What will you do next? I am scared to know! Please, stop this and begin your new life. You are a rich, intelligent and beautiful young woman. I cannot be part of this. I cannot bear to see you do this to yourself and to others.'

'Then don't watch,' said Aurelia shortly, hanging up on Maria. She snapped her phone shut and thrust it into her bag before striding crossly down the street to find a cab. 'What does she know?' she muttered to herself. 'How dare she judge me? She owes her life and freedom to me and she'd do well to remember it.' She stamped down hard on her murmuring conscience and hailed a cab.

Chapter 27

Aurelia called Jenny over the following week for updates on the drinking. 'He can't seem to stop,' said the nanny, worriedly. 'He's been out late a lot, with old friends from college I think, drinking until the small hours. He made an effort to be sober for his wife's funeral yesterday but that only lasted until the wake afterwards, then he was embarrassingly drunk. People were talking.'

'Oh dear,' sighed Aurelia, smiling her thanks at Lauren as she brought in the files Aurelia had requested from Accounts. She spun round in her new chair at Blake's desk to look out at the spectacular view over the city from his office. 'I really hoped that he would hold it together better than this. Thank you for letting me know. Do keep an eye on him, won't you?'

Hanging up on Jenny, she checked that Lauren was occupied somewhere out of hearing then redialled. 'Child Services please,' she directed the switchboard.

The phone in Aurelia's office at 'Miraglo' rang the next evening. She saw that it was the booking counter. 'Yes Michelle?' she answered.

'Aurelia, I'm sorry to bother you. There's a Mr Harrington here to see you, he says it can't wait.' She lowered her voice. 'He appears to be quite drunk.'

'I'll be right out.'

Aurelia sauntered through the kitchens and took the staff corridor to the foyer of the restaurant. Blake sat slumped on the banquette, looking dishevelled. Seeing Aurelia he started to his feet, before falling back.

273

'They've taken him,' he cried brokenly. 'They've taken Edward.' He burst into noisy sobs. The security guard looked embarrassed. 'Do you need a hand with him?' he asked.

'Thank you Simon, would you please help him along to my office?' She held open the door to the corridor while Simon supported Blake. They slowly made their way to the office. Simon lowered Blake into a chair before closing the door quietly on his way out.

Aurelia sat down next to Blake. 'What has happened to Edward?' she asked. 'Who has taken him?'

'Social Services,' sobbed Blake. 'They've taken him into care. They said they can't leave him with me as I'm drinking too much.' He slammed his fist into the chair. 'They're right,' he cried in disgust. 'I'm a hopeless drunk. Look at me! Why would they leave a child with me?'

Aurelia stroked his arm soothingly. 'Oh Blake, I am so sorry,' she said. 'You are not a drunk, you are a man who has had too much to deal with recently. No wonder you are feeling pressured. You look exhausted.'

She put an arm around his shoulders. 'You need to be looked after yourself. Perhaps it is not possible at this moment for you to look after another. We will focus on getting you well, and then Edward will come back,' she soothed.

Blake put his head in his hands. 'I need him back!' he cried.

'Of course you do, he is your son. He should be with you. That is why we must make you strong again. Wait here for a moment, I will be back.'

Aurelia headed for the kitchen, beckoning to her maitre d' to accompany her as she went. She went straight to her head chef and pulled both colleagues into a quiet corner of the kitchen.

'A dear friend of mine is unwell and he needs my help,' she said, looking seriously at them. 'I need to dedicate my free time at the moment to helping him. This means I cannot be here at 'Milagro' very often over the coming weeks.' She smiled at her subordinates. 'I have faith in you both that you can keep this place running smoothly, like the experts that you are. Please feel free to call me at any time, night or day, but understand that I cannot be here as often as I would like.'

Cathy and Pierre confirmed that they would do their best for her and that she need not worry, and she returned to her office. She pulled on her coat. 'Come,' she said to Blake. 'I will take you home.'

They rode across town in a taxi. Blake stared silently out of the window with tears in his eyes. Aurelia left him to his thoughts. As the cab pulled away from his house Blake stood on the pavement as if in a daze. 'Give me your key,' directed Aurelia. Blake wordlessly pulled out his key and handed it to Aurelia, his eyes dull. She helped him up the steps and along the hallway to the kitchen. 'Have you eaten today?'

Blake shook his head. Aurelia pushed him onto a stool at the counter. 'You sit, I cook.'

She took off her coat and rolled up her sleeves before washing her hands briskly. She pulled open the fridge door and surveyed the rather bare contents. 'Aie, aie, aie, you do not make it easy for me!' she smiled, raising her eyebrows. She pulled out some eggs and set about concocting an omelette with various leftovers. Within minutes a hot meal was placed in front of Blake. Aurelia watched him eat. 'You must take care of yourself,' she said gently.

'Why?' he asked bitterly. 'My life is ruined. I have nothing left.'

Aurelia put her hand on his. 'That is not true, do not say that!' she exclaimed. 'You have been through an awful time but you still have your friends, and your shares in the corporation. Your job is waiting for you when you are feeling better, I am just keeping your chair warm for you. And you have your son,' she added. 'You need to get better so that he can come home.' Blake nodded, close to tears.

'What about the ghost?' he whispered fearfully.

Aurelia sighed. 'There is no ghost, it is something your mind is imagining. You are not very well right now,' she said gently. 'It is all a symptom of you needing some help. Look at you,' she continued. 'You are so thin it worries me.' She pulled his face up, forcing him to look at her. 'I think you need somebody to look after you,' she said. 'I am going to come here every evening after work for a little while so that I can at least make sure you have a good meal every day and help you to get better.'

'I can't ask you to do that,' protested Blake.

'You have not asked, I have offered. I insist.' She stood up. 'Come, we start right away. You have eaten, and now you need to sleep.' She sent Blake upstairs with instructions to stay in bed for as long as he liked the next day.

She made up a batch of fresh Danish pastries, leaving them covered on the kitchen table with a note to Blake to eat them for his breakfast the next morning. As she set off back to her hotel she placed a call to her assistant at 'Miraglo', directing him to buy certain foods and have them delivered to Blake's house the next day.

She spent the following day in meetings and on conference calls with certain key clients, impressing them with her expertise in the company. She headed over to Blake's house a little after 8pm. Blake was sprawled on the sofa, staring vacantly at the television, drinking whisky. He raised his head to acknowledge Aurelia then slumped back down.

'Good evening!' Aurelia called cheerfully. 'I am going to make us a delicious dinner.' She carried on through to the kitchen and saw with satisfaction that all of her instructions had been carried out to the letter. The fridge and cupboards were now full of food. 'He even ate his breakfast,' she thought, noting that several of the morning's pastries had gone.

She rustled up a creamy chicken chasseur and served up a sharp apple flan from 'Milagro' to follow. She watched Blake devour it and smiled. 'We will soon have you looking and feeling like your old self,' she said.

'Not if I eat like this every night,' said Blake, swallowing a mouthful of dessert. 'I'll get fat!'

'Do not worry about that,' smiled Aurelia. 'Some good comfort food is exactly what you need right now. Do not think about cholesterol. Enjoy it!'

Aurelia's newly rearranged days soon slipped into a regular pattern. She spent busy and challenging hours at the helm of The Kingsford Corporation but managed most days to fit in at least a brief visit to 'Milagro'. In the evenings she would make dinner for herself and Blake, encouraging him to talk over the wine which always accompanied the meal. She kept her portions small and without sauce, but piled up heaping plates of delicious concoctions for Blake.

As the weeks passed Blake started to fill out again and then began to pack weight onto his middle. Aurelia made sure the drinks cabinet had a constant supply of Scotch and cognac to keep up with his daily drinking.

She started to implement her ideas and procedures at work and slowly but surely The Kingsford Corporation started to recover. Its share price began to rise steeply again as investor confidence grew and the business press began to report favourably on the new leadership. Former clients began to return and new clients approached.

'The company is doing well,' she told Blake one evening as he cut into a thick steak. 'Of course, not as well as when you were in charge, but we're doing our best for you.' She looked over at him. 'I have to meet with the board next week,' she said. 'Do you have any ideas that you would like me to put forward on your

behalf? I am keen for your leadership to be felt still,
even though you are not yet back in the office.'

Blake's eyes filled with the tears which came to
his eyes so readily these days. 'Thank you Aurelia,' he
said gratefully. 'I'll put together some notes for you.   I
do have some ideas that I'm keen for the board to hear.
I haven't given up on my restructuring ideas.' He
looked hopeful. 'I was thinking I might be ready to
rejoin the company some time soon'.

Aurelia smiled at him. 'Well that would be
wonderful. Have you, ah, heard any more from your
ghost?' she asked, toying with her meal.

Fear flashed across Blake's face but he
plastered on a brave smile. 'Oh, I'm sure you're right
about that. It must have been my imagination. Now
that you're here looking after me she hasn't bothered
me again.'

'Well that is wonderful,' smiled Aurelia. 'We
will have you back in the office in no time'.

Inspired by her words, Blake stayed up late
writing out detailed notes for his vision for the
company, and points that he would like the board to
consider at its next meeting. He handed them to Aurelia
before he went up to bed. Aurelia promised him that
she would take care of his wishes.

Arriving in the office the next morning she
headed for the photocopying room and shredded
Blake's notes. 'That's where your input belongs,' she
thought as she watched the ribbons of paper falling
helplessly into the bin. 'I don't want my corporation
restructured.'

279

At the board meeting the following week Aurelia outlined her own plans for the corporation and showed how the company could easily exceed the next six months' targets, to strong praise from her colleagues. 'You remind me of William Kingsford himself,' said David. 'You see right through to the main issue.'

'You're a genius,' smiled Tom. 'I knew we were right to back you. I wish my own company had had a visionary like you back in the day.' Aurelia glowed with delight at the praise.

She told Blake that night that the board had been interested in his ideas, but wanted him to focus on getting better. 'They all sent their best wishes to you,' she said, 'and asked me to make sure that you are taking care of yourself and getting properly better before you head back to your stressful role there.' She topped up his wine glass. 'I suggested that you should focus on getting Edward back first and they agreed.'

'Thank you Aurelia,' smiled Blake. He took a large gulp of his wine and sat back looking sleepy after his large meal.

'I have completed some forms for you,' said Aurelia. 'We can send them to Child Services and apply for Edward to be returned to you.' She pulled a pile of papers and a pen from the sideboard and crossed round to Blake's side of the table. 'If you just sign here,' she indicated and waited for Blake to sign, 'and here...and there, that's it, then I will send them off for you in the morning. Please also sign this cheque for the fee to speed up the process, thanks.' She scooped the papers back up and placed them in her briefcase.

She smiled across the table at Blake. 'We will have him back in no time,' she said.

'Thank you Aurelia,' Blake repeated, reaching for her hand across the table. 'I don't know what I would have done without you over these last weeks,' he confessed. 'You saved my life.'

Aurelia moved away. She cleared away the plates and topped up their wine glasses before sitting down again. 'Do not praise me,' she said to Blake, looking down at the table. She lowered her voice. 'I feel guilt every day in case I was responsible for Paige going mad.' She raised sad eyes to him. 'The truth is, I do think you are a very attractive man, and a very brilliant man, and I wonder if Paige sensed that. Maybe I am to blame. I find you very sexy. Maybe I made her jealous.' She dropped her head as if in shame.

Blake scraped back his chair and strode round the table. Kneeling next to Aurelia he took her face in his hands. 'You're not to blame!' he said earnestly. 'If anybody should feel guilty it's me. I knew Paige was a jealous person but I allowed myself to enjoy flirting a little with you,' he admitted. 'If she sensed anything, it was from me. My visits to your restaurant were the highlights of my week.'

He stared at Aurelia, suddenly very still. He dropped his gaze to her mouth. Aurelia held her breath. Slowly, Blake moved forward to kiss her. As his lips softly touched hers Aurelia fought the urge to recoil in hatred, forcing herself to kiss him back for a moment. She drew back with an embarrassed laugh.

'This is not such a good idea,' she said. 'I confess that I have strong feelings for you but it is inappropriate. This cannot go anywhere, you are newly widowed, and it will only end with my heart broken. I should go. I was foolish to come here so often.'

She stood up but Blake clutched at her wrist. 'No, don't leave,' he cried urgently. 'I need you.'

'I need you too Blake!' she cried, 'but I am in an impossible position!' She gestured despairingly. 'I am tormented by thoughts in my head of how beautiful our life could be together, and perhaps one day in the future providing a happy, stable home for Edward together but I know such thoughts are wrong. Society would frown at us.' She threw back her hair. 'I am a terrible person for even thinking such thoughts out loud and God should punish me. You are not mine and that cannot be my life, however much I wish it.' She sobbed and turned to go.

Blake clambered up off the floor and hastened after her. 'Aurelia, wait!' He caught up with her and pulled her to him. 'It can be your life!' he said feverishly. 'It's a wonderful idea! You are a beautiful woman, inside and out, and you've brought me back to life.' He held her shoulders, staring excitedly into her eyes. 'We can be together!' he said. 'A fresh start.'

Aurelia smiled longingly but then frowned. 'People will talk,' she said, shaking her head. 'Paige died only two months ago. They will say that I have taken advantage of you. It will be a scandal.'

'Let them talk,' said Blake fiercely. 'I'll tell them the truth – that I'm only alive because of you. That you've shown me kindness that Paige hadn't for years. That you know how to look after your man.' He smiled at her. 'In any case, you're rich in your own right – you're not chasing after my money, they'll see that.' He bent to kiss her. 'We'll be a family,' he said excitedly. 'We'll get Edward back. This is the right thing.'

He pulled her close, stroking her back. Aurelia let herself relax against him for a moment, then pulled away. 'I have to think about this,' she said. 'I am confused, I do not know what is right.' She reached for her coat. Blake started at her, aghast.

'You're leaving?'

She stroked his cheek tenderly before donning her coat. 'Yes. I will return to my hotel to think this over. My heart says yes but my head...I must be sensible. Goodbye.' She turned abruptly and dashed from the house.

Chapter 28

Back at her hotel she congratulated herself on a set of moves played well. She pictured Blake wandering aimlessly around his house, not knowing what to do with himself. She reviewed the documents contained in her briefcase. Blake's signature sat decisively on the forms consenting to the immediate adoption of his son. She pulled out the covering letter she had prepared in his name and read it through again.

'I should like to confirm my request for the immediate adoption of my son, Edward Harrington. Edward was taken into care six weeks ago as I was deemed unsuitable to look after him due to my ongoing alcohol abuse problems. I have used the intervening weeks to consider my position carefully and I confirm that I do not want him back. His mother is dead and she was the one who wanted him. I am a busy man and have neither the time nor the inclination to raise a child, particularly now that I am on my own. I want nothing more to do with him.

Please find enclosed the necessary forms to enable you to have him adopted as quickly as possible by a family who will take appropriate care of him. I enclose a cheque for $10,000 to assist with any fees incurred in using a private adoption agency to speed up the process.

I do not need or want any further correspondence on this matter, I just want to forget.'

Aurelia smiled in satisfaction and sealed up the envelope ready for urgent delivery in the morning.

As she was about to get into bed her phone beeped. A text from Blake waited for her. 'I miss you already. Please come back soon xx'. She smiled and turned off the light.

She didn't contact Blake the following day, or the next. A week went by during which she pretended to be busy thinking.

'Oh, you are keen,' she thought, as she received yet another text message from him one evening. A large bouquet of long-stemmed red roses arrived for her at 'Milagro' an hour later, with a card reading *'I need you.'*

'I know what you need,' she said to herself. She picked up her phone and waited for him to answer.

'Hello darling, it's Dante. I will find you. Don't forget me.' She hung up, smiling widely, picturing his fright.

Her phone rang a moment later. 'Aurelia, it's me.' Blake sounded terrified. 'Please, you have to come back, I need you here. I can't be alone.'

'What has happened?' she asked.

'The ghost is back,' he whispered urgently. 'Please, she never bothers me when you're here. I need you with me. Please.'

Aurelia spoke tenderly. 'Blake, I cannot be there knowing your intentions but as an unmarried woman. My reputation matters to me.' She laughed lightly. 'To be honest, I do not fully trust myself when I am with you, and I could not risk something happening between us like this. I am a good Catholic girl after all.'

'Aurelia, I'm going out of my mind. I need you here. I need you,' Blake begged. Aurelia was silent, waiting for him to connect the dots.

'We'll get married!' he cried. 'Let's do it tomorrow.'

'Blake-' began Aurelia.

'No, I mean it.' Blake's voice was determined. 'Come with me tomorrow to Las Vegas. We can get married right there and then. You'll be my wife and we can start our new life together.' He heard Aurelia's pause and continued, his tone beseeching. 'We'll stay in a wonderful hotel; we'll go out for a romantic meal – no cooking for you – just you and me. Please baby. Aurelia, marry me.'

Aurelia smiled into the phone. 'OK. You only live once I hear,' she said. 'Let's do it. Let's go to Las Vegas and get married. I will ask my assistant to book tickets for us.'

'Let me,' said Blake. 'Let me do something for you. I'll arrange flights - we'll take the corporate jet - and get us a beautiful room in the best place in town.'

'Wonderful,' smiled Aurelia. 'Now let me go and get ready. A girl needs to plan for her wedding night!'

She hung up and smiled grimly. 'Just you wait till you see what I've got planned,' she said.

She collected Blake from his house in a company car the next day and they were driven to the airport. Blake clutched her hand as New York flashed by outside the windows. 'This feels right,' he said, closing his eyes in relief. 'You make my head feel less noisy. I feel like you understand me.'

Aurelia smiled. 'Oh, I think I do.'

At the airport she and Blake were driven straight round to the small terminal dedicated to private jets. They waited for a few minutes in the luxurious lounge for their flight to be ready. She sipped thoughtfully on a sparkling water as she watched Blake suck down his double Scotch. She glanced at her efficient carry-on luggage, running through the contents once more in her mind. The flight attendant in the blue and gold Kingsford Corporation flight uniform arrived to usher them the few steps across the tarmac to the Gulfstream jet.

Aurelia settled herself in a silk-covered armchair and accepted a glass of Champagne as they prepared for take-off.

The journey was uneventful and just a few hours later their plane was swooping down parallel to the famous Las Vegas Strip. The afternoon sun glinted off the glass panels of the Luxor's pyramid as the plane taxied to a halt on the tarmac. Aurelia felt a jolt of excitement. 'Sin City,' she thought. 'Perfect.'

A limo was waiting for them, and Blake popped open another bottle of Champagne in the back seat as they were driven along. 'To us,' he toasted. 'To true happiness,' replied Aurelia, taking a small sip.

They drew up outside 'The Wynn', its crème caramel sheen a beacon of luxury among the glitzy neon of The Strip. A doorman helped them inside and their bags were discreetly whisked away. Blake checked them in while Aurelia admired the opulent lobby.

Chandeliers of the finest Venetian glass shimmered exquisitely overhead.

'Your suite is ready, if you'd like to follow me,' said the bell boy. Aurelia and Blake followed him to the lifts to the 39th floor. Arriving on their corridor, he flung open their door with a flourish and Aurelia gasped as she saw the remarkable view outside the window. 'We can see all the way down The Strip!' she exclaimed. 'How wonderful.'

'Enjoy your evening,' smiled the bell boy as he retired with a generous tip in his hand.

Blake looked at his watch. 'I made a booking for us at the Little White Chapel at 5pm,' he said. 'We should set off shortly.'

'Just give me a few minutes to get ready,' said Aurelia, slipping into the bathroom with her bag. She unzipped her luggage and unpacked her shampoo and other personal items. She pulled out a small bundle of clothes wrapped in a plastic bag and hid it behind the pile of fluffy towels above the shower, before changing into a soft cream knee-length dress with plunging neckline. 'It seems a lot quicker and easier to get ready for your wedding the second time around,' she muttered to herself.

She checked her face in the mirror, and retouched her eye make up a little before applying some berry gloss to her lips. She surveyed herself critically. 'So perfect you married me twice,' she thought.

She slipped her feet into high, strappy sandals and stepped out of the bathroom. Blake was tidying his tie in the mirror. He smiled widely at the sight of her. 'You look beautiful,' he breathed.

'Why thank you, señor,' she said, twirling for him in the centre of the room. He caught her hand. 'Are you sure you're happy to get married like this?' he asked her, looking serious. 'Are you sure you don't mind not having the big white wedding that most women want?'

Aurelia smiled at him, adjusting his tie. 'This is exactly what I want,' she said with conviction. She took his arm and they set off for the chapel.

The limo was waiting for them again downstairs and they arrived at the chapel within minutes. 'I booked the full package,' murmured Blake as Aurelia was handed a large bouquet of white roses, and a single bloom was pinned into his buttonhole. They both laughed as they were pressed into position for a photograph under a bower of artificial flowers.

Within minutes the vows had been made, Blake had been directed to kiss his bride, and Mendelssohn's march was playing as the new Mr and Mrs Harrington left the chapel.

'I thought we could head back to our suite before dinner,' said Blake, pulling Aurelia close to him and nuzzling at her neck. She tried to laugh playfully as she pushed him away. 'Can't we please go for cocktails first?' she asked. 'I have always wanted to visit the famous Bellagio – take me there?' She fluttered her eyelashes at him. 'I will make it worth your while later,' she promised seductively.

Blake laughed. 'OK, Mrs Harrington, cocktails it is.' He opened the door of their limo for her. 'I'd like a drink anyhow.'

They stayed on at the hotel's finest restaurant for dinner, feasting on oysters and lobster and accepting the sommelier's recommendations for wine to accompany every course. 'It is a treat for me to eat great seafood prepared by somebody else,' said Aurelia with a satisfied sigh. She nodded at the second empty wine bottle. 'Shall we finish with a cognac?'

'Good idea,' said Blake, motioning to the waiter. He ordered the digestifs then stood up. 'Excuse me for a moment,' he said. Aurelia watched him head to the bathroom looking a little unsteady on his feet and smiled her thanks at the waiter as he delivered their brandy. She quickly delved into her purse and unwrapped a tiny foil packet from inside an empty lipstick case. She glanced casually around to make sure that nobody was near, before pouring the small amount of white powder onto a teaspoon and stirring it into her glass. 'I hope that stuff is as strong as they promised me,' she thought. 'I certainly paid enough for it.' She balled up the foil and slipped it back inside the case, under cover of the table, for disposal later on.

As Blake returned she lifted both glasses and handed her glass to him. 'A toast,' she said. 'To a happy ending.' Blake echoed her words and they both drank deeply. Aurelia's eyes glittered as she noted that Blake had swallowed every drop of the toxic liquid.

'Let's get the check,' said Blake, squinting drunkenly at her. 'We've got a wedding night to enjoy!'

'Great idea,' smiled Aurelia. Blake paid and they stood to leave.

'Are you OK?' Aurelia asked, seeing Blake rubbing his chest as he gripped the back of his chair.

'I'm fine,' he said, frowning. 'Just a touch of indigestion I think. I'll be OK.' They walked slowly out through the large lobby. Well-wishers smiled at them as they passed, noticing Aurelia's bridal bouquet and cream-coloured dress. Aurelia dropped her lipstick case casually into a bin as they went.

As the limo drove away Blake sat back heavily in his seat. 'You are sweating!' exclaimed Aurelia. 'Are you sure you are feeling well?'

'I'm fine,' said Blake. 'Just a little tight in the chest. I'll take some indigestion tablets when we get back, don't worry.' He continued to rub his chest. He smiled sheepishly at Aurelia. 'I've probably had a little too much to drink again,' he confessed.

They rode in the lift up to their suite. Blake sat down on the bed, loosening his tie. Aurelia fetched him some indigestion tablets from his bag and a glass of water. He knocked a couple back and smiled at her. 'There, I'll be good as new in just a moment.'

'Well then,' purred Aurelia seductively. 'Why don't you slip out of your clothes and wait for me on the bed? I am going to change into something more comfortable.'

She sashayed into the bathroom and waved at him before locking the door quietly. She quickly reached up to collect the bag she had hidden earlier. She pulled out a silky shorts and camisole set in cobalt blue. She took off her wedding clothes and slipped into the night gear. She removed her brown contact lenses and wiped her face free of eye make-up. Taking a bobbed blonde wig out of the bag she pulled it on, tucking her long hair under it carefully. She shook her head, making sure the wig was secure. She removed the glittering diamond and platinum wedding ring that Blake had just presented her with.

She stared at herself in the mirror, staggered by the transformation.

'There I am,' she said to herself. 'I wonder if Blake is ready to see his wife.'

Chapter 29

She opened the bathroom door and stepped out from behind it. Blake propped himself up on his elbows. The smile froze on his face as he took in the impossible apparition standing in the doorway.

'Hello darling, it's Dante,' she drawled.

Blake's face drained of colour. He sat bolt upright staring at her in pure terror. He swayed unsteadily, clutching at his chest. 'Dante!' he gasped. 'It's not possible.' He fell onto his side, staring at her with wild eyes full of fear. 'My chest,' he gasped. 'Help me!'

She moved closer to him, watching as he grasped at his chest, struggling to breathe deeply.

'It's not nice, is it, to die before your time?' she asked casually. She sat down in an armchair and crossed her legs, tapping one foot. 'I imagine you don't have long,' she said.

Blake's eyes rolled frantically in his head as he tried to move. 'I can't breathe,' he said. 'Where's Aurelia? Help me.'

'I can't do that darling,' said Dante.

'Why are you here?' croaked Blake. 'How are you here? I thought you were a ghost but you look so real. Is it really you?' He squinted, trying to peer up at her. 'Wait a second...Are you...? Are you Aurelia as well? Was it you all along? What the hell's going on? Why is this happening?'

'Oh, I think you know.'

'Is it because of Paige? Are you angry that I married her?'

295

Dante's temper started to fray. 'No!' she shouted. 'I want you to confess!'

Blake was silent. His throat rasped as he hauled in a breath. 'I always wondered if you suspected,' he said slowly. He raised pleading eyes to Dante. 'You have to understand. It didn't mean anything.'

'It didn't mean anything?' spat Dante.

Blake licked his dry lips. 'No,' he whispered. 'It was before I met you. How could it? I slept with her once and then I met you and everything changed.'

Dante frowned, thrown off track. 'What are you talking about?' she asked.

Blake fought to get the words out. 'I slept with Paige, but only once.' He sighed, closing his eyes. 'I met her at a function a few weeks before I came to speak at your college and we got together. I'm so sorry. I never wanted you to find out. As soon as I met you I knew you were the one.'

Dante's mind raced. 'A likely story,' she sneered. 'You knew you wouldn't have to be married me for long before you could get back with Paige. Cooked it up between you did you?'

'I don't know what you mean,' whispered Blake.

Dante brought her face close to his. 'I know what you did,' she said intently. 'I know you only married me to get at my money and I know you murdered me on our honeymoon. Just admit it to me.'

'I didn't,' said Blake. 'I didn't. Where have you been all this time? I don't understand.'

'You did it!' yelled Dante. 'Just confess!'

Blake shook his head slightly, wincing with pain. 'I didn't,' he whispered. 'I loved you. You killed yourself.'

'I certainly did not,' said Dante, pacing about the room. 'I can't believe you're still clinging to these lies even now. This is your last chance to confess – clear your conscience while you can!'

Blake shook his head, his eyes closed, his breath scratching.

'I know all about it,' said Dante. 'I know you took out an insurance policy on my life just before our wedding. I heard you.'

'That's not true,' whispered Blake. 'I took out a policy on my own life, for your benefit.' He clutched his chest again. 'I knew I was a candidate for heart problems after what happened with my father.' He winced. 'I wanted you to be provided for, and not just by your father.' He looked at Dante sorrowfully. 'It was a policy on my life in case this happened. I should have told you, I'm sorry. I didn't want to upset you.'

'A nice touch,' said Dante sarcastically. 'All designed to make you seem more believable when I suddenly disappeared I suppose.' She began to pace again. She stopped, whirling round to face Blake.

'I'm not stupid,' she said angrily. 'I know you were trying to kill me that night on deck, and you weren't able to as those stewards arrived. I know you drugged me the next night so you could do it properly.'

'I didn't!' cried Blake. 'I knew I'd scared you that night on deck but I explained myself at the time. I'd had a vision of how awful it would be to lose you and I just froze and I couldn't let you go. I'm so sorry I scared you.' A tear trickled from his eye. 'It was the worst day of my life when I woke up in the morning and saw that you weren't in the room with me.' He closed his eyes again. 'My head was sore, as if I'd had too much to drink, and you were gone. I searched for you everywhere I could think of and then reported you missing to the stewards.'

He paused, swallowing painfully. 'They found your robe on the deck, right at the edge of the rail.' His voice cracked. 'I fell onto my knees on the deck and howled. They had to sedate me. My mother flew out to Spain to bring me home and I had to make my life without you.'

Tears ran down his face. 'I don't understand why you left me,' he said. 'Tell me why, please! What should I have done differently? Did you jump? Did somebody push you? Where did you go? Tell me what's happening!' He sighed heavily and tried to drag in another breath. 'Maybe I should have stayed awake to watch over you that night – I knew you weren't well, maybe you weren't thinking straight.'

Dante clapped slowly. 'Bravo,' she said. 'A fine performance. For whatever reason, you're sticking to your story even now. So be it Blake. You had your chance. May you rot in hell for what you did to me,' she said viciously. 'At least you'll be with your darling Paige.'

Blake sobbed. 'Dante, please. You have to believe me. I loved you from the second I met you. After you died, Paige was kind to me and helped me carry on. I didn't want to be alone and I couldn't have you, so I married her. I shouldn't have, it was too soon,

I still loved you and she knew it. Ours wasn't a happy marriage.'

'Oh dear, my heart bleeds,' said Dante scornfully. 'And now here you are, married again to another wealthy woman. You were so quick to flirt with Aurelia, and with Sienna – you showed no loyalty to your wife. What a fickle, greedy man you are.'

Blake closed his eyes. 'It's been a long time since I've been happy,' he whispered. 'For the first time since you died I felt at home when I was with Aurelia, like we could be happy together. I thought maybe at last I deserved some peace in my soul. It must be because it was really you. I felt a connection so quickly. It's because you're my soul mate.'

'Oh please,' sneered Dante. 'I'm sick of your lies. You've clearly repeated them for so long that you even believe them yourself now. I can't take much more of this.' She stood over Blake looking down at his clammy skin and chalky colour. 'Luckily I won't have to.'

Blake struggled to take a breath, staring up at her. 'Where have you been?' he pleaded. 'If you didn't die on the boat, where have you been all this time? Why didn't you come back to me? Why didn't you tell me you were alive?'

He slowly reached a hand out towards her from his sprawled position on the bed. His breathing was wheezy and laboured. 'Help me Dante please,' he begged slowly, trying to drag air into his lungs. 'Please. I always loved you.' His eyes rolled and his last breath shuddered out of him.

'Goodbye Blake,' whispered Dante.

She sat very still for a moment, shaken by the determination with which Blake had clung to his lies. 'Could it be true?' she wondered slowly, picturing his earnest face and desperate tone. She shook her head as if to clear a fog. 'No,' she thought decisively. 'He was desperate because he knew he was going to die. He would have said anything. He's a clever man, he always was a smooth talker.' She thought again of his refusal to change his story. 'I guess if you tell yourself something often enough for long enough you start to believe it,' she thought.

Forcing herself out of her chair she tore off the blonde wig and ran to the phone.

'Oh help me please!' she cried when reception picked up. 'Send an ambulance right away! My husband is having a heart attack! Help me!'

She hung up and raced into the bathroom, throwing the wig back into her suitcase, and reinserting her brown contact lenses before adding lashes of dark mascara. She slid her wedding ring back onto her finger. She placed a towel over Blake to hide his nakedness just as an urgent knock sounded at the door.

She ran to throw it open. 'Oh thank goodness,' she breathed, seeing two paramedics with a stretcher. 'Help me please. I think my husband is dying!' She sobbed, the tears coming quite naturally after the high emotion of the day. The receptionist who had accompanied the paramedics came into the room and put her arm around Aurelia's shoulders. Aurelia crumpled into a chair as she watched one of the medics start emergency CPR while the other unpacked a portable defibrillator.

'We only just got married,' she wailed. 'We have only been married for six hours!'

The receptionist fought back tears herself as she took care of the devastated new wife. She looked up hopefully as the paramedics sat back and started to pack away their things. One of them shook their heads and she clapped a hand over her mouth, her arm tightening around Aurelia's shoulders.

'No!' screamed Aurelia. 'No! He cannot be dead! We just got married!' She rushed across the room and threw herself on Blake's lifeless body. 'Come back, come back!' she cried.

One of the paramedics pulled her away firmly but gently. 'I'm so sorry Mrs Harrington. There's nothing we could do. Your husband has had a massive heart attack.' The two men lifted Blake's body onto the stretcher and covered it with a sheet. They spoke quietly to the receptionist before wheeling the stretcher out of the room. 'Where are they taking him?' cried Aurelia. 'I need him! I must be with him!'

'They're taking him to the Kindred hospital,' said the receptionist. 'We'll take you there right away. Would you like to change into other clothes?' she asked gently.

Aurelia nodded, and staggered into the bathroom. She pulled her wedding dress back on, noting with satisfaction that the mascara had smudged dramatically down her face, giving her a tragic air.

She was led down through private corridors to a back entrance where a saloon with chauffeur was waiting to drive her to the hospital. The receptionist offered to accompany her but Aurelia shook her head. 'I will go alone,' she said sadly.

She leaned her head back and closed her eyes as the car drove her to the hospital. 'I've done it,' she thought. 'All those years of planning and I've finally done it.' She frowned as she waited for a sense of satisfaction to flood through her. She felt flat.

She tried to steer her thoughts away from Blake's insistence that his story was true. 'What if I'm wrong?' she thought slowly. 'His denial was so convincing...What if it was Paige by herself?' She felt hot and flushed as she considered this possibility, then shook her head to clear her sudden panic. 'No, Paige wasn't on the cruise ship with me, Blake was! I could even smell his aftershave on deck that night! Blake wanted me to think it was Paige now she can't deny it. Even if Paige was involved, Blake certainly was too - he was the one who drugged me and threw me overboard after all.' She felt more certain in her mind and took a deep, calming breath. 'He deserved what he got.'

The reception staff at the hospital was expecting her and she was led to the room where Blake's body lay. No instruments hummed or tubes pulsed. All was peaceful. 'He's dead,' whispered Aurelia, staring at the body. The nurse squeezed her hand.

'I'll leave you for a few moments,' she said kindly. 'I'm just outside if you need me.'

Aurelia nodded and moved over to the bed. She stared down at Blake's face. 'So handsome,' she said softly, stroking his cheek. She remembered the night they had met and their wedding day nearly 12 years earlier. She pictured the way that he had looked at her. She smiled sadly. 'It could all have been so different if it had been real,' she murmured. Her heart hardened. 'Three marriages and no-one to mourn you,' she said. 'What a man. Goodbye Blake.'

She turned and walked slowly from the room.

Chapter 30

She placed a call to Donald from the hospital. 'Donald, it is Aurelia. I am sorry to call you so late. So early,' she corrected, acknowledging the time difference between the two cities.

'Has something happened?' asked Donald groggily. Aurelia swallowed.

'Blake is dead,' she said, a tremble in her voice. She heard Donald's shocked gasp.

'No! What? How?' he asked in disbelief.

'Just a little while ago. He had a massive heart attack and died within minutes. The ambulance could not reach him in time.' She forced out a sob. 'Donald, I am calling you from Las Vegas.'

Donald absorbed what she had said and then realised its probable significance. 'Oh God. Aurelia-'

'We were just married!' she cried brokenly. 'It all moved so fast between us from friendship to love, and Blake wanted to marry immediately so we decided to come to Vegas. We were married this afternoon and now, on our wedding night, my husband is dead!' She sobbed into the phone.

'Aurelia, my dear, I'm so very sorry,' Donald sounded tearful himself. 'What can I do? Would you like me to fly out and meet you there? I can leave right away.'

Aurelia took a deep steadying breath. 'Thank you Donald, that is very kind, but no. I will make arrangements for...for us both to return to New York as soon as we can. Later today I hope. I will need to arrange a funeral, but I do not know...' She broke off.

305

'Aurelia, I insist, let me help you with that,' said Donald firmly. 'You're still new to this country, you don't know how everything works. Let me sort out the funeral for you.'

'Thank you Donald,' she replied. 'Would you please inform the board of Blake's death? I cannot bear to tell anyone else.'

'Of course.'

'And Donald? Please do me an important favour. Please do not tell anyone about my marriage to Blake. I do not want to be a tragic news story. Nobody needs to know.' She took a shuddering breath. 'It is news enough that he died so tragically young, so soon after Paige. People will not understand what we had together. I will find it easier if nobody knows.'

'Are you sure?' asked Donald uncertainly. 'Who will help you through this?'

'I will tell my close friends,' she said,' but I do not want this to become public gossip. I would like to be able to grieve in private without the world's press being involved.'

'Of course, I understand completely,' said Donald. 'I won't tell a soul unless you say otherwise.'

Aurelia thanked him and hung up. She signed various forms and made to leave the hospital. 'Mrs Harrington, you'll need to stay at your hotel as the police may need to speak to you in the morning,' said the nurse apologetically. 'It's quite standard when somebody dies so unexpectedly.'

'Of course,' said Aurelia. She took the hotel's car back home where the night manager waited to greet her.

306

'Mrs Harrington, if you would prefer to move to a different room that can be arranged immediately,' he offered. Aurelia shook her head tiredly.

'No, thank you, I would like to sleep in the room I was to share with my husband.'

The manager nodded understandingly. 'If there's anything at all that we can do for you please just call down to reception.'

'I would please just ask for your discretion,' Aurelia requested. 'My marriage to Mr Harrington was a private matter and I am keen to keep it that way.'

'That goes without saying, ma'am,' he confirmed.

Aurelia rode the lifts up to her room, leaning tiredly against the wall. Back in her room she surveyed the scene. 'No-one would know anything much had happened,' she thought, taking in the barely dishevelled bed and the clothes piled neatly where Blake had undressed. Her wedding bouquet sat on the coffee table, the rose petals starting to wilt and curl.

She slipped out of her wedding dress and threw it on top of the pile of clothes, before pulling on her night clothes. She scrubbed her face clean and stared at herself in the mirror. 'And so it ends,' she said to herself.

By the time the two plain clothes police officers arrived at her suite the next morning she had breakfasted and was dressed, sitting forlornly by the window in her suite. She rose to greet the officers as they were shown into her suite.

She smiled ruefully, gesturing at her green silk dress. 'Please do not think I am being inappropriate. I was not expecting to be in mourning,' she explained. 'I do not have anything black with me to wear and I am certainly not in the mood for shopping. Please, sit down.'

The male officer spoke. 'Mrs Harrington, I'm sorry for your loss. I apologise for intruding at this difficult time but we do need to ask you a few questions about last night.' Aurelia nodded, and the officer continued.

'Could you please tell us in your own words exactly what happened yesterday?'

'All day?'

'Yes please.' His colleague waited with a pen and notepad in her hand.

'Well, we travelled from New York, where we live, to Las Vegas by private plane and were collected by a limousine arranged by Blake. We came to the hotel and got ready for our wedding ceremony.' She looked down, swallowing hard. Her voice wobbled as she continued. 'Then we were married at 5pm at the 'Little White Wedding Chapel'. We went afterwards to 'The Bellagio' for cocktails and then for dinner. We came home in our limousine and I changed my clothes while Blake undressed and then we began to...' She blushed. 'Well, it was our wedding night.'

'That's OK, ma'am, we understand,' said the officer. 'Then what happened?'

'We were on the bed together when suddenly Blake clutched at his heart. I did not know what was happening, it was so frightening. He rolled onto his side and was trying to talk to me. I tried to hear what he was saying but it was too difficult.' Her eyes filled with tears and she brushed them away sadly. 'I saw him changing to a dreadful colour and I thought he must be having a heart attack. That is when I called to reception to get an ambulance immediately and they arrived only a few minutes later.' She lowered her head. 'They could not save him,' she whispered.

The officer gave her a moment to collect herself. 'Did your husband complain of feeling unwell at any point?' he asked.

Aurelia considered the question then nodded. 'Yes, he did. He went to the bathroom after dinner and when he came back he complained of indigestion,' she said. 'He was rubbing his chest as we left the restaurant. If only I had recognised the signs,' she said sadly, fiddling with her wedding ring.

'Mrs Harrington, did you and your husband consume any drugs or alcohol yesterday?' he asked.

Aurelia looked surprised. 'Drugs? No.' She gave a small embarrassed smile. 'I confess that we did drink quite a lot. We drank at the airport lounge and on the flight, and also in the limo when we arrived.' She thought back, 'Then after the ceremony we had cocktails, then wine with dinner and also a cognac afterwards.' She watched as the officer with the pad noted the list down. The other officer looked at her. She put her hands to her cheeks. 'It sounds like so much!'

'Mrs Harrington, traces of high-grade cocaine were found in your husband's blood.'

309

Aurelia's jaw dropped, her eyes shocked. 'Cocaine?' she cried. 'Impossible. I do not tolerate drugs and he knows that. In any case, I would have seen if he were doing drugs, I was with him all day.' She shook her head. 'I am sure you are mistaken.'

'There's no mistake. You say he went to the bathroom after dinner. How long was he gone?'

Aurelia stared at the officer. 'A few minutes,' she whispered. 'My God. Was he doing cocaine in there?' She stood up and paced around the room agitatedly. 'What was he thinking?' She turned to stare at the officers, her eyes full of tears. 'Is that what killed him?'

'It seems so,' said the officer. 'That, and a combination of too much alcohol, a rich diet and too little exercise I suspect. I understand he was a big CEO? A stressful job wouldn't help either. His medical notes confirmed that he had a family history of heart disease, were you aware of that?'

Aurelia shook her head. 'We have not known each other for very long,' she said. 'Only a few months. It was love at first sight. We thought we had the rest of our lives to get to know each other.' She sank down into a chair and put her head in her hands. 'There is so much I did not know,' she cried.

The police officers stood up. 'Thank you for your time Mrs Harrington, we'll leave you now. Is there anyone we can call for you?'

Aurelia shook her head and waited until the officers closed the door quietly behind them. She wiped her eyes and started to pack her suitcase. 'Time to go home,' she said.

Chapter 31

'Ms Santa Maria? This is Lawrence Kessler, Mr Harrington's attorney.'

Aurelia motioned to Lauren to close the office door as she left and turned to survey her view as she spoke into the phone. 'Hello Mr Kessler, thank you for calling. I understand from Donald that you are aware of everything that has happened over the last week?'

'I am,' confirmed Lawrence. 'Mr Waterman was kind enough to fill me in at the funeral yesterday. My apologies for not speaking to you at the service, I thought it more appropriate to call you separately. I'm very sorry for your loss. Mr Waterman tells me that you are keeping your maiden name?'

'Yes. I want as few people as possible to know about this further tragedy. I cannot bear the looks of pity and sympathy – I prefer to try and carry on without people knowing of my private heartache,' said Aurelia.

'Of course.' Lawrence paused delicately. 'We do need to discuss the issue of your husband's will. Are you happy to talk about it now? If not, I can come in and see you at your convenience?'

Aurelia's heart quickened and she took a deep breath. 'No, that is fine. I prefer to settle everything as soon as possible so that I can grieve in peace.'

'Quite so,' said Lawrence. 'I'm not sure how much you know about Mr Harrington's finances?'

'Very little,' said Aurelia. 'Ours was a match of passion and I am a little embarrassed to tell you that we did not yet know many things about each other.'

She sniffed, adding sadly. 'We hoped to have many years to teach other everything about ourselves.'

'Quite,' murmured Lawrence. He coughed and moved away from unsteady emotional ground to firmer facts. 'Well, Mr Harrington was a wealthy man,' he explained. 'After the death of his first wife, Dante Kingsford, he inherited her estate. Ms Kingsford was only 22 at the time of her death – a tragic story – and Mr Harrington inherited her modest private savings account and few personal items – jewellery, the apartment her father had given her, her car and so on. However, the grief of losing his only daughter caused Mr Kingsford himself to die soon afterwards. As his will left everything to his daughter, that wealth also passed to Mr Harrington.'

Lawrence paused, and Aurelia could hear him moving some papers in front of him. 'Mr Harrington sold the various properties and other assets, keeping only the renowned art collection and the most valuable asset of all, the 26% shareholding in The Kingsford Corporation.'

Aurelia smiled bitterly at Blake's callous sale of her childhood home and other items precious to her. 'And he used his new shareholding to insist on a place on the board,' she stated, trying to keep her tone neutral.

'Not at all,' said Lawrence, sounding surprised. 'William Kingsford gave up his role running the company as soon as his daughter disappeared. He was never the same again.' Lawrence paused, remembering. 'It was a great shame.' He continued. 'No, it was Mr Kingsford who nominated Blake as his successor as CEO.' He chuckled quietly. 'There were some hot tempers which flared at the decision, and several older board members railed against it, but William – Mr Kingsford – was insistent that Blake should take over.'

Aurelia was silent, digesting this new piece of information. 'Blake must have conned my father too,' she thought, reminded irresistibly for a moment of Luis Alvarez. 'Whatever it took to get him where he needed to be.'

She prompted Lawrence. 'So where does that leave us now?'

'Well, as you know, Mr Harrington went on to marry again.'

'Paige,' said Aurelia flatly.

'That's right. Mr Harrington had spoken to me about writing a will at the time of his marriage, leaving everything to Mrs Paige Harrington.' He sighed. 'I did suggest to him several times that we should indeed do so but it never seemed to be a priority for Blake, and he in fact never created a will.' He continued briskly. 'What this means is that your husband died intestate.'

'Intestate?' asked Aurelia, knowing well what the word meant and smiling into the receiver as she congratulated herself on a probate battle she would not now have to fight with Paige's relatives.

'Yes,' continued Lawrence. 'It means he died without leaving a valid will. As such, we pass into the realms of probate law and, as his wife, you are deemed to be his sole heir.'

Aurelia was silent for moment, pretending to digest this information. 'What about Edward?' she asked.

Lawrence sighed sadly. 'The adoption of his son was finalised before Mr Harrington's death. As such, Edward no longer qualifies for the list of beneficiaries under probate.'

'Poor Edward,' said Aurelia softly. 'I begged Blake to reconsider the adoption but he was insistent that he wanted to do it. He told me that he did not want to see the reminder of Paige every day. It was hard for me to hear that, but I think he did love me too in his own way.'

'I'm sure he did,' said Lawrence kindly. 'What will you do now? You do realise that this inheritance, combined with your already sizeable shareholding, means that you now own over 51% of the corporation? To all intents and purposes it is your company.'

Aurelia smiled as she surveyed the setting afternoon sun glinting on windows across the city. A plane slipped across the sky, leaving a perfect white vapour trail in its wake.

'I will have to do my best to live up to him,' she said huskily. 'I will make a success of this company for him.'

'I wish you the best of luck,' said Lawrence. 'I'm sure he would be very proud of you.'

Aurelia pulled open her desk drawer and looked down at the photograph of her father. 'I hope he would,' she said softly.

Chapter 32

Three months later Aurelia strode into the kitchens at 'Milagro.'

'Hello everybody,' she called. 'How is everything?' Her head chef welcomed her with a kiss on each cheek.

'Aurelia! Wonderful to see you. We missed you these last two weeks.'

Aurelia smiled, shrugging off her stylish jacket. 'Thanks Cathy. It is great to be back. All of the 'Milagro' restaurants in Europe are doing wonderfully well and it was so fantastic to see all of my friends and build on some relationships.'

She delved into her large bag and brought out a large box of chocolates and a luxury selection of shortbread. 'Presents from Europe!' she announced. 'Please help yourselves.'

Her staff crowded round eagerly, opening up the boxes and cooing over the contents. Aurelia popped a chocolate into her mouth and looked around. 'So, what have I missed?'

Cathy nodded at the counter. 'Oh, same old, same old. We kept this morning's papers for you – we know what a news junkie you are!'

Aurelia smiled her thanks. 'Wonderful.' She scooped the pile of newspapers into her arms and grabbed her jacket. 'I will be in my office, I need to make a few calls. I can stay here until after the lunchtime rush then I must head across town – I have a corporation to run!'

317

She glanced at the papers as she walked down the corridor, slowing down as she started to read an item on the front page. 'No,' she gasped, her hand flying to her throat. She stopped dead in the corridor, her eyes tearing frantically across the page.

The newspapers fell from her arms and she collapsed against the wall, her face white. 'No!' she screamed. 'No!'

The workers in the kitchen looked up, startled as they heard the piercing screams. They ran into the corridor, crowding around the scattered newspapers and Aurelia's jacket lying abandoned on the floor. They could hear her vomiting in the nearby bathroom.

Cathy bent down to pick up the top newspaper and scanned the main article.

'What is it?' asked one of the waitresses.

Cathy shook her head, confused. 'I don't know,' she said. 'Something must have upset her.' She heard violent crying from the bathroom and shooed everyone back into the kitchen. 'Let's get back to work.'

She entered Aurelia's office, hanging up her jacket and placing the papers on her desk. She looked in puzzlement once more at the main article, unable to understand Aurelia's distress.

'Robert Osborne, 38, was today charged with the murder of Mrs Dante Harrington 12 years ago.

Mrs Harrington, the daughter of millionaire New York businessman William Kingsford, was previously believed to have committed suicide on her honeymoon on board the cruise ship 'The Diamond Sunrise' after her unexplained disappearance.

Mr Harrington, who was reportedly devastated by his young bride's death, died himself of a heart attack three months ago while holidaying in Las Vegas. Eye witness reports of the extent of his grief at the time of his wife's untimely death, meant that he was never considered by police as a suspect for foul play.

Mr Osborne has now come forward to confess that he was asked to carry out the murder by his cousin, Paige, who went on to become the next Mrs Harrington some months after Dante's death. Paige Harrington herself died five months ago, after suffering from mental health problems. Mr Osborne released a statement to reporters before he was taken into custody:

'Now that Paige and Blake are both dead and I can't hurt her by speaking up, I feel an overwhelming urge to confess what we did. I was very close to Paige and would have done anything for her. I worked as a steward on 'The Diamond Sunrise'. Paige found out that the Harringtons would be honeymooning on board my ship. She was jealous of Dante and desperate to be wealthy. We didn't have much money when we were growing up - Paige had to work three jobs for two years before even being able to afford to go to college. She asked me to make sure Dante disappeared without trace while we were out at sea. I drugged Dante while she was at dinner one night so that she would be weak. I crept into her suite at around 2am and held a cloth covered in chloroform over Mr Harrington's nose until he was unconscious, so that he wouldn't wake up and disturb me. I walked Dante up onto the deck and threw her overboard. I feel ashamed and disgusted by what I

did. I need to clear my conscience. Prison is too good for me. I'm so sorry.'

Detective Inspector Fullerton, who ran the investigation at the time of Dante's death and who reports that he was never fully convinced by the coroner's verdict of suicide, also commented for us. 'I am pleased at last to be able to have justice for Dante. Her tragic murder is a devastating story of the depths that are possible in human nature. My only relief is that Mr Harrington himself is not alive to find out the truth about his wife. He was a good man. He deserved better.'